lie to me

A Touched Trilogy

ANGELA FRISTOE

LITTLE PRINCE PUBLISHING

NANAIMO, CANADA

LITTLE PRINCE PUBLISHING
NANAIMO, CANADA

Publisher's Note: This is a work of fiction. Names, characters, places, and incidents are a product of the author's imagination. Locales and public names are sometimes used for atmospheric purposes. Any resemblance to actual people, living or dead, or to businesses, companies, events, institutions, or locales is completely coincidental.

LIE TO ME/ ANGELA FRISTOE. -- 1st ed.
ISBN: 978-0-9949544-7-3

Dedicated to Calleigh

The truth is rarely pure and never simple.

—OSCAR WILDE

PROLOGUE

"I WANT TO SEE them." Zoe winced, and a hoarse croak struggled from her lips. Hours of laboring had ravaged her throat. She fought against the urge to close her weary eyes. "I want to see them. I need to."

Michael went to the door and spoke to a nurse outside the room. Zoe gazed at his strong features when he returned to her side. "They're bringing them now." Even as he said the words, three nurses entered the room rolling the carts.

Her babies.

He handed her the first baby, and she cradled the infant in her arms, smoothing a hand over short raven curls. "Phoebe, my little truth teller." The baby's eyes opened, and the deep blue twinkled as Zoe whispered, "I love you." She knew.

"Truth teller?" Michael asked. He nuzzled Phoebe's hand wrapped around his finger.

"She knows I'm telling her the truth. It's her gift. To hear the truth of the words."

Phoebe would be a challenge for Michael. Her gift was rare and a difficult one to understand. Zoe smoothed a finger along the baby's soft, gently wrinkled face. Little Phoebe was so at peace knowing her mother spoke with love and truth. She would be spared what was to come, and Zoe was grateful that at least one of them would be. She gave Phoebe another kiss on the forehead.

"Tomorrow and always, I'll be with you." Zoe looked up at

Michael, his face lined with worry. "Don't worry. Everything is fine."

Phoebe's little face scrunched up, and she gave a small whimper.

He carefully lifted her and put her back in the rolling crib, then picked up the next baby, placing her against Zoe's chest.

"Chloe, my sweet seer." Their eyes met, and Chloe gave a cry filled with fear and sadness, her fingers clutching desperately at Zoe.

This time she ignored Michael's questioning gaze. She couldn't share with him what Chloe had seen. It hurt too much. She pressed a kiss to Chloe's head and passed her to the nurse, then leaned over to take the last baby from Michael's arms.

"Lily," she said, placing her hand over her heart. Warmth flooded Zoe, and she smiled weakly. "My healer." Lily's little heart beat fiercely, and Zoe rubbed her hand along Lily's back as she began to wail. "I'm sorry, little one. You're not strong enough yet."

Gradually Lily's wail subsided into a soft mewing, and her eyes fluttered closed. Michael lifted her from Zoe's arms, placing her back on her mobile bed and the nurses wheeled the babies out of the room. Zoe wanted to scream and cry for them to come back, to let her hold her girls just one more time, but there was no strength left in her.

When her eyes closed, she didn't fight. She let them fall as a tear slipped down her cheek. A hand gripped hers, and a panicked voice began shouting. Michael. Girls. Be strong.

CHAPTER 1

THE NOTE SAILED THROUGH the air, rushing past me on the way to its destination. I turned my head to the side, watching the perfectly formed square land on his desk. He palmed the note and glanced up. His grey eyes made contact with mine for just a moment before he leaned forward to look around me. I sighed in boredom, sinking back in my seat. Twenty minutes to go then I never had to worry about sitting through another of Mr. Mason's lectures again. Unless, of course, he decided to teach senior level Spanish next semester.

I blinked, trying desperately to clear the haze forming before me, and focused on the guy next to me. I met those steely eyes again, and in spite of my lack of embarrassment, heat rose in my cheeks. Not that I let that stop me from looking. It wasn't the first time Nathan Lauer caught me staring, and, considering the way he'd been bulking up at the gym, it wasn't going to be the last time. My lips twitched as the red flush on his cheeks overshadowed my pink face.

"Phoebe," Tonya hissed from behind me. I ignored her, enjoying Nathan's discomfort too much to acknowledge her.

My desk jerked, and I turned to glare at my best friend. She gave me one of those are-you-an-idiot looks and nodded to the front of the class.

"Ms. Matlin?" Mr. Mason's voice filtered through the remaining haze. "Ms. Matlin?"

I spun around.

"Yes?" I said, hating that everyone was watching me.

He gestured to the door. "You're needed in the office."

I threw Tonya a smirk, knowing she was dying to leave the class as much as I was. Gathering my things, I shoved them in my backpack, making sure I took everything. Even if they only needed me for a minute, I wasn't coming back for the rest of Mr. Mason's lecture.

The hallway was quiet as only a few students lingered at their lockers. With it being the last day before Christmas break, I wasn't surprised to see people leaving early. Hell. I wished I was one of them. Most of my classes were only half-full, but after Dad caught me skipping the previous week, I knew I couldn't risk it.

I made a pit stop at my locker, which was on the way to the office. Twisting the lock, I banged the side of my fist against the orange door to loosen it enough to pull open. I unzipped my bag and pulled out my cell phone. A new message flashed across the screen. I shoved my bag in to the locker, and, closing the door with one hand, started pressing buttons to get the message.

Where r u? C

A groan slipped out, and I glanced around to see if anyone heard. Thankfully, the closest person, a guy halfway down the hall, looked more interested in his cell than my moaning. I tried to remember what I'd apparently forgotten. Chloe might have been obsessed with texting, but she only used it with me in extreme situations.

I fumbled with the buttons, trying to text her back. Walking while typing wasn't my forte, so a jumble of letters filled the screen as I walked to the office. I paused outside the glass door, and at the end of the message typed **here** then hit send. It was safer to imply I was where I was supposed to be than risk her asking why I wasn't.

Chloe was the perfect one. Organized, precise, and peppy. She was enough to make me puke. How we were sisters, let alone two-thirds of a set of triplets, was beyond me. That we weren't related was one of my greatest fantasies.

I flipped the phone closed and looked up in time to see the office door flying at me. I jerked back, and my hand lashed out to stop it from smacking me in the face. Deep blue eyes, identical to my own, stared back at me.

"Where've you been?" Chloe demanded. Her perfectly sculpted brows arched with indignation.

"Shoveling shit." I ignored her rolling eyes. "In class. Where else?"

"You weren't even supposed to come to school today. We're going to be late." Milk chocolatey waves of hair flowed around her face as she turned back in to the office and waved to the secretary.

"It'll be okay," Lily said, and stepped out from behind Chloe. At just over five feet, she always managed to find the perfect hiding spot until she was ready to speak. If it weren't for her copper curls, she'd probably be able to disappear entirely.

"Late for what?" I asked. The two of them just stared at me—Lily with compassion, while Chloe's face filled with dismay. "What?"

"Oh, Phoebs." Lily sighed. "I'm so sorry. I didn't think you'd be like this."

She reached for my arm, and even before she could touch me, I felt the heat radiating from her. I stepped back, evading her grasp. "Like what?"

Her head dipped, and she let her hand fall. Guilt flooded

me before I shook it off. Lily was a master at emotions and manipulating them. Not that she made me feel guilty. No. That was my conscience. Still, I resented her attempts at controlling me even if she was doing it with the best intentions. Her sole purpose in life seemed to be to make sure that everyone felt okay. I can't even say good, because when she touched you, it was like she sucked out all the bad stuff, and if there was nothing good to take its place, it was the most bizarre feeling of emptiness.

"Get over it, Phoebe." Chloe grabbed Lily's hand and started dragging her down the hall, leaving me to follow. "You should have remembered."

"Remembered what exactly?"

"Mom's birthday."

She threw the words at me, knowing full well what it would do to me. Every muscle in me tightened, and I froze mid-step. Lily stopped with me, and Chloe had no choice but to do the same.

"Let's go," Chloe said. "Nanna is just getting there, and she's wondering where we are." Her eyes focused on me then fluttered for a moment, looking in to my future. "She has something for you. You'll love it."

I hated when she did that, even more than Lily trying to fix me.

"I'm not going. I never go. Why would you even think I'd go this year?" I asked.

Chloe's face scrunched in confusion. "I saw..."

I struck while she was down. "Well, maybe there's something wrong with you because that's something that's never going to happen."

Anger and pain burned my throat, and my nose tingled. I swirled around, intent on going back to class. Anywhere but here with the two of them. Or worse ... there with her. I sensed Lily moving toward me, and tried to twist away, but her palm fell on my back. Soothing heat flooded me, drowning the pain and anger with a numbing calm.

"Damn it, Lily. You know I hate it when you do that!" I stomped off, no longer angry with Chloe for trying to direct my future, or with Nanna for wanting to use me as a substitute for my dead mother. Instead, my forced anger was with Lily for not healing what was really wrong with me—my lack of a gift.

I reached Mr. Mason's class and yanked the door. It flew open and crashed against the wall. I stood in the doorway under the intense scrutiny of the entire class, Mr. Mason included.

"I'm back," I said, and breezed in to the class, moving straight to my seat.

My friend, Owen, chuckled, and I shot him a cocky smile. I evaded Tonya's curious look and concentrated on the swirling wood pattern of my desktop. Normally, I talked to Tonya about pretty much everything, but not this.

Our family was different, and even if I didn't have a gift, Dad had drilled in to me the need to protect my sisters. Even when we were younger, I was the one telling them not to freak people out. Not that they ever listened. Chloe would constantly make her little predictions, and Lily couldn't keep her hands to herself.

Mr. Mason droned on, and I watched the second hand on the clock tick slowly around the face. Five minutes. I could have skipped out early, but the chance of getting sucked in to Lily and Chloe's plans was too great. It was safer to die of boredom.

A twitch of black cloth out of the corner of my eye drew

my attention to Nathan. He was refolding a piece of wrinkled paper into its original intricate square. He looked past me and nodded to the person on my left side. Vivian, his girlfriend. I didn't bother looking at her. Mainly because the sight of her caused me to gag more than Chloe did. He tucked the last corner in and flicked his hand, letting the note fly to her.

As the note crossed in front of me, I reached out and snatched it mid-flight. I wasn't sure what possessed me to do it, but Nathan's shocked expression combined with Vivian's gasp of outrage made it worth the effort.

I gave Nathan a smile and a wink, then blew him a kiss, loving the answering blush. Owen and Tonya's snickers almost covered Vivian's hiss. Mr. Mason shot them a look, and I hid the note in the palm of my hand until he'd refocused on the board. I peeled open the note, a smirk on my face. I'd never been a note passer before, and I wondered just what was so secretive that they couldn't just whisper. Most of the time, Tonya and I didn't even bother to lower our voices when we wanted to say something.

I looked at the note. Vivian's bubbly writing alternated with Nathan's scrawl. Her perfect script started the note.

~ *Where were you last night?*
home
~ *I thought you were coming over*
no
~ *What about tonight?*
no
~ *What the hell is wrong with you?*
I need some space
~ *What does that mean?*
I think we should break up

I looked up at Nathan. This time, though, he didn't meet my gaze. His face flamed, and now I understood why he'd looked so horrified when I'd nabbed the note. Vivian tried to grab it from me, but I clenched my fingers around the small square, refusing to give it to her. The bell rang, and people started moving all at once.

"Give it to me," Vivian said, making another grab for the paper. I shook my head and slid out of my seat, moving quickly to give Tonya a chance to get between us. I ran from the room, oblivious to the shrieking calls of Vivian.

"Phoebe!" Nathan raced through the hall behind me.

I turned in to the art room. He followed me, closing the door behind him. The last art class of the day had already finished. Ms. Steward, the art teacher, was known for leaving early. The large space reeked of paint fumes and dust that floated in the air, highlighted by the sunlight pouring through the windows lining the wall. It had been more than a year since I'd last been in the room, but the smell took me back. Every insecurity within me rose, instantly deflating me.

"Give it to me, Phoebs." Any embarrassment he'd felt before vanished from his face, leaving anger and frustration glaring back at me.

I lifted my hand, the note still clenched in my fist. "What is this?"

"A note," he said.

"No shit. How can you do that?"

My heart beat frantically. What did I want him to say? It seemed that no matter what he said, it wouldn't negate the fact that he had just dumped his girlfriend in a note. Or, he would have if I hadn't intercepted it.

"You don't get it." He sank against a table, lifting one leg off the ground to kick at the air.

"Then explain it to me." Anger forced the words from my lips, and they echoed in the empty room.

"Why? Why should I have to explain it to you?"

"Because you—we..." Because you chose her over me. I didn't need to say it. The fact was there between us, and had been every day for over a year.

"This isn't about you," he said, standing up. He took a step toward me, tearing the note from my hands. He was at the door when I finally got the courage to speak.

"You need to tell her to her face. Grow up and be a man." Only the stiffening of his shoulders let me know my dig bothered him, then he was out the door and it drifted closed with a gentle click, leaving me alone again.

With elbows on the table, I plowed my fingers in to my dark curls. I wasn't mad for Vivian. I was mad for me. That he had picked her instead of me, and that a year of pretending he hadn't broken my heart had done nothing to actually heal it. It was easier to smile and flirt than to let him know how much it had hurt. He hadn't told me to my face either. That was what hurt the worst. He'd chosen her, yet he was treating her even crappier than he'd treated me.

When Nathan had first moved to town two years ago, I'd fallen in lust. He was hot, smart, and, best of all, he was new. He'd never dated Chloe, he didn't know about the weird things Lily could do to a person, and he never questioned why I hated being with my sisters. Absolutely perfect. Except he'd never acted on the interest he'd shown in me. I spent weeks pursuing him until I finally cornered him in the art room. After giving him our first kiss, my first kiss, I asked him to Homecoming.

Too bad for me, he'd already asked Vivian. That he

obviously told her about the kiss made it even more humiliating when she and her groupies laughed about it in front of me.

Cringing at the memory, I dropped my head on to the table, letting it roll back and forth. Reliving that incident was nearly as mortifying as this. I'd acted jealous—okay, I was jealous—but what was worse was now he knew it.

The gentle swish of the door opening brought my head up. Chloe stood framed in the doorway. Just what I needed. An overbearing sister relishing in the I-told-you-so moment. Something Chloe and her all-seeing eye did way too often.

"Don't say it," I snapped, moving past her in to the hall.

"Say what?" she asked, catching up to me.

I arched a brow. "I told you so."

"Why would I say that?" Her brow creased.

"Because you knew he'd never like me." I wondered if she'd enjoyed bursting that bubble when she'd told me. I picked up my pace, hoping she'd get lost in the rapidly thinning crowd, but I just didn't have that kind of luck.

"I never said he didn't like you. I only told you I saw him with Vivian." She swerved around a couple that had stopped in the middle of the hallway then was back at my side. "Besides, didn't he just ask you out?"

"Yeah right. You've already told me that wasn't going to happen." Having all my fantasies squashed by Chloe the Fortune Teller was just one reason why I avoided spending time with her.

Her face paled, and her mouth dropped open. "I never said it wouldn't happen. Besides, I saw him ... I mean, I saw you go back to class. Then he followed you to the art room and asked you out."

"Uh. Yeah. Didn't happen." We reached my locker, and I

swung it open, throwing in my jacket and grabbing my binder for Biology class. When I glanced at her, she seemed completely unaware of anything going on around her. "Aren't you supposed to be meeting Nanna?"

"She plans on being there for a while. Besides, you're going with us." She gave a smirk and leaned against the neighboring locker. "I saw it."

I grit my teeth. "Well, it ain't gonna happen, so maybe your vision isn't as clear as you thought. Look at how wrong you were about Nathan. What happened in the art room was about as far from him asking me out as you can possibly get. You can't be right all the time, Chloe."

I slammed the locker closed and turned my back on her, walking to class. After a few steps, I stopped and glanced back. Her pale face was disturbing. She really was freaked out about her vision not happening.

"I'm sorry, Chloe, but maybe you just got the message wrong." As much as I hated her constant knowing look, I hated the idea I'd hurt her even more.

"I've never been wrong before." Her normally confident voice whispered softly through the air, trailing behind her as she walked off.

I wanted to call after her, to reassure her, but didn't know how. I'd never had a gift, so how would I understand suddenly not having one?

Lily, the Healer, Chloe, the Seer, and Phoebe, the Truth Teller. That was what my mom called us minutes before she died. She'd been right about Lily and Chloe. Me, on the other hand, ... well, it hadn't happened yet. I couldn't even say I knew what I was supposed to do as a truth teller. I definitely didn't have a problem lying. Not that I was a chronic liar. Sometimes, though, it was just easier.

So just what does a Truth Teller do? The only person around to ask was Nanna, and I wasn't in the mood for her today.

I pushed thoughts of my supposed gift aside and headed for my biology class.

"Hey, girl," Bianca called as I entered the biology lab.

I gave her a goofy smile, trying my best to lighten my mood. Thoughts of what had happened with Nathan were bringing me down. If I wanted to survive the boredom of the day, I definitely needed to focus on something else. I flopped in to my seat next to Tonya, flinging my binder on to our table.

"God. Isn't this day over yet?" I groaned, choosing to discount the fact that I could have left with Chloe and Lily. Going with them would have been even worse than sitting through an hour of Mrs. Schaeffer's video montage of her favorite dissections.

"Please tell me we have plans every day for the next two weeks," Bianca said, twisting in her chair to face us across the aisle. "My parents want Karin to tutor me."

Bianca's parents considered her a disgrace. They were a very traditional Chinese family, and while her older brother was entering medical school, and her younger sister was some kind of cello or violin prodigy, Bianca was, well ... Bianca. She tinged her pixie cut hair with purple streaks and wore a bit too much eye shadow. According to her parents, she had no interests that would lead to any future employment. Apparently, being able to scout out hot guys with her eyes closed wasn't going to help her cut it in the real world.

"In what?" I asked, knowing that, despite her apparent rebel look, she had the highest GPA of all my friends.

"Mandarin."

"Isn't that, like, Chinese?" Tonya asked.

"Yes."

"And aren't you Chinese?"

Bianca rolled her eyes. "So? Just because I'm Chinese, doesn't mean I speak all Chinese dialects. My family speaks Cantonese, but my parents say Mandarin will be more useful in the business world. Last time Karin came over, she blabbed to my mom about this Mandarin class she's taking at the community college."

"Hey. Karin's not so bad," Owen spoke up from the other side of Bianca.

Tonya made a barfing sound. Her dislike of Karin was well known to everyone, including Karin, despite the fact she was part of our group of friends.

"I have family coming in, but I should be able to get away some of the time." I rolled my pencil back and forth along the table. "I can do something tomorrow."

"Let's go shopping. We can have a girls' day," Bianca said.

"What about me?" Owen flicked her head, and she gave him a gentle elbow back.

"Okay. A girls, plus one, day then," she said.

"Nah. I have better things to do." He turned back to his stack of books and pulled one out, flipping to a dog-eared page. Bianca and I rolled our eyes. Owen was just plain weird sometimes.

"I might have some time after Christmas," Tonya said, then pulled out her cell and started punching away at some text.

I leaned over, trying to see what she was typing. She knew I didn't do texts, and the only other people I could think she'd want to message sat across the aisle from us.

She shot me a dirty look and tilted her phone away from my eyes. I stuck my tongue out at her and settled back in my chair. She'd been acting strange the past few months; always busy with some vague thing she had to do with her grandma. Then again, she had a grandma who wasn't always nosing around in to everything you'd done since you'd last seen her, so maybe she didn't mind.

Mrs. Schaeffer came in then, so any questioning would have to wait. After ten minutes of lecturing about the importance of dissection as a method of learning more about organisms and the humane treatment of the specimens, the lights dimmed and the computerized video projector started. Normally, movie time was an opportunity to catch up on some of my sleep, but Tonya began kicking me under the table.

"So?" she whispered.

"What?" I looked at her and smiled at the expectant expression she wore.

"Come on, Phoebs. You know you can't not tell me what the note said." She leaned closer, her eyes growing wide. "You took off with it like the room was on fire. It must have been really juicy. Sex talk, right? I always knew Vivian was a little skanky. And Nathan has always been a bit too quiet."

Her eyebrows wiggled, and I broke out in a laugh. Mrs. Schaeffer gave a sharp cough from her desk in the front corner of the room, and I stifled my chuckles. No way did I need an office referral the day before Christmas break.

"No sex talk," I whispered. "Honest. It was just some stupid stuff. Their reaction was too much. Did you see Nathan's face when I grabbed it?" My soft laugh sounded forced even to my ears. I opened my binder and focused on drawing a swirling flower pattern on a blank sheet of paper, avoiding her gaze.

I didn't want her to know what the note said. Although I

couldn't figure out why it would matter, the idea of her knowing that he had tried to break up with Vivian in a note just didn't sit right. Hell. I didn't even want Vivian to know.

"He looked like he was gonna piss his pants. You sure it wasn't something important?" Tonya asked.

She eyed me suspiciously, and I tried to relax my smile into something more natural. Considering I was supposed to be the one with some kind of internal lie detector, she was a lot better at finding fibs than I was.

"Can you imagine Nathan and Vivian ever having a meaningful conversation, let alone in a note?" I arched a brow. This time, it wasn't as difficult coming up with a believable expression. Until I snatched the white missile, I hadn't thought it possible either.

"Ladies..." Mrs. Schaeffer's voice boomed over the droning commentator from the video.

Our heads whipped up to find her glaring at us. Most of the time, a dirty look from a teacher didn't faze us, but Mrs. Schaeffer had a wonky eye and a husband nobody had seen in five years.

"You're more than welcome to watch the video after class with me, or you can stop your chatting and watch it now."

Knowing from experience she was serious, our heads bobbed frantically. The dissections continued, and I slouched back in my chair, tipping the hard plastic seat back on two legs. I had no interest in biology, and even less in chemistry or physics. If Dad hadn't made two science classes mandatory, I'd have enrolled in three sessions of art. Closing my eyes, I let myself drift off, blocking out Tonya's groan of dissatisfaction. The noises around me faded, and I imagined Nathan at the beach, decked out in his surfing gear. Fantasies were so much easier than real life.

I was almost asleep when something hit the back of my head, causing me to jerk up and nearly fall out of my seat as it skidded backward with a grating screech of protest along the tiled floor. Two dozen sets of eyes focused on me. Only the darkened room concealed my embarrassment. I gave a grin and waved at my gawkers, putting in a little extra smirk for Owen and Bianca, who tried so hard not to laugh.

Once everyone, other than Tonya, had diverted their attention away from me and back to the screen, I glanced behind me to see what had ended my nap. Resting inches from my black boot was a balled up piece of paper. My eyes shifted around, looking for who had decided I was the new trash can, and they came to rest on Vivian. Figured. How was it possible to have been in class with her for an entire semester and not even realize she was there? I didn't skip that often.

I picked up the paper, and then swiveled back around to face Tonya. "When did she start coming to this class?"

"This is the first time. Maybe she's stalking you."

Shaking my head in denial, or maybe in defeat, I smoothed out the crumpled paper.

Leave Nathan alone.

I looked back at Vivian, and she made an ugly face that I guessed was supposed to be threatening, then grabbed her things and stomped out of class. Mrs. Schaffer harrumphed, and someone giggled. Probably Bianca.

Vivian was such a drama queen. What did Nathan ever see in her? I rolled my eyes then slid the note over to Tonya. Her soaring eyebrows made me wish I hadn't. No way now would she believe me about the first note. My best chance against her questioning was a quick escape after class before she started the interrogation.

Luck, however, deserted me. The bell rang, and Tonya grabbed my bag, holding it hostage behind her as she stood with the table between us. That was the problem with having a best friend; they always knew what you were going to do. She was almost as bad, or good depending on your point of view, as Chloe sometimes. I'd never say that to Chloe, though. Doing that would just open Chloe's vision floodgates, and I'd be constantly bombarded with every detail of every soon-to-be minute of my life.

I refused to struggle for my bag. Tonya would only take it as confirmation that I was hiding something from her. Instead, I screwed my face up in confusion and hoped she'd buy it.

"What's wrong?" I sank further in to my chair, tipping it up on its back legs again as Mrs. Schaeffer went out the door, following the rest of the students. Owen and Bianca stopped behind Tonya, waiting. Owen was mildly disinterested while Bianca looked confused.

"What are you hiding?" Tonya asked, her head tilting to the side.

"Noth—"

"Cut the crap, Phoebs. Vivian is pissed, and you've been looking guilty all class—well, at least the part where you were awake." She crossed her arms over her chest, ignoring my bag as it swung around and bumped her hip. There was no way to get out of it, but if I told her now, it'd be all over campus within an hour.

"Fine, but not at school. I'll tell you when you come over tomorrow."

"I can't tomorrow." Her face shuttered, and she spun around, tossing my bag to me in a quick motion. I caught it as it slammed in to my chest.

"Why? I thought we were gonna go Christmas shopping? You already ditched me last weekend." There were only six days left to shop, and I needed to get, well, everything, and Tonya was one of those people that managed to find the best things the instant she walked in to a store.

She shrugged and twisted a strand of her straightened hair.

"I've gotta go see my mom."

Liar. It whispered through me, my stomach churning to the point I thought I'd puke. There was a moment when my brain tried to make sense of what I was hearing, what I was feeling, then it came again. *Liar.*

"Liar." The word slipped out, unrestrained in its harshness, and almost instantly my stomach settled. Then I saw Tonya's face.

"What did you call me?" Her back stiffened, and her head reared back. Shit. Owen and Bianca went bug-eyed behind her. Tonya's lips pursed, and her eyes narrowed, darkening from brown to black.

"I ... I..." My voice faded, unsure if I should call her on it again, or try and fib my way out of it. It wasn't the first time I'd called her a liar, and she'd always laughed it off before. Her reaction and the flush coloring the soft brown of her cheeks told me I'd actually caught her.

"Screw you," she snapped as I stood there with my mouth moving like a gasping fish. "I don't need to tell you every move I make, and I don't need my best friend calling me a liar." She spun, shoved Owen out of her way, and took off out of the room, slamming the door behind her.

My bag thudded to the floor. Owen and Bianca stared at me, the question in their faces a reflection I was sure of my own. What the hell had just happened?

CHAPTER 2

I PULLED UP IN front of the house after school and groaned. Every hope of evading Nanna vanished. Her old blue *Plymouth* was parked in the driveway. I hesitated before putting my *Sunfire* in to park. The urge to simply drive away overwhelmed me, pushing me to switch gears and press my foot back on the gas, but her head had already peeked out the screen door. I turned the car off and grabbed my bag. Sliding out of the front seat, I barely controlled the urge to get back in and speed off.

There'd been a time when I loved Nanna's visits ... before I realized she was using me. Every hug and smile she gave weren't really for me, but for who I reminded her of. Oh, sure. A part of her loved me for me, but, mostly, I was her favorite because I was the living image of my mother.

"Phoebe, dear, I missed you this afternoon." She smiled sweetly and came out on to the front porch as if she didn't know how much I wanted to avoid her, which, of course, she did know. I tried to shake off the guilt flooding me. She hadn't missed me. She'd missed seeing Mom.

"Hey, Nanna," I said, walking up the path to the house. There was a chance that if I could ignore her suffocating presence, she might just leave me alone. I didn't need her trying to analyze me. Especially when I was still confused about what had happened with Tonya.

"You shouldn't be out without your jacket." She reached

for me as I made it to the top of the steps, enfolding me in a hug that felt like the warm fuzzies we practiced giving in kindergarten. It was always like that with Nanna. No matter how crappy I felt seeing her or talking to her, her hugs were like magic. I used to wonder if she had a bit of Lily's gift to make people feel better, then I'd learned she could give some nasty cold pricklies on the side. Something I didn't think Lily could ever do. "You're shivering. Have you told your father about the heater in your car not working? What would happen if you were caught in some bad weather? You'd freeze."

"Nanna, we live in Southern California. I don't think we need to worry about snowstorms. Besides, I'm pretty sure Chloe would see it coming."

I pulled out of the comforting hug, and then, following her through the front door, glanced around the living room for my sisters. Not surprisingly, they were nowhere around. The two of them were determined to get me to talk to Nanna. Lily probably thought it would make me feel better about 'things', even if she wasn't sure what those 'things' were. Chloe would just want me to do it because she had to make sure her vision was still right.

Nothing about our house had changed in the seventeen years since Mom and Dad bought the place. Dad repainted every few years—the exact shade of green Mom had picked out, despite it being a vile lima bean color and completely out of step with anything remotely resembling good taste by today's standards. Even the porch swing was identical to the one Mom bought, although Dad had replaced it after I broke it doing one of my gymnastics routines. Of course, that was before I'd realized gymnastics actually required some discipline and just a hint of athleticism.

"I'd like to speak with you," Nanna said, turning to face me with her business face. Her hands propped on her hips, and there was a slight tap to her right foot.

"I'm not in the mood. Tonya and I had a fight." I walked around her, intent on going down to my room.

"Well, what can you expect? You called her a liar," she said, exasperated.

My head dropped back in defeat. No way would she let this slide. As annoying as it was for Chloe to always tell you your future, Nanna could always make it worse by bringing up the past.

I went to the kitchen table, pulled out a chair, and sat, my eyes following my fingers as they began tracing the intricate lace flower pattern of the tablecloth.

"Phoebe, what happened?" she asked, sitting across from me, the chair creaking in protest under her heavy frame.

Gnarled hands stretched across the table to grasp mine. The warmth of her grip was soothing. It reminded me of how, when I was little, she would read my past, making me feel secure in the knowledge that even if I didn't know what the future held for me, I knew what the past did. I'd always loved that until she'd started calling me on things I didn't want to be brought back up, like the time I stole Chloe's favorite Barbie and tested out my hairstyling skills.

Nanna needed a connection in order for her gift to work. Touching a person could let her see all the memories they left open, even those little-forgotten ones. When she'd moved to the old folks' home five years ago, I'd thought I was a bit safer. Then I found out she'd taken one of my hairbrushes. It was far enough removed from me that it didn't let her see everything, but what I couldn't contain hidden behind a mental wall was enough for her to get an idea of what I was usually up to. I always felt like someone was watching over my shoulder.

She waited for an answer, but I didn't give her one. She would see everything anyway. At my lack of response, she sighed and let my fingers slip from hers, obviously finished with my memory. She shook her head, and said, "You're just like your mother."

I stiffened in my seat. That was not what I wanted to hear. Not because I didn't love my mother, or at least the idea of her, or even that I didn't want to be like her. I just didn't want to be a replacement for her, which was exactly what Nanna wanted.

"Before she met your father, she didn't want to accept her gift either. Once she met Michael, she realized the benefits of giving hope. She never listened to her heart, how it wanted her to help the people around her, but Michael's problems went beyond what she'd seen before. That was when she started—"

"It's not the same, Nanna." I pushed my chair back, intent on ending the conversation. "Mom made a choice not to use her gift. Mine hasn't appeared."

"It's there, Phoebe. Otherwise, why would you call Tonya a liar?"

Defeated, I sank back on to the hard seat. She wouldn't leave me alone until I told her, and if I tried not telling her, she'd just watch me harder. Sometimes, I wish that, along with seeing the past, she could hear and feel everything I did at that time as well so I wouldn't have to go through the process of explaining myself.

"I don't know," I said. "I mean, one second, she's telling me she's going to see her mom and, the next, I called her a liar."

"There must have been something. What were you feeling?"

"My stomach cramped," I said, and her head nodded.

"Your Aunt Ava had similar symptoms when she suspected someone was lying. But you sounded so sure when you said it, as if you knew she was lying. Not simply suspected she was."

"I wasn't sure. I mean, I wasn't actually calling her a liar. I was just repeating it."

"Repeating who?" She leaned forward, the creases scoring her forehead deepening.

"I don't know. Just some voice in my head." My words seemed to echo through the room, and her eyes widened impossibly. "Is that wrong?"

I had no idea how these gifts worked. Especially since Lily and Chloe both had different experiences. Chloe explained her visions as a blurry still-frame movie playing over top of what she saw in front of her while Lily said she would get a tingling in her hands when she felt someone in pain. Neither of them had talked about voices. In fact, none of my mom's relatives had ever mentioned voices, and considering the look Nanna was giving me, hearing them wasn't a good sign.

"I ... I'm not sure, dear. Honestly, you're the first truth teller we've had in the family since before my time."

"What about Aunt Ava?"

"Oh. She wasn't a truth teller. She was more of an empath. She'd feel the guilt people experienced when they lied."

"Great. So first, I'm the family freak with no gift, and now I'm going to be the freak that hears voices."

The basement door opened behind me, and I spun around to see Chloe coming up. "Oh, please," she said, and levered herself up on to the counter. "You really think anyone in this family is going to judge you because your gift is unusual?"

"Yeah, well, it's not like I can do anything with it anyways. What good does it do to know that someone's lying?" I gave her the evil eye. "You could have at least warned me I was going to get in to it with Tonya."

"You know my visions don't work that way, Phoebs. Besides, it's not like I want to see everything you're going to do. I'm just glad you're not planning on having sex anytime soon." She shuddered and made a gagging sound. And that was the perfect example of why I could hate her so much.

"Shut up," I snapped, turning back to Nanna. "So, what now? I'm supposed to listen to this voice and do what?"

"It not that simple, dear," Nanna said, finally recovered from her shock. "Let me do a bit of thinking on it. We need to know how to approach this, and we need to move quickly. Controlling your gift is essential."

Chloe snorted, and I spun back around. She had a smirk on her face.

"Is that a problem?" I asked while every nerve inside of me itched to yank her long brown hair.

"For the rest of us, no. For you, yeah. I don't think I've ever seen you have much control." Chloe slid off the counter and bent her arms back to rest along the edge.

"Oh. You have no idea how much control I'm exerting right now."

She rolled her eyes. "Phoebs, I love you, but when have you ever kept your mouth shut?"

"I can keep a frickin' secret." Hadn't I kept my mouth shut about Charlie Schmidt being her first kiss way back in fourth grade? I didn't tell anyone—well, except Tonya and maybe Bianca a couple years ago.

"I'm not talking secrets," she said. "I'm talking about your opinions. You spew words without thinking. That's why I didn't tell you about the fight with Tonya. I enjoy seeing you dig your own grave."

"Chloe, that's enough," Nanna interrupted. "Today isn't a day for fighting. Your mother would hate to think of you fighting on her birthday."

"I'm sorry, Nanna." Chloe swept to her side and pressed a kiss to her cheek. "I'm going back to the cemetery to get Lily. She's almost ready to come home."

"Why don't you take Phoebe with you? She hasn't been yet."

As much as I relished the idea of escaping Nanna, a visit to my mother's grave wasn't going to happen. Especially not with the two of them pressuring me.

"No thanks."

I pushed away from the table and walked to the stairs leading down to my room.

"Why are you such a bitch?" Chloe asked as I started down the steps.

"Chloe!" Nanna's voice was clearly audible over the whack I heard her give Chloe's arm.

I glanced back and looked from Chloe to Nanna. "Maybe I just don't like living in the past. Especially one I can't remember."

"That's not fair. Mom loved you," Chloe said. "You know that."

"Maybe, but it doesn't change the fact that she's dead, and everyone expects me to be just like her."

"Phoebe Lynn, that is not true." Nanna stood gingerly, leaning heavily on the table.

"Really? Tell me that you don't think of her when you look at me. Tell me you don't wish I was her."

The slow exhale of Nanna's breath filled the room. "I'm not going to dignify that with an answer, young lady. I loved your mother, and I love you. You're the Truth Teller, Phoebe, and unless you accept the truth within your own heart, you'll never be able to use your gift."

CHAPTER 3

CHRISTMAS SUCKED. OKAY, SO maybe not all of Christmas, but the whole 'we're a happy family' thing did. I'd managed to avoid most of the relatives as they'd descended on our home by claiming an excessive amount of homework that didn't exist, but total escape was never possible. The gift of prophecy was the most common one among my cousins, so hiding out rarely worked for long.

"Phoebe?" Lily's soft voice followed a knock on my door.

"Come in," I called from my bed where I was stretched out on my stomach with a worn copy of *The Hunger Games*. Reading wasn't my thing, though, occasionally, I liked to surprise myself. "What's up?" I asked as she glided in to my room.

How she could be related to Chloe and me always amazed me. As loud and out there as Chloe and I were sometimes, Lily was quiet and serene. Not that she didn't speak her mind. She just didn't ever seem to feel the need to do it in public or for everyone to hear.

"How are you doing?" She sat on the edge of the bed and curled her fingers in to the bright green duvet.

"Fine. Why?"

"I..." She shifted restlessly, her fingers clenching the blanket.

Crap. She wanted to heal me. I scooted up into a sitting position as far from her as I could get without falling off the bed.

"I know you and Tonya haven't been talking, and Chloe mentioned Nathan—"

"Chloe should have kept her mouth shut," I snapped. "Nathan is nothing to me. Besides, that was almost a year ago."

"And Tonya?" Lily was still tense, barely moving except for the constant wringing of her hands.

I shrugged. "Who knows? She's the one who lied to me."

"Would you call her? For me?" Her eyes turned pleading, and I would swear tears gathered in them.

"Why?"

"You don't understand what it's like to be a healer and know that the person in pain doesn't want your help." Her voice trembled, making me feel guilty all over again. "If you don't want to talk to her then at least let me—"

"Forget it, Lils. You always say you'll just do a little bit, and then you're digging for more."

Her shoulders sagged, making me want to wrap her delicate frame in my arms. I would have if I hadn't learned from experience that Lily's gift wasn't just in her hands. Her healing energy radiated out of every pore.

"But I'll call her," I conceded.

"Thank you." She smiled, and the heavy air around her vanished, or at least lifted a bit.

"How's Dylan?" I asked, trying to deflect her concern. Even though Lily's boyfriend was an honorary member of the family, I hadn't seen him since school let out for vacation, which, considering his crappy attitude lately, wasn't a bad thing.

"His parents took him up to Colorado to go skiing. He's supposed to be home in time for Nadine's New Year's party."

I nodded absently, not interested in Dylan. I didn't know of anything else to talk to her about. We'd never been close, and, unlike Chloe, she never told me what went on in her head. That she'd asked me to talk to Tonya made me wonder just how bad she had it. I'd always assumed that she had the best gift. She made people feel better, and if she didn't want to, then she didn't touch them. Now I wondered if there was more to it than she'd told us.

"Is everything okay?" I asked.

She nodded solemnly, and, for a moment, seemed about to say something, but, instead, bobbed her head again and made a quick exit from my room.

I thought about my agreement to talk to Tonya. I'd avoided calling her. Not because I was angry, but because she was hiding something from me. And that was what Lily knew was really wrong with me. I rolled off the bed, grabbed my cell phone from my desk, and sank in to my computer chair. I pulled up Tonya's number, and while waiting for her to answer, booted up my laptop, knowing that conversations with Tonya could go on forever.

"Hello?" Tonya answered curtly. Guess all was not forgiven.

"Hey. What's up?" I rolled my eyes at my lameness. The silence on the other end told me pretending nothing had happened wasn't going to work. "Look, I'm sorry. I shouldn't have called you a liar. I didn't mean it."

"Then why would you even say it?"

The defensiveness was still there, and even though the voice in my head hadn't surfaced since our fight, I didn't doubt the truth of it. Her reaction had proven I was right, but I wasn't going to call her out on it again. Better just to shift the focus. Poor Nathan was about to become my fall guy.

"I didn't want to talk about Nathan anymore. Especially in front of Bianca and Owen. So, I just said it. I swear I didn't mean it."

"What's up with that, anyway? I thought you were over him."

The change in topic signaled the end of our fight. That was one of the things I loved most about Tonya; she got over things quickly. The only problem now was I had to 'fess up' to the note.

"I was—am. He was dumping her."

"In a freakin' note? That's as lame as a text. What a prick."

My back straightened, and, as pathetic as it was, I rose to his defense. "Any other girl, yeah, but this was Vivian."

"True. Still, that was pretty low. Man. I can still see her face when you grabbed it. Then in Bio, she looked like she was gonna kill you."

We laughed at the memory.

"So, how was your mom?" I wasn't trying to catch her lying again. Though even as the words left my mouth, I wondered if that was what she'd think.

"Bitch," she said, her voice trembling with humor. "Okay, so I wasn't going to see my mom."

"So? Spill."

"Don't freak or anything, but I've been seeing this guy from San Diego."

She couldn't hold in her giggle.

"What?! How? What?!" I sputtered.

"We met online over the summer, and right before school started, we got together."

"Girl, are you crazy? What if he'd been a perv or something?"

"Whatever. I'm not stupid, Phoebs. I met him at the mall

the first time, and we just talked."

"The first time? You've seen him more than once?"

"We've been dating. He's not a perv. He is so awesome."

I contained my groan. Tonya didn't have the greatest track record with guys, and with her grandmother raising her, she got away with a lot more than I ever would. I pulled up *Google* on my computer. "What's his name?"

"Trevor Sanders, and, oh my god, he is so hot."

She went on about him for another five minutes, and I let my fingers fly across the keyboard, switching search engines, trying to find out anything about the guy. An inactive *Twitter* account and a private *Facebook* page were the only results I could find. Not even an *Instagram* page. But, considering my lack of tech skills, missing something would have been pretty easy.

"We've been seeing each other on the weekends," she said.

"So he's why you've been ditching me lately. I can't believe you didn't tell me."

"Yeah, well, I wanted to be sure about him, you know? I knew you'd flip, which you did, but if you met him, you would so get why I did. He's been driving up here every day over the break." She sighed, and I resisted the urge to gag. I loved romance and all that crap, but not when I was in this kind of funk. The whole thing with Nathan and the note had only made me crabbier.

"What does Gran think about him?"

Gran was the ultimate test. She'd kicked a few of Tonya's monthly flavors to the curb.

"She doesn't know about him yet. I wanted to see if I'd like him first. Now I'm worried that she won't, and you know what she's like," she said.

Yeah. She'd called out every loser Tonya or her mother brought home. Not that it had helped Shondra James from getting involved with a local drug dealer. She was sitting in prison while Gran tried to keep Tonya from suffering a similar fate.

"Besides, I want you to meet him before she does. You're going to Nadine's party, right?" The begging in her voice was obvious.

Nadine was a friend of Chloe's and probably the most likable of them all, other than Bianca, and she always included Lily and me, even though we rarely took her up on it. Of course, she always invited everyone to everything.

"I wasn't planning on it, but if it means I get to meet this guy then yeah, I suppose I'll be there."

"Thank you! Thank you! I'll owe you major."

"I'll just add it to your bill. Hey. Want to go shopping tomorrow?" I asked. "Bianca and I were going to go to Town Square."

"Is Karin going?"

I'd purposely left off mentioning Karin. Tonya couldn't stand her. Mainly because Karin was one of those ultra, annoyingly nice people.

"Yes, but if it's the four of us, you'll hardly notice her."

"What? She's not bringing her lap dog with her?"

"No. Owen isn't coming. And he's not her lap dog."

I had to defend him. Owen was one of those guys that couldn't catch a break—way too laid back and never seeming to notice things going on around him, even though he pretended well. Like how he'd seen everything that happened between Tonya and me, but he hadn't realized until a couple days ago that we'd had a fight.

"He may not be yet, but Karin would love it if he was."

"Yeah, well, he's not coming. So am I picking you up, or not?"

"Yes, but you better keep that thing away from me."

We spent another twenty minutes catching up, and I'd just hung up when there was another knock on my door. Before I could even call out to see who was there, the door swung open and Chloe sauntered in.

"Finally," she said, and flopped on to my bed face first. She lifted her upper body and rested her chin on her hands. "Lily's been cowering in her room the past week, trying to stay as far away from you as possible. I don't know why she bothered. If I was her, I'd have just done it while you were sleeping."

Her words did make me feel a little guilty, but I squashed the feeling before Lily could pick up on it and appear beside Chloe.

"Maybe that's why I like Lily better than you." I swirled my chair around in circles, her angry face flashing by me again and again.

"Now who's the liar? You spend less time with Lily than with me."

"That's because Lily doesn't barge in to my room uninvited, nor does she know where I'm going before I'm actually there."

"Whatev'," she said, rolling her eyes.

"Did you come here for a reason other than to annoy me?" I asked. The spinning chair slowed to a stop, and I lifted my feet to rest them on the corner of the bed, enjoying the utterly annoyed expression crinkling her face.

"Nanna said you haven't 'heard' the voice again," she said.

"Nope. So, either our family members always tell the truth, or it was a fluke."

"Maybe we should test it." She flipped over on to her back, preventing me from seeing her whole face.

"Why do you care if it works or not?" My suspicion was obvious in my tone.

"Because I know you, Phoebs. You'll start obsessing and get all upset. Lily will be moaning about how she just needs to touch you for a second, and then everything will be fine. And, to top it off, you'd start doing stupid things, and I can't block them out."

God. I hated when she was right.

"So just how am I supposed to test this? I can't just ask a person if they're lying to me. Just look at what happened with Tonya."

"You can ask me some questions, and I'll answer. Sometimes I'll tell the truth, and sometimes I'll lie." She tipped her head up so I could see her eyes. "Do it for Lily. You know how upset she gets when you're stressed or unhappy, which, considering your natural personality, is pretty much all the time."

I reached over, grabbed one of the pillows off the floor, and tossed it at her. She swatted it away before it even came near her face.

"You really thought I wouldn't see that one coming?" she asked.

"Fine. Go ahead. Test me." There wasn't any point in fighting it. She already knew I would do it. Otherwise, she wouldn't have wasted her time.

"Okay. Ask me some questions. Ones you don't know the answer to."

I sighed in resignation. "What did you do this morning?"

That was the first in a string of questions I asked, and it proved just as useless as the next twenty. Not once did I hear or feel anything telling me she was lying, no matter how ridiculous her responses got.

"I give up," I said. Dropping my feet to the floor, I braced my elbows on my knees and let my head drop to my hands. I was tired and irritated. The whole thing was pointless.

Chloe huffed, scooting off the bed. "I don't get it."

"Get what?"

"My vision showed you doing it. Using your gift." Her words brought my head popping up in time to see her eyes narrowed slightly as she turned to the door, and I wondered what she was thinking. I stared at her back as she headed in to the hall.

"You're wrong again. Does that bother you?"

She glanced back and smiled. "Not at all."

My stomach cramped. *Liar.*

I kept my mouth shut. Every impulse inside of me throbbed with the desire to scream the word at her departing back, but I didn't. Having Chloe know she'd been right wasn't something I wanted her holding over my head. It was better to savor my knowledge that I'd actually caught her in a lie she didn't want me to know. So, instead, I rose from my chair and swung the door shut, enclosing myself in my sanctuary.

What was it about that lie that had made it get called out? She'd lied about a bunch of stuff over the past half-hour, yet the one thing she didn't want me to know about was the only thing that called to me. I spun in a circle and let myself drop to the bed. Flinging my arms out to the side, I squeezed my eyes closed, and, for once in my life, prayed that I didn't really have this stupid gift. That it was all in my head.

My hand groped along the comforter until I found my iPod. I snagged the headphones and dragged it to me, then flicked my finger across the touch screen, finding a song that fit my miserable mood. After putting in the earbuds, I turned the volume up, trying to drown out the stupid voice still echoing through my head.

* * *

I woke the next morning to the sound of little pitter-pattering feet in the hall, followed by giggles as my door slowly creaked open. I yanked the comforter over my head, hoping if I stayed still, the little brats would think I was gone.

"Fee-Fee? Fee-Fee? Are you awake?" Tiny hands smacked down on my face. I grimaced, holding in my groan of pain as one made contact with my nose.

"Emma, I don't fink she's here."

"But, Ella, her feet are still here."

Icy fingers circled my toes, and my feet involuntarily jerked away, exposing my legs. No use trying to hide now. At three years old, my cousins, Ella and Emma, might have believed I left my feet in bed, but they'd never believe I left my legs, too.

"Boo!" I flung the blanket off my head and sat up.

Matching green eyes widened into giant orbs before the two of them turned tail and ran. The pounding going up the stairs reassured me of some privacy to get up—for a little while.

I climbed out of my warm bed and made a mad dash for the shower just as those little feet started their way back down the stairs. Locking the door behind me, I relished an extra minute of darkness, letting my body believe I might be going back to bed, before flicking on the lights. I needed to get ready to go shopping, and those two rug rats would latch on to my legs and make it impossible.

In a town as small as Beachgrove, going to Town Center was about as exciting as going to school. Yet, it was the only place to go, and everyone I knew would be there. I contemplated talking Tonya in to driving to San Diego, but nixed the idea. Since my job at the local golf course ended a couple months back, I was running short on gas money, and, if I wanted to buy a new outfit, I'd need the extra cash. Besides, Bianca would kill me if I ditched her with Karin.

Two hours and a game of hide-and-seek later, I pulled up to Tonya's house. She rushed the car before I even shifted to park and swung open the door. She slid in and then slammed it shut.

"Girl, what took you so long?" she asked.

"The demon twins. They attacked me when I got out of the shower and tied me up until I played hide-and-seek."

She gave me a skeptical look.

"Okay, so I volunteered, but in my defense, you know how cute they are."

"How much longer is your family staying for?"

"I think they're leaving tomorrow or the day after. It'll be nice to have things back to normal," I said. That Nanna had already left had been my one constant wish for the past week.

"I'm so tired of normal. I've been bored out of my mind. Seeing Trevor has been the only thing keeping me sane."

"You could have come over," I said. She gave me a nasty look. "Right. Sorry."

"That's okay. You can buy me a venti hot chocolate to make up for being so mean to me."

"Hey. You admitted you lied."

"Well ... damn."

We laughed, and it felt good to have things right between us again. Something that, despite our call last night, I hadn't been too sure of.

"Are we picking up Bianca and the thing?" she asked.

"No. They're meeting us there."

I stepped on the gas and made a u-turn for the center of town, driving slowly to take in the massive houses. Tonya lived in the damn-you're-rich area of town, and every time I drove through, I liked to pretend I actually lived there. Maybe the one on the corner with the huge palm trees perfectly arranged in the yard.

My dad was a lawyer and made decent money, but I wasn't holding out hope that we'd be moving here. It always seemed strange to think that Tonya lived in a mansion while her mom served time for selling drugs and theft, but her grandpa had been a successful artist until he'd died, and her gran had been a university professor.

We turned out of her neighborhood, and the home sizes shrunk. Five minutes later, we were surrounded by the masses. I found a parking spot and zipped in, cutting off another car that had its blinker flashing. I gave a careless wave and parked.

Getting out of the car, I caught a glimpse of the car I'd stolen my spot from parking a row over. The driver's side door opened, and a tall guy stepped out. He turned around to glare at me, and I nearly choked on my own spit. Nathan.

Why the hell did I have such crappy luck with him?

"You okay?" Tonya asked, coming around to my side of the car.

"What? Yeah. Why?" I was barely able to pull my eyes away from Nathan to look at Tonya.

"You look totally spaced out."

"No. I'm fine. Let's go." Before she could see Nathan, I grabbed her hand and dragged her in the opposite direction. Not because it had been him. No. I always avoided the people

I cut in front of.

Somehow, in the two weeks since our fight, I'd forgotten how much fun shopping with Tonya was. Bianca and Karin met us outside *The Gap*. We went in, furiously trying on anything that looked even remotely decent before heading to the next place. By lunch, we were exhausted.

"Let's grab something to eat," I suggested as we left what seemed like the hundredth shop we'd been in.

"Definitely! I'm starving," Karin said.

Tonya opened her mouth, to make some snide comment I'm sure, and I managed to stomp on her foot just in time. Karin was stick-thin, despite constantly stuffing her face. Any complaints she made about eating and weight pretty much pissed off every female around her. Especially Tonya, who was a bit on the bootylicious side even if she did love her curves.

"Let's dump our bags in the car first," Bianca said to Karin, then turned to us. "We'll meet you guys at the food court."

The two of them took off for Karin's car while Tonya and I followed the scent of food to the food court. Tonya and I had yet to buy anything, but Bianca had nearly bought out the last three shops we'd gone in to. With my tighter budget, I wasn't so willing to jump on the first thing I found.

"Oh! Wait a minute. I want to look in here." She started toward the shoe store.

"I'll meet you by the tables," I said, knowing that if I went in with her, I'd leave with another pair of shoes I didn't need and couldn't afford. She threw her hand up behind her, and I took it for an agreement.

The beautiful weather had drawn nearly everyone in town outside to the courtyard, and the tables were crowded. I searched for an empty spot, deliberately passing over that table holding Chloe and her friends. They had room, but spending quality time with her after last night held no appeal. Then again, it never appealed to me.

Wandering through the maze of tables, I spotted an elderly couple rising, and I rushed forward, reaching for a chair just as someone slid in on the opposite side. Nathan.

Great. My eyes flew up to stare at the sky in disbelief. What the hell?

"Are you stalking me or something?" I asked, unwilling to believe these meetings were just coincidence, and not wanting him to think I was the one doing the following.

"I could ask you the same thing. You're the one with an interest in my love life."

I tried to think of a witty comeback. "Whatever. This is my table." Oh. I could be so brilliant sometimes.

"Since I'm the one sitting, it looks like it's mine," he said, a little smirk tipping up his lips.

It was a side of him I rarely saw. He always seemed so passive. Like I could push him around if I really wanted. He let Vivian do just that for almost a year.

I sat, refusing to give up my table. The staring contest started. He had gorgeous eyes; a deep gray, like rolling rain clouds drifting in from over the ocean. And they twinkled like there was some private joke going on that only he knew and he was laughing inside. Laughing at me.

"Look, Phoebe. I don't know what your problem is with me." He paused and then blushed. "Okay. Maybe I do. But, that was a year ago. Do you want me to apologize or something?"

"No."

I did, but what would be the point?

"So..."

An awkward pause slid between us.

"I shouldn't have taken the note," I admitted reluctantly.

He shrugged. "Doesn't matter. I shouldn't have written it, but she was bugging the hell out of me."

"So you didn't break up with her?" Hopefully, I didn't sound as disappointed as I felt.

"I did, just not in a note."

"Wait. Are you admitting I was right?"

God. How could my heart be beating so fast?

"That I needed to man up? Yeah, guess I am, but that was a low blow. God. You sounded just like my dad whenever I try to get out of doing anything." He shook his head with a lopsided smile. "You going to Nadine's party tomorrow?"

"Yeah. You?"

He nodded, and then glanced behind me before standing.

"I thought you were ready to fight for your table?" I said, wanting him to stay.

"I've seen you play dirty, and I'm not sure I wanna do that in public with you. Now, privately..."

I couldn't help the stupid grin that caused my cheeks to strain. He was definitely flirting. There was no way he wasn't. He turned to leave, but I needed to make sure; to know if what he'd said about me being right was really the truth.

"Was I right about the rest? Was it because of...?"

"You? Us?" His brows arched, and it was my turn to blush. "No. It had nothing to do with you."

Liar. I clutched at my stomach, trying to control the sudden cramps. I didn't call him on it. That was one lie I could happily live with knowing.

I stared after him as he walked away, my entire body buzzing with something unnamable.

"Hello?" A hand flashed in front of my face.

"Hey," I said. My eyes focused on Tonya. She sat next to me just as Bianca and Karin arrived at the table.

"Girl, you got it bad." Tonya picked up a fry from her plate and pointed it at me. "You know Vivian will kill you, right?"

"Nothing happened, and nothing will. Remember? He had his chance, and he chose her."

"Phoebe Matlin, do we look that dumb? You were practically drooling all over him."

"I was not! Okay. So maybe a little. But you have to admit, he's looking fine."

She rolled her eyes and stuck the fry in her mouth.

"He's okay, I guess," Karin said, and took a sip from her soda. "I prefer a leaner body. Someone who looks more intelligent than beefcake."

"Owen," Bianca coughed in to her hand. Tonya and I laughed at Karin's blush.

"You have to admit that Nathan is getting a bit big," she said in her defense.

"Yeah. Muscular big. Strong, powerful, hot." Bianca wiggled her eyebrows and sighed. "Too bad he's got a thing for Phoebe. Otherwise, I'd be jumping him every chance I got."

"He doesn't have a thing for me." That came out sounding way too hopeful.

"Sure, Phoebs. You keep telling yourself that, and maybe Vivian won't kill you," Tonya said.

"Well, I expect you guys to have my back if she comes after me." I glanced between their faces.

"Catfights are beneath me," Karin said, shaking her head.

Bianca was grinning away. "My parents would officially disown me if I got caught fighting. Unless, of course, it was some ancient art form that would honor my ancestors."

"Uh. Yu know I don't fight anymore. Not after Melanie tore my weave out." Tonya rubbed her scalp at the painful memory from freshman year.

I just shook my head. Melanie was an entirely different crazy than Vivian, although Tonya always said you can't judge a girl by her talk. And Tonya had been involved in four girl fights, which was exactly four more than me.

"I'm going to grab some food." I stood and headed for the Chinese food counter.

"Watch your back," Tonya called after me, with Bianca and Karin laughing along with her. "I'm pretty sure I saw Viv around here earlier."

"Whatever," I yelled back.

* * *

Three hours later, Tonya and I waved bye to Karin and Bianca and dragged ourselves back to the car. I'd managed to find something for the party, so the sore feet had been worth it. We put our bags in the trunk and got in the car. I'd already started it when a piece of paper under the driver's side wiper caught my eye.

I rolled down my window, and, reaching through, I grabbed for it three times before managing to snag it. Thinking it was an ad, I tossed it on Tonya's lap and started pulling out of the parking space.

"You were right," Tonya said.

"About what?"

"I don't know. That's what the paper says." She held the paper up, looking to see if she'd missed anything else. I slammed on the brakes and snatched the paper from her.

It was Nathan's handwriting. I wanted to do a happy dance, but Tonya was already giving me a strange look, and I wasn't ready for a lecture on going boy crazy from her. Especially since I was usually the one giving them to her.

I was right. The stupid grin stretched across my face lasted the entire way home and maybe a bit longer.

CHAPTER 4

NORMALLY, NEW YEAR'S EVE wasn't that big of a deal for me. I didn't see any point in it other than a good excuse for a party. This time, though, I was still riding the high from Nathan's note, and I had at least the hope of seeing him without Vivian.

"Fee-Fee, why you dwessed pwetty?" Ella asked from where she lay on my bed. Emma sat next to her, and both of them watched wide-eyed as I got ready. Why they didn't hover around Chloe or Lily was unexplainable, considering how mean I could be to them. Then again, they were holy terrors in training, so maybe they felt more comfortable with one of their own.

"I'm going out to a party."

I swept the mascara across my lashes, determined not to smudge them.

"On a date?" Emma asked.

"No. Just with a friend."

Eyes blinking, I took in my reflection, satisfied with my latest attempt.

"Cwoe and Wiwy haf dates." Ella looked at me with the pity only a three-year old could give.

"Gee. Thanks for pointing that out," I said, then dove on to the bed to tickle them. I might have taken offense if they actually knew what a date was.

My cell beeped, and I abandoned the girls to check it. I

flipped it open and saw Tonya's name as sender.

Itz 10. Where r u? U left yet?

I spent a couple moments struggling to reply. Finally getting the word **now** to fill the screen, I quickly pressed send.

"Do you hafta go?" Emma tipped her head to the side, her blonde Shirley Temple curls falling across her face.

"Yes, and isn't it past your bed time?" I lifted first one then the other girl to the floor and guided them out of my room.

"No. We stayin' up 'till minnite," Ella said, a sneaky grin on her face.

"It's midnight, you little stinker, and I bet Nanna's already looking for you."

The girls stalled on the steps until I started tickling them again. Then they shrieked as they ran the rest of the way up to where Nanna stood at the door to the basement.

"I should have guessed they'd be down there with you," she said, grasping their hands before they could take off on her. "You look nice, dear. Have a good night."

I watched her walk down the hall with the girls until she turned the corner. Things had been more strained than usual between us since our argument, and, as much as I loved her, it was nice to have a break from her nagging.

Earlier that morning, Owen had begged a ride for tonight since he had yet to get his license. He lived halfway between my house and Nadine's, so it hadn't been a big deal, although Karin probably would have spazzed. Bianca had already spilled that Karin had called him about ten times the past few days to offer a ride, and he kept turning her down.

He was sitting on the front steps, his house dark behind him, when I pulled in to his driveway. Despite being friends for three years, I'd never been inside his place or met his parents. When he came to my sixteenth birthday party, Nanna had met him, and afterward, told me to let go of any questions I had about his family. That it wasn't worth the loss of friendship.

Her words had driven me crazy for weeks. I wanted to know what she'd seen and why I shouldn't ask him. Then I just kind of lost interest. Or, more accurately, Nathan arrived and I got a bit distracted. Besides, Owen didn't look like a sexy, mysterious, stranger that would be hiding juicy secrets. He was more of a spaced, tree hugger.

"Hey," he said, climbing in. His curly black hair was pulled back in a short ponytail that always made me think he should be playing soccer for some European team. "Thanks again for the ride. My dad had to work and couldn't drop me off. I thought I was going to be stranded at home."

"You could have always asked Karin." I grinned as I reversed back on to the road.

"That's not funny."

"Oh, come on. You need to loosen up a bit." I nudged him with my elbow. He was so weird sometimes. He went from spacey to deadly serious to hilarious all in the space of minutes sometimes.

"I just don't feel comfortable with it being a joke. Karin's my friend. That's all."

"Have you told her that? Because she spends a lot of time crushing on you."

"I told her, which is why it's not funny anymore." He shot me a look. "That means no more encouraging her. Please."

"You know, the best way to deter her would be to get yourself a girlfriend." I ignored his groan of disgust. "We know there's a girl you like. Who is she? Obviously, it's not Karin." I started running through mental pictures of every girl I knew at school. "Is it that blonde who sits behind you in History? I saw you talking to her the other day."

"No! No. Can you please just drive and leave my life to me?" His normally olive complexion was just a hint darker, and he squirmed in his seat.

Nanna's words about not questioning him came back, and I grit my teeth to hold in the next barrage of questions. I figured I could live without knowing everything about Owen, even if it was juicy gossip Tonya would kill for.

"Fine. Spoilsport. What did you do for Christmas?"

"Nothing much." He gave a one-shoulder shrug, and when he smiled, I knew I'd managed to stop before putting my foot in my mouth. "Worked a bit at the hotel and hung out at the library."

"Sounds exciting. Read anything interesting?" The library was the last place I was interested in going.

"Just the entire collection of *The Walking Dead*." His smile grew to a full-blown grin.

"Oh my God! You're joking, right?" My entire body jerked upright. "I've been saving my money to buy it online. How did I not know they had that?"

"Maybe if you'd ever actually been to the library, you'd have seen it."

"Can I borrow it?"

"It's at the library, Phoebe. I would hope you understand the basic workings of the place even if you've never been inside."

"Shut up," I said, rolling my eyes and turning the radio up to drown out any more possible digs.

By the time we got to Nadine's place, cars already lined the street. I pulled around to the next block and parked under a street light. The first few houses were dark, so I figured I'd gotten lucky that the owners had gone out.

Owen's cell rang as we climbed out of the car, and he glanced at the caller ID. "It's my dad. I better take it."

"Want me to wait?"

I shifted from one foot to the other, hoping he'd say no. I wanted to see Nathan, even though I wasn't sure what I planned to say, or, more importantly, what I wanted him to say to me. That he was dying of love for me and had made the biggest mistake of his life by dating Vivian would be a start.

"Nah. Go ahead." Owen waved me on and answered his call.

Walking down the street, I glanced nervously behind me. It was silly really; being afraid of the dark. Owen was somewhere back there in the darkness. Besides, we lived in a small suburb of San Diego. Not downtown LA. Of course, that hadn't stopped my dad from doing the best possible job of instilling a fear of dark streets in to my heart with tales of murder, rape, and robbery.

Seeing no one else around, I wrapped my arms around myself and walked faster, wishing I hadn't been too vain to bring a coat. Despite the warm days we'd been having, the evenings still cooled down considerably, and goose bumps covered my exposed arms. I rounded the corner, and the thumping sound of music and people reached me. Even before reaching the door, I could see the windows vibrating in sync with the boom of the bass. I entered the house, and a wave of human heat bombarded me.

Winding my way through the crowd, I searched for someone I'd actually want to talk to. It wasn't that I didn't like the other kids at school, but I just figured why waste time talking to them? Because we obviously had nothing in common. Otherwise, we'd be friends. I guessed they didn't take offense, because most of them never tried to talk to me either. My little group of friends was enough. Any more than the three of them, four if I counted Karin, and I'd be too distracted. Nathan, of course, would be a totally necessary exception to that. Mainly because he already was a distraction.

I spotted Nathan leaning against the banister, talking to his best friend, Andrew. Our eyes met as I passed by and winked at him, just to see the color flood his cheeks. He was almost too easy to embarrass. Andrew gave him a knowing nudge, and Nathan broke eye contact. The temptation to stop and talk was there, but I resisted. Leaving him behind, a smile stretched across my face.

Tonya sidled up to me. She wore a short black skirt and a sparkly blue tank top, making me feel a bit underdressed in my skinny jeans and retro tee shirt, but I was probably a lot more comfortable.

"What are you so happy about?" she asked me.

"Nothing."

"Weren't you driving Owen?" She glanced behind me in search for him.

"Yeah. He got a call when we arrived, so I left him back at the car." I grabbed a pretzel stick from a bowl on a nearby table and started to suck all the salt off it.

"I almost wish Karin was here to see you come with him. She would totally flip; then she'd be all over him."

"Well, don't tease him about it. I tried that earlier, and he wasn't impressed."

"You mean he was actually awake to hear what you said? That boy is so freakin' strange."

"Sometimes I think he just chooses what he's aware of," I

said, trying to defend him, even if it was a feeble attempt.

"My point exactly. Freakin' strange. He's just lucky that he's pretty to look at, or I'd kick him out of our little circle."

"We have a circle? And Owen's pretty to look at?" I tried to hold back my laugh, and, instead, it came out as a strangled snort.

"I just made our little circle," she said, flipping her hair over her shoulder before she joined me in laughing. "And, yes. Owen's hot. If you weren't completely obsessed with Nathan, you might actually notice these things."

Owen was hot? I looked back in to the living room, trying to spot him, finally finding him still near the entrance. He was taller than most of the people, and, yeah, I could see how someone would be attracted. He had that lean body type that maybe hid some muscles underneath. Hot, but not my type. Now, Nathan, I could see his muscles. I'd been fantasizing all day about touching those muscles. Waves of shivers ran through me, and I forced him from my mind.

"Sooo? Where's this Trevor?" I asked, tired of talking about Owen. He wasn't really an interesting topic.

"Getting us drinks," she said, motioning to the kitchen. "God, Phoebs. I think I'm in love."

I resisted the urge to roll my eyes. "He's that wonderful, huh?"

"You have no clue. He's amazing! There he is," she gushed, pointing out a tall guy with a deep brown complexion and short dreads. I could see why she'd fallen for him. Three letters were all that was needed to describe him. H-O-T.

"He's cute," I said when she looked at me with her eyebrows raised.

Grabbing my arm, she tugged me through the room

toward him, and once we reached him, she dropped my arm in order to twine her fingers through his. When he turned his attention to her, she practically glowed. She was way more in to him than any of the other guys she'd dated.

"Trevor, this is my best friend, Phoebe."

"Hi," I said, and gave a weird hand wave.

"Hey," he said, bobbing his head while he curved an arm around Tonya's shoulders.

There was an awkward lull as we took each other in, maybe in some kind of attempt to see what Tonya saw in the other.

"So, you live in San Diego?" I asked when I couldn't stand it anymore.

"Yeah." Head bobbed again.

Great. A real conversationalist. Tonya stared up at him with adoration, and I had to suppress a chuckle. She obviously didn't care about his ability to carry on a conversation. Not that I blamed her. He was gorgeous. Dark creamy skin, piercing brown eyes, broad shoulders. Hell. I could appreciate a gorgeous guy even if there wasn't a brain attached.

"Trevor's going to UCSD next fall," Tonya said like a proud mama.

"Really? What's your major gonna be?" I asked.

"Law."

My stomach cramped, and I waited for the whisper, but nothing came, or at least nothing I could hear over the music. Maybe it was just my period.

"You okay, Phoebs?" Tonya ducked out from under Trevor's arm and stepped closer to me.

"Yeah. Just not feeling well all of a sudden. I'll be alright in a minute."

"Why don't we find a spot to sit?" She started to guide me to the kitchen, but Trevor grasped her arm.

"She'll be fine. Let's dance." He didn't look at me. Just gazed hard at Tonya.

"But—" She glanced back and forth between us.

"I came here to be with you. I didn't drive almost an hour to sit in a kitchen." Trevor dropped Tonya's arm then took a step closer. "If you want to spend the night with your friend, I can find someone else to be with."

Wow. I didn't even know what to say. Apparently, Tonya didn't either, because we both just stared at him.

"I'm gonna get another drink." He headed to a table at the back of the room where a beer keg had been set up.

"What the hell's his problem?" I asked, rubbing a hand across my stomach as the cramps eased.

Tonya glared at me. "Nothing's his problem. He's disappointed that he can't be alone with me. That's what boyfriends want."

"Whatever," I said. "I'm gonna go sit."

I wasn't expecting her to follow me, but it still kind of hurt that she left me pretty eagerly to join Trevor on the sofa where he was working on a beer. Instead of staying in the kitchen, I wandered through and went out the back door. The yard was dark except for where the indoor lights filtered through the windows, and the moon glinted off the dark water of the swimming pool. I sat on one of the pool lounge chairs and rubbed my hands along my arms.

What did the cramps mean? Was it a warning? It could have been just a false alarm. It wasn't like before when the whisper followed the cramps.

"You have a serious problem, you know." Nathan's voice came from right beside my ear. I swirled around to see him crouched beside me, thoughts of my gift completely vanishing as I met his stormy eyes.

"A problem?"

Did my voice just quiver? I swear he got hotter each day.

"Yeah. You're a terrible flirt."

He smiled, and I couldn't help myself. I smiled back and leaned in closer to him, inhaling deeply. He smelled amazing, like the ocean, or at least what the ocean should smell like. Fresh and cool, with a breeze that sent tingles up your arms. I didn't know what cologne it was, but, damn, it was worth whatever he paid for it.

"Am I really that bad at it?" I asked.

He straightened up and came around to sit in the chair beside mine.

"Oh. I wouldn't say you're bad at it. I'd just say you're bad."

Heat filled my cheeks, yet he looked entirely unfazed.

"How do you do that?" I asked.

"What?"

"Anytime someone else is around, you blush like a little girl, but the second we're alone, you have no shame."

He laughed. "I guess it's the same way you have no shame in public, but the second we're alone, you blush like a little girl."

I pursed my lips in a failed attempt to stop a smile from forming.

He raised a knee to rest his arm on. "So, why are you out here? Normally, you're joined at the hip to Tonya or Bianca."

I shrugged a shoulder. "Bianca isn't here, and Tonya's got a new boyfriend and, apparently, he doesn't want to share her."

"Ah. So you're sulking."

"I am not sulking. I wasn't feeling well, so I came out for some fresh air."

He leaned his head back, looking up at the sky. He had one of those strong profiles that should only belong in marble. A year ago, he'd been a bit on the scrawny side, but, now, well, I was pretty sure he hid a six-pack under his shirt.

His lips curled up; he knew I was staring. Even knowing that he was aware of my gaze, I didn't take my eyes off him. When he was surrounded by his friends, there always seemed to be a part of him hiding, yet there, alone with me, he was relaxed, like he was the real Nathan.

"Enjoying the view?" Chloe's voice came from behind us.

"Yes, and you're interrupting," I snapped, and then swatted at Nathan when he gave a laugh. Both of us turned to watch her walk across the patio.

"I need to talk to you. It's important." She raised her eyebrows and motioned her head to the corner of the yard. She crossed her arms, and I knew refusing was pointless. She'd just keep bugging me.

I pushed up out of the chair and followed her to a far corner of the yard. I turned back to see Nathan watching me. I blew him a kiss and gave a small wave. He just shook his head, looking back up at the stars.

"Have you ever considered that Nathan just doesn't take you seriously?" Chloe asked, and slapped my hand down.

"Maybe, but it's a hell of a lot better than him not thinking about me at all." I gave her my full attention. "You said it was important. Is this it?"

"How are you getting home tonight?"

"I'm driving," I said, confusion drawing my eyebrows low.

"Are you taking Tonya?"

"No. She came with her boyfriend, Trevor. Why? What's

this about?" I watched as she shifted her weight back and forth on her feet.

"I saw you in your car, and Tonya was beside you right before it crashed." Her voice trembled, making me wonder how detailed her vision of the accident had been. A strong stomach never had been her strong point.

"Shit. You sure?"

Her head tilted to the side as she raised an eyebrow. "I saw it, Phoebs."

"Yeah, well, you saw a few other things that never happened, didn't you?"

"This isn't a joke. You know how accurate these visions are."

"Again, you're batting zero with me lately." Maybe it was a lame attempt at brushing her off, but if she was right, then there was absolutely nothing I could do about it, anyway, so worrying wasn't worth the effort. We'd both learned that changing her visions wasn't possible.

"So what? Two mistakes out of millions I've had?" Her voice shook.

Obviously, the vision had scared the crap out of her. I just didn't know what to do or say. Maybe she was wrong about this. I wanted to brush it off again, but her pale face gave me pause. Taking a deep breath, I said the only thing I could.

"I promise not to give a ride to Tonya."

"Will you go home now? I'll follow you back." She crossed her arms, rubbing them slightly as if she could brush away the vision she'd had.

"Chloe, I'm not going to leave early." I looked back at Nathan where he sat, pretending not to be watching us.

"Come on, Phoebs. It's not like this thing with you and Nathan ever seems to go anywhere," she said, letting the snarky sister I knew loose.

"That's not what you said a few weeks ago. You told me you had a vision of him asking me out."

Her mouth opened and closed like a fish out of water. She knew if she admitted she'd been wrong then it was possible she was wrong again. She'd always known her visions were the future; I had her wondering if they really were.

"Stop worrying." I gave her a half hug then deserted her. I had better things to do—namely Nathan—than go home with Chloe because of some vision.

Walking across the yard, I went straight back to him while Chloe stomped back inside. I needed to get my thoughts focused and off Chloe's vision. If she was right about her gift, that it was always right, then there was nothing to do. I slid on to my chair and gazed up at the stars, not wanting to talk. Just being near Nathan was enough to get my body humming.

Finally, when my racing thoughts settled, I turned to him. His eyes were closed. For a moment, I thought he was asleep until a devilish smile bore dimples in to his cheeks.

"You're staring again," he said so softly I almost didn't hear it over the music carrying out to us from the house.

"Are you complaining?"

"No. Maybe." He sighed. "I just never know where I stand with you."

"What do you mean?" I sat up, swinging my legs over the side to face him.

"You play hot and cold. One minute, you're practically panting over me and the next, you're insulting me." His eyes glanced off mine before focusing on the stars above us.

I tried to think of something witty to say to make it easy between us again. I didn't want him to know why I teased him. When he'd taken Vivian to that dance and then spent the next year dating her, I'd tried to salvage some dignity.

That day in the art room when I asked him to Homecoming, I had thrown myself at him, kissed him, and he'd rejected me. Because he thought Vivian was better. After that, I figured it was just better to make him think it was all a big joke. That I didn't take it seriously, and he shouldn't either.

"Forget it," he said when my silence continued.

"What do you want me to say?" I snapped. "How about I don't know where I stand with you. When you first moved here, I did everything I could to show I liked you. I kissed you and asked you out, and what did you do? You started dating Vivian. Vivian. That pretty much said it all. Vivian and I are about as different as a dog and a … an elephant." I stood up, too angry to care that he could probably see up my nose. "What did you want me to do? Pine over you? Pout and cry every time I saw you kiss her or hold her hand. Excuse me for wanting to puke instead. Vivian. I mean, the least you could have done was have some good taste."

He rose from the chair to stand toe to toe with me. I crossed my arms over my chest.

"There's nothing wrong with Vivian."

"Really? Then why break up with her? I'm surprised you had the balls to do it. You've spent the last year letting her tell you what to do. She probably even told you when to kiss her."

"Gee. Who else does that remind me of?" He looked pointedly at me.

"Yeah, well, that's not a mistake I'll make again." I suddenly regretted starting this whole argument.

"Well, maybe that's why I broke up with her, and maybe it's why I never bothered to go out with you."

"What's that supposed to mean?"

Hurt was pulsing through my chest. Why the hell did I even like this guy? He obviously didn't like me.

"It means that I don't like being chased around, and maybe if you hadn't come on so strong last year, I would have asked you to the dance myself."

My mind had already been racing to find some attack response, but his words stopped my mouth from forming it.

"You push and push, and then when I give the slightest push back, you take off or make some flippant comment. I just don't know when you're being serious." He threw Chloe's words at me. God. I hated it when Chloe was right. Why didn't she just tell me that was what she'd seen?

My shoulders sagged, and my eyes dropped to focus on where the tips of our shoes met. It wasn't Chloe's fault. It was my own. I'd acted like a little girl with her first crush and did what I normally do. I bit my nose off to spite my face.

Nathan's hand wrapped around one of my arms, then slid his fingers down to wrap around mine.

"Do you think we could start over? Pretend I'm the new guy again? Only this time, maybe you could leave the chasing to me?" His eyes widened in a cute attempt at puppy dog eyes.

My heart was thudding, and it was difficult to draw in a deep breath. Then my nose started to tingle. What the hell?! No way would I cry 'cause Nathan wanted to chase me. If I'd seen this in a movie, I'd have fast-forwarded because I was embarrassed for the actors forced to repeat the ridiculous lines. Thankfully, my natural instincts kicked back in.

"Does that mean I can't flirt? I'd miss that." I looked up at him, for once, loving that I was tall. It made it easier to see the small blue flecks mingled with the gray in his eyes.

"I think I could handle a bit of flirting. Just maybe not in front of the guys." His fingers danced across my palm before trailing up my arm.

"But that's the best part," I teased.

"Is it?"

He cupped the back of my head and leaned toward me.

"Hey. It's not midnight yet!" a voice called out from the doorway, breaking us apart.

The voice was followed almost instantly by calls of "Fight! Fight!" from inside the house.

CHAPTER 5

NATHAN AND I SPRINTED inside. As much as I hated fights and sickened at the sound of fists pounding on flesh, the instinct to see who was fighting overrode the threat of puking. Everyone had crowded in to the living room to the point where Nathan and I were trapped in the kitchen doorway. No way could we see anything.

"Who's fighting?" I yelled at some guy next to me, hoping he could hear over the music.

He shrugged his shoulders. "Dylan and some guy I don't know."

"What happened?" I asked. Again, he shrugged then moved away from me, trying to get a better view.

"It's Dylan," I said, turning to Nathan.

"Shit."

Dylan was one of Nathan's best friends, and Lily's boyfriend. Nathan guided me along the wall toward the dining room table then pulled out two chairs with pale suede seat covers. Climbing on top, we stood heads above the swarm of spectators.

One punch was enough for me. I'd seen the fighters. Dylan and Trevor were swinging and grappling in the center of the room. Tonya stood at one end of the circle, encasing them, tears streaming down her face. Lily was nowhere to be seen.

I jumped down from my vantage point and started shoving my way through, Nathan following right behind me.

The closer I got to them, the louder things became. Amid the roars of "Fight! Fight!", poor Nadine screamed at them to stop. Her parents didn't mind the occasional party, but destroying their home would mean the end of the school's party house.

I reached Tonya's side just as Nathan burst in to the circle and stepped between the two guys. Both of them kept jabbing at each other until a couple more guys helped break it up, grabbing arms and dragging them in opposite directions. The end of the fight sent a mass of people to the beer kegs.

"What happened?" I asked Tonya, wrapping an arm around her.

"I don't know. Trevor and Dylan were talking, so I went to get a drink. When I got back, they were arguing about something and then they were hitting each other." Tonya pulled away from me and ran to Trevor, where he'd wrestled himself free from the guy holding him back. I started to follow her when Lily entered the room. She was deathly pale and went straight for Dylan.

I couldn't let her heal him here in front of everyone. I snagged her arm as she passed me, ignoring her struggles to get to her boyfriend.

"Lils, not here," I whispered, taking in her pursed lips and glistening eyes. "Wait outside. We'll bring Dylan out." I gave her a gentle push toward the door then went over to where Dylan and Nathan stood talking. Or, at least, Nathan was talking. Dylan was sulking in a chair, cradling a bloody hand to his chest.

"Dylan, Lily's outside waiting for you."

"Great. Even she doesn't want to be seen with a loser."

Above Dylan's head, Nathan rolled his eyes and made a drinking motion with his hand.

"Get your ass up, or I'll drag you out there. Then everyone'll be talking about how not only did Trevor beat the shit out of you, but I did, too." I spun on my heel and left.

The cool air did little to dampen my anger. Lily sat huddled on the steps, head resting on her raised knees. I smoothed a hand over her red curls and down her back. Dylan was being such an idiot, and, because of him, Lily was hurting. I wanted to smack him upside the head, but that would only make it worse for Lily.

"We should go to the hospital, man," Nathan said to Dylan as they eventually made their way outside.

"I'm alright," Dylan snapped, shrugging off Nathan's hand from his shoulder. "Lily, let's go."

He pulled his keys from his pocket and took off down the street to his car. Lily watched him, unmoving. When he realized she wasn't coming, he stopped to look at her.

"Let's go," he said, again.

There was no way Lily would get in his car with him behind the wheel drunk, but I also knew she didn't want to upset him.

"Forget it, bro." Nathan walked up to Dylan and grabbed the keys from him before Dylan even realized his intent. "You're not driving."

"God. You're just like your dad."

"Yeah, well, when it's my dad who would be putting your ass in jail for drunk driving, that's a good thing." Nathan shoved the keys in his pocket and came back to where Lily and I stood, waiting for Dylan to react.

"So, who's driving?" Nathan asked, giving me a sheepish smile.

"You?" I suggested.

He grimaced. "Yeah. I don't think so. Not only would my

dad kill me for driving after having a few drinks, he'd kill me if he even knew I'd been drinking. I'm crashing at Dylan's tonight."

I was so tempted to give him some smart remark, but Lily clutched at my hand as Dylan approached. I looked down at her, wishing I knew why she was so apprehensive about healing Dylan. Her internal struggle caused her body to practically vibrate. Odd, since Lily was usually a bit over-eager to use her gift. She gradually released my hand and went over to Dylan, but even then, I noticed she didn't touch him.

"Guess it's me then. I'm parked around the block," I said, motioning with my hand. "I'll catch up with you guys. I need to talk to Tonya for a minute, and let Owen know I'm leaving."

"Owen?" Nathan raised his eyebrows at me.

"Yeah. I picked him up on the way here, but I don't know if he has a ride home."

"Want me to wait?" he asked.

"Nah. I'll just be a minute."

I watched the three of them head off down the street then turned back to the house. As much as I wanted to make sure Lily was okay, I couldn't just ditch Tonya or Owen.

Everyone inside seemed to have already forgotten the brawl and were back to full party mode. Even Tonya and Trevor had moved past it, and were grinding each other in beat to the music. Squeezing between clusters of people, I wound my way over to them.

"I'm taking off," I yelled, hoping to be heard over the music. She stopped moving, letting go of Trevor to face me.

"What? Why?"

I stared at her in shocked realization. She really was

obsessing over this guy. He'd pretty much just humiliated my sister's boyfriend by beating the crap out of him, probably scaring the crap out of Lily, and she wondered why I was leaving? Maybe I'd have stayed if it had been one of Chloe's flavor of the month boyfriends, but this was Lils.

"How am I supposed to get home?" Anger bit her words short. "You were supposed to drive me home."

I cocked an eyebrow. "Since when?"

She glanced at Trevor, then back to me. "You know Gran can't see Trevor drop me off, and you never drink, so I figured..."

"Yeah, well, maybe you should have stopped your new boyfriend from beating up Dylan. Now I have to drive him and Lily home."

"Why can't she just drive his car?" she asked.

Trevor moved in closer and settled an arm around her shoulder, pulling her to his side. She gave him a smile so sweet I wanted to puke. Just wait till the honeymoon phase was over. Then she'd be back to her bitchy self.

"I'm leaving. If you want a ride, then let's go. Otherwise, I'll call you tomorrow."

"Fine," she snapped. "Let's go."

"We ain't ready to go," Trevor said, finally opening his mouth. I rolled my eyes, groaning in frustration. "We'll get a cab."

"Bye," I said, and turned away, ignoring Tonya's call of my name. I wasn't going to spend my night listening to them argue. Owen stood over by the kitchen, talking to Nadine and a couple of guys from our biology class last semester.

"Hey," I said when I reached him. "I've got to take Lily home, and I'm going to drop off Nathan and Dylan, too. I can give you a ride, but we're leaving now."

"That's okay," he said. "I'll catch one with someone."

"You sure?"

"Yeah. Your car is freakin' small, and I don't want to see Lily in action."

"I'll see you Tuesday then. Happy New Year."

Waving bye over my shoulder to Owen, I scanned the living room for Tonya, but she and Trevor had disappeared. I noticed a guy Tonya had dated briefly last year sitting on the couch and nudged him.

"Have you seen Tonya?" I asked.

"She just left with her latest boyfriend," he said, and took a swig of beer.

Left? After making a big stink about me leaving, she was gone before I'd even made it out of the house. I stomped toward the door.

"Phoebe!" Chloe called out, working her way to me. I stepped outside, letting her follow me. "What happened?"

"I'm taking Nathan, Dylan, and Lily home." I wrapped my arms around me, seriously debating if I should just make her follow me all the way to the car.

"What about Tonya?"

"What about her? She and Trevor already bailed."

"But, I saw..."

"Do you realize how often you've been saying that? 'But, I saw!' Maybe you need to talk to Nanna about your visions."

Part of me felt horrible for calling out Chloe on her misguided visions again, but I squished that feeling fast. I started down the street, rubbing my hands along my arms. It was darker than I thought it'd be. Only a few of the streetlamps worked. The rest were turned off to save the town money. Tall bushes lined the sidewalk, so I edged my way to the far side of the pavement, just in case. Dad always said it was better to look stupid than to be caught actually being stupid.

"Boo!" A huge blob jumped out from the bush.

I jerked back, and a scream ripped through my throat, echoing down the street. My body turned instinctively to run in the opposite direction. It took only a moment to recognize the hysterical laughs coming from the blob. Nathan. I swung my arm out, hitting him, and enjoyed seeing him struggle to cover the side of his head.

"You ass! I can't believe you did that!" Another smack. "You scared the crap out of me." Smack.

"Okay. I'm sorry," he said between his continued chuckles and attempts to evade my hand.

"No you're not."

"You're right. I'm not sorry. The look on your face was priceless." His smile was so cute I just deflated. He glanced behind me. "Did you talk to Owen and Tonya?"

"Owen's gonna catch a ride from someone else."

"What about Tonya?"

Anger gnawed at my insides, thinking of how rude Trevor had been, so I decided to keep it simple. "She and Trevor left while I was talking to Owen."

A gentle breeze swept down the street, and a shiver ran through me.

"Here," Nathan said, tugging his hoodie off. He tossed it to me, momentarily blinding me as it flopped over my head before I could yank it off.

I considered throwing it back. No way did I want him to think I was one of those sissy girls. On the other hand, he gave me the shirt off his back. I pulled it over my head, instantly glad I'd taken his offer. The fleece was still warm from his body, and it smelled just like him. Which was completely unfair, because it totally destroyed my anger.

"Thanks," I said. His smile grew. Damn. I was blushing. "Where are Lily and Dylan?"

"They went ahead. I thought you might get scared walking in the dark—you know, with all the boogiemen around."

"Boogiemen, huh? Well, I always knew there was something weird about you." I took a step forward, closing the distance between us.

"Oh. There's definitely something weird about me." He came to me this time, stopping when only an inch or two separated us.

"And what's that?" I whispered.

"That it's taken me a year to get up the nerve to kiss you a second time." His hands wove through my hair. I leaned closer, glad I stood nearly eye-to-eye with him.

"That's not entirely true. I kissed you the first time."

"Do you really want to fight about this?"

"No."

I didn't move. He'd said he wanted to do the chasing, so it was his chance.

I gazed up at him, loving the shadows flickering across his eyes. Why wasn't he kissing me? Was he going to? Was he chickening out? Maybe I should do it. I would do it. I inhaled and let my eyes start to drift closed.

Then he kissed me.

There were fireworks. Really. They exploded through the night sky, illuminating the street in blues and greens, followed by reds and oranges. My eyes finished closing, because as beautiful as the sparkling lights were, nothing was going to stop me from totally enjoying the feel of Nathan's lips on mine.

It was better than I remembered, or maybe he was better,

or maybe a year of waiting had simply faded the memory. His lips were soft and warm and tasted of chocolate. My heart raced, and little shivers ran up my arms. I pressed closer to him, loving the way his hard chest felt against mine. His hands dropped from my face, slid down my ribs, and wrapped around my waist until they came to rest at the base of my spine.

The flirty side of me wanted to reach back and drag his hands lower, but his words from earlier had stuck. I had to let him make the move no matter how frustrating it was to wait. I curled my fingers around the back of his neck and tangled them in his hair. Trying to catch my breath, I drew back, pulling in deep breaths that mingled with his until his lips followed mine. The tip of his tongue swept across the seam of my lips, and I sighed. God. He tasted as good as he smelled. It wasn't fair that I'd missed out on a whole year of this.

Finally, we broke apart, and he rested his forehead against mine, placing a gentle kiss at the corner of my mouth.

"Wow," he said. "Why the hell did I wait so long?"

The words were innocent, but they stung nonetheless. It had been his choice to wait that long. He'd chosen Vivian over this. Over me. I tried brushing it off. Wasn't I getting him now? Wasn't that what was really important? Brushing it off didn't work.

I dropped my hands and stepped back so I wasn't touching him. The feel of him was way too tempting, and I knew there was something I should remember. "Lily." She and Dylan were waiting for us. I abruptly turned and headed for my car. Behind me, I could feel Nathan watching for a moment before he sprinted after me.

"What was that about?" he asked when he caught up to me.

"What?"

I gave him a sideways, confused look while, somehow, managing to avoid any real eye contact. No way would I admit again that I was still hurt by him turning me down. I would just play dumb. But how long could I keep it up for? It didn't seem too hard for Vivian. Then again, I doubted she was playing.

"The taking off thing. What else?"

It was hard to read his face in the darkness, but he sounded angry and more than a little confused. Another illuminating flash of purple in the sky revealed I was right. Not exactly the reaction I was going for. Apparently, dumb wasn't going to work, so flirty was my next best option.

"You wanted to do the chasing, so I'm letting you." I smiled and found that it didn't feel as forced as I expected.

"Don't do this, Phoebe." He grabbed my hand and gently pulled me to a stop. "I don't know what I said to piss you off, but don't start with the games again."

I sighed. "Okay. Then let's just say I don't want to talk about it. Let's go. Lily and Dylan are probably wondering where we are."

When I walked away, he kept his grasp on me. We ended up walking hand in hand. There was something really sweet about that simple action that I'd never considered. I'd dated a few guys over the past year—just because I wanted Nathan, didn't mean I'd been a complete monk, or whatever they called female monks—but never anyone I liked as much as Nathan. Holding hands had always felt awkward, and the touch of sweaty palms just didn't do anything for me. But this was different. This was Nathan, and I couldn't feel anything other than the soft glide of his skin against mine.

Turning the corner was all it took to bring back reality.

Under the streetlight, Dylan leaned against the hood of my car, Lily standing before him, his hand clutched between hers. She was working her magic.

Dylan's face was devoid of pain, relief sagging his shoulders. Lily, though, was beyond pale. Even from three houses down, I could see her shaking, the gray tinge to her complexion.

"Lily!" I cried out, rushing forward, Nathan forgotten as I watched my sister crumple. Dylan tried to hold her up, but the drinks he'd consumed showed in his lack of balance, and she hit the grass lining the roadway.

I reached her side as she struggled to sit up. I sank to my knees and lifted her head, cradling her in my arms. "Lils? Are you okay?"

She cleared her throat, somehow managing to look deathly ill and mortified at the same time. "I'm alright. Just help me up."

Nathan took one of her arms, helping me get her on her feet. She pressed in to the side of the car.

"Hold her up," I told him, and let go of her arm to take my keys from my pocket.

Once the doors were unlocked, Nathan helped her in to the back. Dylan managed to get in on the other side, smiling and giving the occasional drunken giggle, having turned into a happy drunk. I wanted to shove my fist in his face, but then Lily would feel the need to heal him again.

I started the car, and *Taylor Swift*'s voice filled the small space at an ear-splitting volume. Three cringing faces glared at me. I fumbled with the control until it was blessedly silent, making a mental note to avoid that station from now on.

"He's gotta get his hand checked out. It looks pretty bad," Nathan said, gesturing back to Dylan. I nodded, and put the car in drive and pulled out, heading for the hospital.

"Hey. You're going the wrong way," Dylan complained after a few blocks. "I live the other way."

"I'm not going the wrong way, because I'm not taking your stupid ass home," I said. "This is the way to the hospital."

"I don't need to go to the hospital. I'm fine." He waved his hand through the gap between the seats, practically shoving it in my face. I caught a glimpse of his mangled fingers and nearly puked.

"Dude, your hand's broken." Nathan stared at the crooked digits in fascinated horror. He glanced at me and whispered, "He must be in shock."

"Nope. Lils here just fixed me up. Right, babe?"

He tried to wrap an arm around her, but she sat squished up against the door as far from him as possible, her eyes already closed in a deep sleep. I was surprised she'd lasted even that long. Her reactions to healing were erratic. Sometimes, she seemed to be uplifted and energized. Then there were times like this—when her body was almost drained of life. She'd probably sleep straight through till morning. I had no idea how I'd get her inside without Nanna or Dad noticing.

Nathan twisted in his seat to check on her. "You sure she's okay? Maybe she should get checked out, too."

"She's fine. Just dandy," Dylan said with a slur. When he saw Nathan's doubtful look, he laughed. "Don't tell me you don't know."

"Know what?"

My hands tightened on the steering wheel. "Shut up, Dylan."

"Oh. No way." He laughed again. "This is too good. How could you live here for this long and not know about the freaky Matlins?"

"Shut the hell up, or you'll walk to the hospital." I forced the words through clenched teeth. That Nathan didn't know about us was one of the things I liked about him.

"I already told you to take me home." Dylan shot me a dirty look and leaned between the seats so he could talk to Nathan easier. "Ever since kindergarten, they've done weird shit—well, at least Lily and Chloe did. Phoebe's only one of them 'cause she's just plain freaky."

Nathan gave me a smile. He didn't seem to be taking it seriously, but, still, I didn't want Dylan to tell Nathan anything else. Not when I was just getting a shot with him.

"Weird, huh? Like what? Voodoo stuff?" He cocked an eyebrow at Dylan, clearly trying to play along with what I hoped he saw as Dylan's drunken ramblings.

"No, man. Like Chloe can see the future and shit. She told Andrew once that his dog was gonna get hit by a car and POW! Two days later, the dog's dead."

"You'd think he would've put the thing on a leash." Eyes rolling, he obviously didn't believe anything Dylan said.

"Whatever. Now, Lily..." He reached over to stroke her cheek with his unbroken hand. "She's a healer. She can heal people. Like she did with me tonight."

"Yeah. Have you looked at your hand, bro? It's still looking broken."

"But I ain't feeling it. I ain't feeling it." He waved the hand in front of Nathan's face to prove his point. "That's how she works. I'm tellin' ya; a freaky Matlin." Whatever else he was about to say was cut off when I slammed on the breaks, causing him to jerk forward and smack his face on the back of Nathan's seat.

"Get out." The trembling in my hands transferred to my

voice.

"What the hell, Phoebe?" Dylan rubbed the pink spot on his head from where he'd banged it.

"I said get out of my car, ass wipe. My sister may not know what a prick you are, but I do. Get out."

"Come on, Phoebe. I was just joking. You know I love Lily."

I stared at him in the rearview mirror, refusing to respond. Finally, he got the hint, opening the door to climb out and then slamming it shut behind him.

He began his stumbling trek home, flipping me the middle finger from his good hand as he passed by the front end of the car. Anger burned my insides, and I sat there a few minutes, watching him walk away. He'd been a nice guy once, but now I wished Lily could see the dick he'd become. He reached the end of the block and turned the corner, disappearing from view. Maybe I should have taken him home at least. No. He deserved to suffer.

Nathan stared at me, and I was starting to feel like a freak. Pulling the car back on to the roadway, I took a quick glance back at Lily. She was seriously out of it. Whatever she'd done to Dylan had drained her.

"That was awkward," Nathan said in a drawn out voice.

I shrugged, exaggerating my attention to the road as I drove a winding path back out of the neighborhood, hoping he'd drop it. But my luck sucked, because he kept staring at me. Waiting. I sucked at the waiting game.

"He deserves to walk," I said, cracking under the pressure of his curious gaze. "Too bad Lily wasn't awake to hear him. I hate it that she does this to herself for him." I stole another look at her, and was glad to see she'd slept through it.

"What do you mean?"

"Over the past couple months, every time she's healed him, she crashes like this."

"Heals him? You're playing me, right? To see if I fell for his crap?"

He leaned away from me, slightly, but I saw it. Not for the first time, I wished my sisters had kept their mouths shut and hands to themselves. But, no, they'd never seen the problem with helping people out, even if it meant some stupid nickname. I never wanted to be included in it.

"It's not a big deal. Chloe's good at predicting what people will do. And Lily, well, she only makes people feel better." Downplaying it always seemed to work best, and made people a little less freaked out. "You saw Dylan's hand. It's still broken. He just doesn't feel it."

"So why'd he call her a healer?"

He'd relaxed a bit, and wasn't giving me strange looks anymore.

I debated on how honest to be. Having people make assumptions about us or even benefiting from us was one thing, but to actually explain it was entirely different.

"Lily's gift is mainly emotional and sensory. She can stop pain, and sometimes she can heal minor physical problems, like a little cut. But the big stuff she can't do. If you're dying, then you're shit out of luck unless you want to go with a smile on your face."

"So, Lily heals, and Chloe can guess the future, but what about you?"

I shifted in my seat, wishing for some distraction on the roads, but no other vehicles appeared to save me. "I'm supposed to be able to tell when someone is lying."

"Supposed to?"

"Yeah, well, it doesn't seem to work right for me. I've only been able to catch a couple of people, and it didn't work out so well." I flashed a wicked grin his way as we waited for a light to change. "But you really shouldn't try lying to me anymore."

"I haven't lied to you," he said, but his blush called him a liar before any voice in my head did.

"Uh huh. If you say so."

He said something in response, but the light changed and I revved the engine, drowning out his voice. We passed by Nadine's place again, and a few blocks down, I turned the corner, planning to take a short cut through Tonya's neighborhood to the other side of town.

There were flashing emergency vehicles ahead of us. As the lights grew closer, I slowed down, initially for safety, and then because of my uncontrollable urge to rubberneck.

A silver pickup truck was curved around a tree, its entire hood bunched up. Glass sparkled on the black pavement, glinting red and blue with each turn of the emergency lights. I hit the brakes when I saw the figure sitting on the ground near the ambulance.

Tonya.

The streetlight above her shone down, highlighting the blood that matted her dark hair and trailed down her cheek, mingling with tears. I shoved the car in to park and practically leapt out.

"Tonya! What happened? Are you okay?"

"Oh my God, Phoebs. I...I don't know. Everything happened so quick." She trembled violently, and I sank down beside her, wrapping an arm around her shoulders, ignoring the paramedic who squatted beside her, making notes.

"Are you hurt? Was anyone else hurt?" I asked.

"They said I just scraped my forehead, but Trevor hurt his

foot." She lifted a hand to her head, and her fingers grazed over a bandage hidden beneath her curls.

I glanced back at Nathan. He stood watching us, his arms folded on the roof of the car. Lily still slept in the backseat, her head against the window. Even from here, I could see her restless movements. She could feel something wasn't right. I didn't want her to get any worse, but this was Tonya.

"Are you in pain? Lily could..."

"I'm okay now. They said it looks worse than it feels. But Trevor's foot looked pretty bad."

I didn't volunteer Lily for that one. Helping my best friend was one thing. Expecting Lily to heal the guy who'd beaten the crap out of her boyfriend would be too much, even if Dylan was a dick and deserved it.

"I thought you guys were gonna call a cab?"

I tried to keep the accusation from my voice; the judgment that she'd get into a vehicle with a drunk driver.

"Spare me the lecture, Phoebs. Trevor wanted to spend some time with just me, so we left right after we talked to you."

"How could you get in the car with him?" I blurted out, unable to hold it in any longer. "You knew he'd been drinking."

She pulled away from me, crossing her arms over her upraised knees. "He wasn't driving. I was."

Liar.

My stomach clenched, and I fought the urge to vomit. I wanted to call her out. I couldn't believe that she would cover for the guy. Her eyes shifted between me and one of the cops with panic I couldn't ignore. For whatever reason, she was lying. I couldn't betray my best friend. Not after just fixing up our last fight.

"Do you want me to drive you home?" The words choked out of me, burning my throat like acid with the lingering taste of her lie.

She shook her head. "I'm going to go with Trevor to the hospital and wait for his parents to pick him up. I'll call a cab. Hopefully, Gran will be sleeping when I get back."

"You don't think she's going to notice that on your head tomorrow?" I asked, gesturing to the bandage.

"I'll just tell her you dragged me in to some girl fight over Nathan." She cracked a smile, and I tried to do the same, but it was hard with the knowledge that she'd lied to me again.

"Didn't you blame your last fight on me?"

"Phoebe, I've blamed you for all of my fights."

Did she find lying to me as easy as she did with Gran? It wasn't a question I wanted an answer to, so I gave her an awkward pat on the back. I didn't know how to deal with the fact she was lying to me and the police about what had happened. We stood as the paramedics loaded Trevor in to the ambulance.

"I'll call you tomorrow."

Lily was awake by the time I got back in the car. Nathan slid in to the passenger seat, and we shared a glance before putting on our seat belts.

"Who's hurt?" Lily asked, her usual sweet voice filled with dread.

I pulled away from the accident, peeking in to my side mirror to see Tonya joining Trevor in the ambulance.

"Nobody," I said. She snorted, and I sighed with resignation. "Nobody who needs your help. We'll drop off Nathan and then head home, okay?"

She gave a slight nod, staring out the window. I was surprised that she didn't ask about Dylan, and, possibly, it was my wishful thinking, but maybe she was so glad he was gone that she didn't want to ask about him.

"Hey. Aren't you crashing at Dylan's?" I asked Nathan.

"Not now. He's so smashed he'll wake his parents up, and I don't think I want to be around to see that. I'm safer facing my dad than worrying about Dylan's parents calling him at the station. So, what happened back there?" Nathan asked.

"The truck they were in smashed in to a tree."

"Who was driving?" He was starting to sound like his father.

"Tonya said she was."

Nathan raised his brows. "She said she was? Does that mean you don't believe her?"

"I think she's covering for Trevor because he'd been drinking." As soon as I said it, I wanted to pull the words back in to my mouth and swallow them. Why would I tell the police chief's son that my best friend was lying to the cops and her boyfriend should be arrested for DUI?

"Chill, Phoebe. I don't tell my dad everything. You think I would've been at the party if I'd told him there was going to be alcohol?" He gave me a slight smile. "You may just want to head home. Unless you want your dad to start asking questions about what went down tonight."

"What? Why?"

"Lily's asleep again, and I doubt you can carry her all the way to her room."

I resisted the urge to smack him. He had a way of knowing just what to say to nettle me. But he was right. Lily was out of it, and, small as she was, I wouldn't even be able to get her out of the car, let alone to her room. Waking Dad up to help wasn't an option. At least not if the three of us wanted to have any social life for the rest of our lives.

Strange as it was, Dad would have been okay with us drinking, but using our gifts in public? No way. While Nanna and the rest of the family had no problem with using their gifts, Dad was more protective, which Lily and Chloe didn't make easy for him. Maybe it had to do with losing Mom, but if he knew what was happening to Lily when she healed Dylan, we'd all be grounded from using our gifts for life.

"I know; you hate it," he said, and laughed as I sighed and made a turn, changing directions from his place to mine.

"Hate what?" I asked.

"That I'm right, but that's okay." He gave me a wickedly smug smile. "One day you'll love that about me."

I rolled my eyes. I refused to consider the idea that, of all the things that I already liked about him, that him being right would be something I'd love. His cute butt and stormy eyes definitely. Being a know it all? No way.

"Whatever."

God. Was that the best I could do? But any smart remark I might have come up with was gone. I shot him a glance. Then followed it up with a smack on the arm when I saw his smug smile.

He laughed, and a bit of the stress I'd been feeling ever since the fight left me. We pulled up to my house, and I shut the engine off.

"This is your place?" he asked in surprise as he looked at the house, and I realized that he'd never been over before.

"Yeah. Why?"

"I don't know. I just thought with your dad being some fancy lawyer, you'd live in a bigger place."

"Nope. Dad is big on the pro bono cases. Nanna calls him a bleeding heart. Besides, Mom picked the place out, and Dad said this is where she would have wanted us to grow up. He even let Nanna help decorate it. So be prepared to get bombarded with lace and flowers."

We got out of the car, and Nathan opened Lily's door, catching her in his arms when she slumped out. He shifted her carefully as he lifted her out of the car with her head flopped back. Watching how gently he held her, a stab of jealousy hit me before realizing how ridiculous it was to be jealous of my sister's ability to pass out simply by touching someone. I shut the door softly as she gave a loud snore, and both of us had to muffle our laughs. As delicate as Lily was, she could pull in a snore like a linebacker.

Nathan followed me to the front door, and I opened it slowly, lifting it slightly to avoid the loud shriek of protest it would let out when opened at the wrong angle.

Inside was dark; the only light coming from a lamp either Dad or Nanna had left on in the living room. I didn't want to disturb Lily or risk waking anyone. I left the other upstairs lights off and led Nathan down the steps, flicking on the hallway light in the basement as we went, and then in to Lily's room. The light in her room revealed what a perfect reflection of her it was—perfect. Everything neatly put away and no dirty laundry piled on the floor. Even her desk was meticulously organized—three pencils sticking out of a mug in a perfect tripod.

After laying Lily on her bed, we left and closed the door behind us. I walked in to the small sitting area that Dad had designated as our area and switched on the light.

"Thanks for helping me. Dad would have killed me if he'd seen her like that," I said, turning around to face him. He nodded absently, his mind clearly somewhere else.

"That stuff Dylan was talking about...he was just joking, right? And you were only going along with it to tease me? To see if I would fall for the freaky Matlin thing, right?" He sat on the arm of the couch, crossing his arms over his chest. The doubt was there; not just in his question, but in his eyes and defensive stance. I couldn't tell if it was because he was worried it was true, or if he was a bit put out by the idea that I would try and mess with him.

I considered telling him it was a joke, but to what end? Even if, so far, I was able to control my new urge to call people liars, my sisters had no problem sharing their gifts despite Dad's and my best efforts.

"No. It's the truth." I tried to give a smile, but it slipped from my face too quickly to be believable. "My mom's side of the family is all like us. My great-great-grandmother was the first, as far as we know. She was a healer, like Lily."

"Come on, Phoebe. You really expect me to believe this?" His doubtful look grew, a hint of anger slipping through. Apparently, he figured I was messing with him.

"It doesn't matter if you believe it or not. I don't care," I snapped, and turned on my heel to walk down the hall. Nathan caught me near the bottom of the stairs.

"I'm sor—"

"Shh!"

Light footsteps sounded overhead. I grabbed his arm, dragging him to my room. I shoved him in and closed the door before making my way to the bathroom.

"Phoebe, dear, is that you?" Nanna called from the top of the stairs.

"Yeah. Lily and I just got home. She's crashed already. I'm just going to brush my teeth then go to bed."

"You're home early. Didn't you have a good time?"

My eyes rolled. "It was great, Nanna. Lily and I were tired, so we came home. G'night." I popped my head in to the stairway and gave her a brief smile and wave before disappearing behind the wall.

"Goodnight, dear," she said, not moving. I wondered if she knew Nathan was down there with me. All she needed to do was touch something of mine, and she'd see everything that had happened tonight. Eventually, she moved away, and I let out a deep puff of air.

I went in to the bathroom and brushed my teeth, listening to her shuffling steps above me in the kitchen until, finally, they drifted off to her room. Once it was quiet again, I put up my toothbrush then nearly ran to my bedroom.

I flung the door open and caught Nathan doing exactly what I suspected he'd do. The ass was going through my underwear drawer. I made an inarticulate sound of outrage, and he looked up, eyes bugged out and a pair of hot pink panties in his hand.

"Oh my God!" I rushed forward, snatching the panties from his hand. I shoved them back in a drawer then slammed it shut. "I can't believe you'd look at my—my..."

"Panties?" He laughed, and I whacked his arm. If he didn't watch his mouth, I was going to get arrested for assault.

"Yes!"

Another whack.

"I was just playing with you. Swear. I didn't go through your—your ... stuff. I was looking at your books, and they were right there in the middle."

I waited for the voice or at least the cramps, but nothing came. Considering the state of my room, there was a high probability his story was true. My temper settled, yet nothing could lessen the flaming heat that pulsed through my cheeks.

"Come on, Phoebs." He gave me one of those twinkling smiles, and I felt my lips twitch in return. Then his eyes turned back to serious. He moved in closer and looped his arms around my waist. I ran my hands up his arms and clasped them around his neck. I could get used to this.

"I'm sorry I pissed you off before, and then just now. I didn't mean to. It's just a bit hard to believe something like what you're telling me." His voice seemed softer than usual, or maybe the sound of my quickened breathing muffled the normal gruffness.

"I guess that's understandable." My eyelashes fluttered, and I struggled to control them when I remembered how stupid I'd looked practicing in front of the mirror earlier.

"Is that how you knew Tonya was lying about driving?"

"Yeah," I said, letting my head drop to his chest. "Until a few weeks ago, I'd never had any hint of my gift. I'd always assumed Mom had been wrong, or even lied about it. Then Tonya lied to me and it happened. My stomach started to hurt, and a voice in my head said liar."

"And was she?"

"Yeah. She finally admitted it, but she didn't talk to me for almost two weeks. And that's what happened again tonight when she told me she was driving. Except, this time, I didn't say anything to her."

He stared at me for what seemed like the longest minute ever, before cocking his eyebrow.

"So that's it, right? I mean, you're not going to read my mind or anything?"

"No. That would be my cousin Kevin. Which I have to say is exceptionally disturbing. Especially when he has yet to learn how to keep his ten-year-old mouth shut."

"It may be best if I don't meet Kevin until he's a little older." He flashed a sexy smile, and I laughed, rolling my eyes.

"Trust me, I avoid the kid as much as possible, so the chances of you meeting him are pretty slim. Although, I could use some dirt on you, so I might just arrange a special meeting between you guys."

"Yeah. I don't think so," he said, and tugged me a bit closer. "Why do you think Tonya did it? Why lie about being the driver? If she gets caught, she'll be in even more trouble than he would have been."

"I don't know. It was not like her at all. Trevor's actually what started the whole voice in my head thing. That first time I heard it was when she lied about meeting him. I don't think she's ever lied to me before. At least not about anything important." I shrugged, hating the idea that Tonya could be changing so much because of some guy. "Maybe I'm wrong. She could have been driving. I mean, it's not like this Truth Teller thing has been working all the time."

"What do you mean?"

"Chloe tried to test me, and I pretty much failed. I didn't pick up on a single lie until she was done. I've only managed to pick up on a couple of lies from other people—mostly my little cousins, who, I'm sure, are compulsive liars."

He was quiet for a moment, as if trying to process everything, then quirked his eyebrow at me. "So, apart from me not being able to lie to you, you're basically normal, right?"

"Yes." I bugged my eyes out and then rolled them.

"Good." He dipped his head down and brushed his lips across mine. I sucked in a deep breath and leaned in to deepen the pressure.

"What the hell, Phoebe?!"

Nathan and I broke apart, and I twisted around to see Chloe standing in my door. Her hands were on her hips in the typical holier-than-thou stance she took anytime she felt she had the upper hand on me.

"You know Dad will kill you if he catches Nathan down here," Chloe said.

"Well, if you keep your voice down, that won't happen. I thought you were going to spend the night at Nadine's."

"You truly believed I'd stay after what I saw?"

"Saw?" Nathan interrupted. "You mean like saw saw or saw saw?"

Chloe and I flashed him matching are-you-serious looks.

"What?" he asked, a sheepish smile creeping across his face.

Chloe shook her head and turned her attention back to me. "What happened with the accident? How are you okay?"

"I wasn't there."

"What do you mean you weren't there?"

"Exactly that. After the fight, we left with Lily and Dylan in my car. Lily passed out after healing Dylan, and then I kicked him out. We were heading to Nathan's place when we saw it."

"It?"

"Well, Tonya really. She and her new boyfriend, Trevor, were the ones you saw in the accident. He—she wrapped the truck around a tree," I said.

"Whoa-whoa. You knew about the accident before it happened?" Nathan stepped closer up, trying to get in to the conversation.

"Yeah, but it's not right." Chloe's voice trembled. "Phoebe, you were supposed to be driving. I saw it."

"So you just get flashes of the future?" Nathan asked, interrupting again.

"No. Well, yes. At least with Lily and Phoebe since they're

my sisters. With others, I have to be physically close to a person, and then I'd need to let it happen," she explained impatiently before addressing me again. "Why didn't you drive Tonya home?"

"She wanted to stay with Trevor, but I couldn't leave Lily to deal with Dylan alone. He was smashed and trying to get her in the car with him."

"I just don't understand." She sank on to my bed, her pale complexion and squinted eyes giving me a glimpse of her utter confusion, and it froze me. This was not typical Chloe behavior.

"I better get going," Nathan said, looking from Chloe to me.

"Do you want me to drive you home?" I asked.

"Nah. The walk will give me time to air out before my dad gets a whiff of me. Although, I could use a bit of mouthwash."

We left Chloe in my room, and after Nathan gargled in the restroom, I led him upstairs to the door, making sure to keep the lights off. Caution kept us from talking, even to say goodnight. At the top of the steps, he paused while I tugged off his hoodie and handed it back. He dipped his head and gave me a peck on my cheek.

Then he was gone, leaping over the porch steps. He walked down the path, glancing back once. A cocky smile flashed when he saw me watching. After that, he started doing an exaggerated swagger, and I barely managed to hold in my giggle.

Back in my room, I found Chloe precisely where I'd left her. The giddy feeling Nathan had planted in me vanished. Her hands hung limp, dangling over her knees, and her head drooped. I sat beside her and wrapped my arms around her.

"I'm so glad you're okay, but I don't get it. What's wrong

with me?" she asked as she looked up at me.

"Nothing's wrong with you, Chloe. You saw an accident, and there was an accident."

"I didn't just see an accident. I saw you in an accident. Something's wrong. I'm not working right." She shuddered, and I felt a tear splash on my arm.

"Welcome to the club."

Once sarcasm would have dripped from those words, but now they were said with sympathy and fear. If Chloe's gift, one that had worked without fail for seventeen years, wasn't working, then what hope did I have of every knowing how to use mine?

CHAPTER 6

A TAP AT THE door woke me the next morning. I rolled over and gave Chloe a shove. We'd spent the night talking about little things, avoiding anything to do with our gifts until finally giving in to our weariness. It was kind of nice having a reminder that Chloe didn't annoy me all the time. I shuffled across my room, opened the door, and saw Dad.

"Morning," I said.

"Are you coming up to say goodbye? Nanna's taking the twins home. I think she'd like you to be there when they leave." His expectant look suggested I didn't really have an option.

"Yeah. Sure."

I suppressed the groan threatening to erupt. Saying bye to the twins and Nanna wasn't the issue. It was the talk I knew Nanna would insist on giving me first. Every visit was the same. I gave up trying to avoid it years ago. Now I just let it go in one ear and out the other.

"I saw Chloe's car outside. Did she come home with you?"

"I'm here, Dad." Chloe came up beside me. "Phoebe and I decided to have some sister time."

"Oookay." His surprise was probably a mirror of what mine would have been yesterday if Chloe had said the same thing. "Well, hurry up."

He headed back upstairs, and I searched for my slippers. I could have sworn they'd been in my room a few days ago, but I'd worn them since then. I sank to my knees and began pulling junk out from under the bed.

"Are you going to talk to Nanna?" Chloe asked.

I shoved my head under the bed. Maybe she'd give up if I pretended I couldn't hear her. "What?"

"You do this every time, you know. You stall and stall, hoping she'll run out of time, and she never does. Why don't you just go talk to her? And, for once in your life, actually listen." She grabbed my arm and pulled me up from the floor.

"Maybe because I don't want to listen to lies."

I yanked free and started searching in a pile under my desk.

"Are they lies? Until a few weeks ago, your gift didn't even work. So test it out on her. See if she's lying."

"Well, why don't you just tell me where I'm going to find my stinking slippers? Then I won't have an excuse."

Chloe walked over to the closet, opened the door, and gestured to the fluffy pink slippers hanging neatly on the shoe rack Dad had put up last summer.

I glowered at her and snatched the stupid things off the rack. "Who put those there?"

"I did, when I found them on my bed. If you want to leave your room a mess, fine, but keep it out of mine." She walked out to the hall and pointed to the stairs. "Now go."

I pursed my lips and brushed past her, barely making it without giving her a shove just because.

"Fee-Fee! We leaving." Ella charged at me with Emma close behind. I gripped the doorframe to steady myself to avoid crashing back down the stairs. A tempting idea since I'd take Chloe down with me.

"I know, girlies. That's why I came up. I need to give some raspberries." Despite the cries of no, they lifted their shirts for the juicy belly kisses, before giggling and shoving my head away.

"Girls, why don't you go and check that you have all of your toys packed up? Nanna wants to say goodbye to Phoebe," Nanna said, giving Chloe a sideways nod over their heads.

"I'll help," Chloe said, and grabbed the girls' hands. "Besides, I give much better raspberries than Phoebe."

"How come?" I heard Emma say as they left the kitchen.

"Oh. Because I'm nicer."

I didn't hear a response to that, but figured they were much better judges of character than Chloe.

"I thought you two were getting along?" Dad commented, eyebrows raised.

"Yeah, well, you know us."

Dad shook his head, and left Nanna and me alone. I wandered over to the table and sat in a chair. It seemed like every serious conversation Nanna and I had took place at that table.

She stepped forward, but, instead of sitting, she stopped behind me, cupped the sides of my face in her hands, and then kissed the top of my head. Once done, she dropped her hands and shifted so I could see her.

"You're just like your mother," she said, a smile curving her lips.

My own pursed in a sour response.

"Can't we skip this and get to what you really want to say?"

"And what might that be, dear?" Her smile dimmed, her brow creased, and eyes squinted.

"That I need to accept my gift. I need to be just like Mom. I need to go see her grave. Blah, blah, blah." It poured from my mouth, without a single thought to how horrible it sounded until after the words had already spewed forth.

"That's not what I was going to say."

"Liar." The word burst forth at the same moment it rang through my head. "It's what you always say."

Nanna sucked in a harsh breath, then pulled out a chair and sat heavily. "Alright. I want you to go see her, but I don't want you to be just like her."

My fingers dug in to the delicate lace tablecloth. I waited for the voice, but it didn't come. My heart squeezed tightly in my chest. It didn't matter if it didn't come. I knew she was lying. She had to be.

"Zoe was a beautiful person. She had a gift that helped many people, and once she knew how to use it, she never looked for ways to get out of it," Nanna said. "I see that same selflessness in Lily. But Zoe was also scared of what it would do to her. How it might control her. Chloe's been having that same fear. Yes, you have her eyes, her face, and, Lord help me, you have her mouthiness. All of you remind me of her, so get off your high horse, because it's not all about you."

She placed both hands on the table and pushed up, leaning in close to me. My eyes widened as I took in her suddenly fiery expression. She didn't look like a pushover anymore.

"I have asked you to go to your mother's grave enough times, but no more. I'm tired. Tired of having an ungrateful granddaughter who won't listen to the stories I want to tell about her mother. Tired of a snotty granddaughter who is repeatedly disrespectful to the memory of her mother. And I'm tired of the pouty granddaughter who isn't willing to accept the God-given gift she's been graced with and is too selfish to figure out how to use it to help anyone."

She backed away, and her features softened into the

familiar Nanna face. "Now, I'm dropping the girls off and going home. Chloe said I'll see you in a couple weeks." She paused in the doorway. "I love you, Phoebe, but sometimes you can be a donkey."

I almost smiled at her refusal to cuss, but the fact she was right made my lips curl into what was anything but a smile. I somehow made it through the goodbyes with the girls and then back down to my room. The instant I hit my bed, the tears welled up.

It was stupid to be upset. Nanna had finally admitted defeat. She wouldn't be pestering me about seeing Mom's grave. She didn't understand; nobody did. Going to the cemetery to stare at Mom's grave wasn't going to help me accept my gift, or make me feel closer to her.

Until I was twelve, going to the cemetery hadn't bothered me. Mainly because I'd thought I wasn't alone in my lack of memories. Then, on one trip, for what would have been Mom's fortieth birthday, Chloe said she could remember images of her from while she was carrying us. Chloe had seen every action our mother was going to take. Had even seen her last breath. Lily had chimed in that she could remember the feel of her, the love, the warmth, and comfort. Not distinct memories, but enough that she'd smiled as she softly admitted that visiting Mom's grave helped her remember that feeling.

Knowing they remembered while I had nothing but a nauseous ache, made it an even emptier pit inside of me.

With Nanna and the girls gone, I spent the rest of the day watching television and avoiding Chloe's looks of disappointment. I stayed up long past my usual bedtime, randomly flipping through the channels, trying to block out the expression that had been on Nanna's face.

* * *

The next morning, the beep of my alarm was exceedingly annoying. I'd already pushed the snooze button twice and was tempted in to hitting it a third time. Topping my list of least favorite days had to be the day after Winter Break ended. New classes always meant a whole crapload of homework. I rolled over, trying to get back in to the warm, comfy spot that would lull me back to sleep for another five minutes. My eyes had just drifted closed when my door banged open, bouncing off the wall.

"Get your butt moving," Chloe said as she marched over to my closet and rummaged through the clothes hanging there.

"You do understand the concept of privacy, don't you?" I reluctantly sat up, swinging my legs over the edge of the bed. "What are you looking for?"

"I know you borrowed my black cardigan." She yanked out a pink top, along with a few more shirts, and threw them over her arm. "I should have known you were the one taking all of my clothes."

"Hey! That's not yours," I said as she added a dark blue blouse to her collection.

"No, but it's Lily's, and she's going to wear it this weekend."

"Do you honestly think you're going to find the sweater in there?" My closet was notoriously bare.

"You're right," she said, and walked over to a pile of laundry I'd yet to put away.

I watched her dig through for a moment before dragging myself out of bed. There was no avoiding it. The aroma of freshly brewed coffee drifted in to my room. Dad was awake, and any chance I had of ditching school was out the window.

"Can I ask you something?" I glanced back at her as she made her way to the door, the clothes dangling from her arm.

"Go ahead," she said, turning around.

"Do you think it's strange that Tonya lied to me about Trevor?"

She seemed to consider it for a moment. "No."

"Care to elaborate?"

"Phoebs, you're not the best person to discuss relationships with."

"What does that mean?"

"Come on. You and Nathan have been flirting for almost two years and, until the other night, neither of you did anything about it. And even then, you couldn't keep your smart mouth closed."

"Gee. I always knew you loved me."

I brushed past her and stomped out of the room.

"Phoebe," Chloe said, following me down the hall. "Tonya has a reason for lying about it."

That stopped me. I swirled around to face her. "Did you see something?"

"No. Well ... not really. I saw the two of you at the hospital. That was it, but I know it's connected somehow."

I wanted to ask for specifics, but knew she wouldn't say anything else. For the longest time, Chloe had basked in the joy of telling us everything that was going to happen, but over the past year or so, she'd chilled on sharing the more serious stuff. Maybe she'd realized how frustrating it was for us to know and not be able to change it.

"You're going to be late," she said, brushing past me to head upstairs. "Mr. Arnold's gonna be pissed."

"Thanks for the warning," I grumbled at her departing back. It would have been nice to be able to do something about it, but there was no way I'd be showered, dressed, and at school on time. What good was a sister who could see the future if she didn't wake you up on time?

* * *

Forty minutes later, I wandered down the hall to Mr. Arnold's class, refusing to run when I was already late. I neared his door and wondered about Chloe's warning. Mr. Arnold was a pretty cool teacher, even if he was almost forty. I'd been late lots of times when I had him for chemistry during sophomore year, and he'd simply seemed glad I'd shown up at all.

"Bitch."

I spun around at the snarled word. Vivian stood a few feet away. So not what I needed. I turned back around, intent on getting to class.

"Don't walk away from me!" she yelled.

Her heels clicked behind me, closing the distance. Crap. I felt her hand on my shoulder, and then, with a shove, she sent me flying forward. My books scattered across the hall, and I slammed in to Mr. Arnold's door, bracing myself with my hands.

I wasn't a fighter. Sure, I mouthed off a lot, but somewhere inside of me hid a chicken that had managed to avoid anything resembling a catfight. But she'd attacked me first. I pushed away from the door and faced her. I didn't even have time to think of what I was going to say. She came at me like some crazed ghetto girl, arms flying, and she got in a few whacks before I clued in enough to raise my arms in defense.

I grabbed a chunk of her hair and yanked. She screamed, and her fist hit my eye. Letting her hair go, I placed both hands on her chest and pushed as hard as I could. She fell back, landing on her ass just as people poured out from the surrounding classrooms.

"Phoebe, what is going on?" Mr. Arnold asked. I didn't need to see his face to know that Chloe had been right. He was pissed. And what was worse was that I knew I looked guilty.

"She started it!" I pointed to Vivian, who was still on the floor, trying her best to look innocent.

"Everyone back to class," he said, waving his hand around at the mass of people who had gathered in hopes of a brawl, and then waited for them to clear the hall. "Ladies, you know we have a zero tolerance policy for fighting here on campus. Would either of you like to tell me what you were arguing about?"

Nathan appeared in the door, and my already hot face seemed to burst with fire. No way was I going to admit I'd been fighting over a boy. How many times had I laughed at other girls who did that? Technically, I'd only been defending myself, but, still. If Nathan hadn't dumped Vivian like he had, there was no way she'd have come after me. Looking at him now, I wondered what he thought. I could see concern as he took in my eye, which was already swelling shut, but there was also humor. He wasn't going to let this go.

"It was nothing," I said when Vivian remained silent. "Just a misunderstanding."

"Well, both of you are going to the office."

Vivian seemed to finally realize the trouble we were about to get in to, because she stood up and rushed over to us.

"Mr. Arnold, please. It was just a mistake. It won't happen again. Please!" she said, and when I saw the tears in her eyes, I could actually believe they were real.

"I'll let it slide for now—"

"Thank you, thank you!" Her voice grated on my nerves.

"But, after school, I expect both of you here for detention."

I barely contained the snort of laughter as horror swept across Vivian's face. Unlike me, I doubted she'd ever had even the threat of detention before.

"But—"

"Your other option, Ms. Winters, is to take this to Mrs. Peters and your parents."

"We'll be here," I said before Vivian could say anything stupid.

"Good. Now, inside. Both of you are late." Mr. Arnold turned around and looked at Nathan standing alone in the doorway. "Mr. Lauer, I trust you're not encouraging these ladies?"

"No, sir." He turned tail and practically ran back to his desk. Definitely not one to stand up for his girl. Then again, was I even his girl?

Walking to my desk, I was surprised not to see Tonya. We'd compared our second-semester schedules the day before, so I knew she was supposed to be there. I sank in to an empty seat, ignoring a smirk from Chloe when our eyes met. As if Vivian's presence wasn't enough to make me hate the class already. I gave Chloe my best evil eye and winced at the pain in my right one. She could have at least warned me that I was going to get socked in the eye.

I probed gently at the tender flesh, sucking in a breath at the pain.

"Phoebe, do you need to go to the nurse?" Mr. Arnold asked.

"No. I'm fine." The nurse meant going through the office and having to explain just how I ended up with a black eye. I preferred to suffer until I found Lily.

When the bell rang, I slid out of my desk and headed for Lily's locker. I was almost there before realizing someone was following me. Twisting my head around, I found Nathan right behind me. I turned back, ignoring him.

"Are you really okay?" he finally asked when I stopped at Lily's locker. I rested my back against the cool metal, and he leaned his shoulder on the one beside me.

"I will be."

"Then what's wrong? You seem pissed about something."

"Gee. I wonder."

"What does that mean?"

"Well, your ex-girlfriend attempted to beat the crap out of me, and you didn't even try to defend me."

"Seriously?"

His shock seemed genuine, but could he actually be that dense?

"Yes, seriously. I thought we ... you..." I didn't know what I thought we were, but, still. He should have done something.

"I'm sorry. I guess I should have hit her or something?"

"No." I sighed.

"Maybe I should have told Mr. Arnold you and Vivian needed to go to the office and be suspended or even expelled."

"No."

I cracked a smile.

"Oh. Then I should have started yelling that you're my new girlfriend and Vivian is a jealous bitch."

I wanted to say yes, but I was in shock. "Am I your new girlfriend?"

"Yeah. Sure. I mean, you're a girl and you're a friend, right?" His lips twitched, and I slugged his arm. "I'm kidding!"

He leaned in and pressed his lips to mine, lighter than last time, but the shivers that ran through me were the same. I could so get used to being his girlfriend.

"Is there a reason you guys are making out in front of my locker?"

We pulled apart at Lily's words. I ran my fingers along my lips as if I could hide the fact that my sister had caught us kissing.

"Wow. That's a nice shiner," Lily said.

"Yeah. I was hoping you might be able to fix that."

Lily stepped closer and laid her fingers lightly on my eye. I watched her as the pain faded. She grew quiet and still, her face growing even paler. I wondered what she felt as she healed me, but it was a subject she always managed to avoid talking about.

After a moment, she dropped her hand. "Better?"

"Much." I poked at it gently to check for tenderness. She swatted my hand down.

"Don't touch. It's still a bit pink, but if you leave it alone, it'll probably be fine in about an hour. It's a good thing Chloe warned me this morning. Otherwise, I wouldn't have come back to my locker."

"She told you Vivian was going to punch me?"

"No. Just that you'd need me. Why did Vivian punch you? Never mind. I think I can figure that one out." She looked pointedly at Nathan.

"I'm hoping to avoid a repeat," I said.

Nathan chuckled. "Apparently, you don't know Vivian very well."

I managed to put the thought of detention right out of my mind until the last bell rang. It helped that Nathan was in a couple of my classes and ate lunch with me. Wondering about Tonya took up a good chunk of time as well. After a series of painfully typed texts done under my desk went unanswered, I decided to call before heading to detention.

"Hello?" Tonya answered.

"Hey. Where are you? You should have told me you were skipping. I so could've ditched today. Vivian went ape-shit on me this morning, and Nathan totally flaked out."

"I'm not skipping."

Liar.

Crap. I was getting sick of these cramps.

"What's wrong then?" I asked.

"I'm sick."

Liar.

Forget about it. It didn't matter.

"Oh. Well, I'll talk to you later."

"Sure."

She disconnected before I could even say bye.

She was lying again, and I had no clue why. A hollow pit in my stomach formed. Maybe it had to do with her mom. The last time Shondra James was released from jail, Tonya missed almost two weeks of school before her gran got her back. Of course, Tonya could be sick. I could be hearing things. If she truly was sick, then her gran would know. I scrolled through my phone's contact list for Mrs. Robinson's home number.

"Miss Matlin, don't you have somewhere to be?"

My shoulders sagged as Mr. Arnold appeared at my side.

"I'm coming right now."

I shoved the phone in to my pocket and closed my locker.

I barely remembered the last time I'd had detention. A year ago? Definitely not the daily occurrence like in elementary and middle school. Dad liked to think it was because I grew up. I thought it had more to do with the teachers in high school realizing they couldn't actually make you stay after school.

Mr. Arnold walked down the hall, with me following. As much as I wanted to skip out, I couldn't risk him taking it to the principal if I didn't show. Then again, if Vivian didn't come, I was definitely going to bail. There was no point in wasting an afternoon if my Dad was just going to kill me for getting expelled.

Walking in to the room, I found Vivian already at her desk, a sheet of loose-leaf paper in front of her. On another desk was an identical paper with a pencil sitting next to it.

"Have a seat, Phoebe. The two of you are going to write an essay about what happened, why it happened, and what you'll do to avoid a similar situation in the future."

I sank in to my seat and started.

Nathan dumped Vivian, and she's pissed at me for it. She called me a bitch then pushed me into the door. I pushed her back, and she fell. From now on, I'm going to stay the hell away from her.

I wondered if he was going to give me shit for cussing in it, but, really, I was just being factual. Satisfied with my paper, I placed my pencil on the desk and glanced over at Vivian. She was working on the backside of what looked like her second page. She was probably going to make me out to be the bad guy. I picked up my pencil and began writing again.

Thirty minutes later, Mr. Arnold collected our papers. I'd managed another paragraph at least. Not my greatest work, but it at least looked like I made an effort. Although, compared to the novel Vivian handed in, it wasn't much.

Mr. Arnold sat on top of a desk at the front of the class, looking back and forth between us.

"I've given the two of you girls an opportunity here, because I believe that both of you know better than to do something like this again. But, if I ever see one of you even speak harshly to the other, you'll both be in Mrs. Peter's office so fast you'll leave skid marks of fear behind you."

I dutifully nodded and kept my eyes averted. The best practice was to show shame and fear. Vivian, stupid as she was, smiled at him, then waltzed out the door ahead of me. Starting toward the exit, I looked over my shoulder. Mr. Arnold turned back in to his classroom and tossed the papers in the trash. At least I hadn't slaved over the thing.

I pushed through the outside door, welcoming the cool breeze. Some school district idiot figured since it was winter, the heating should be on, despite the mild southern Cali climate.

"Hey," Nathan said from where he lounged on the steps.

"Hey, yourself." I bounced down the steps. "Who're you waiting for? Me or Vivian?"

"Ha-ha." He followed behind me and slung an arm over my shoulder when he caught up. "I don't double back."

"Good to know."

"So, I was thinking, maybe we should go out on a date or something." He shrugged, and the shy Nathan I typically saw around other people peeked out for just a moment.

"Ya think?"

He gave a crooked grin, shyness completely gone. "Yeah. What about a movie? There's some girly movie coming out this weekend."

"I'd rather see the new *Wes Craven* movie."

"Horror? God. Why did I wait so long?" He pressed a kiss to my cheek.

When we arrived at my car, he reached around and

hugged me close. Our lips met, and my entire body tingled. The gentle sweep of his hands along my back made me press closer. Only the sound of an approaching car pulled us apart. Engine revving, Vivian's sporty red convertible sped past us.

Laughing, I dropped my head to his chest, feeling his matching chuckles against my forehead.

"I need to go," I said.

"Hot date?"

"Yeah; with my trig text."

"Well, I was thinking of chasing, but I suck at math. I'll see you tomorrow."

I gave him a quick kiss and got in my car. Through the window, I watched him walk to his vehicle and wondered if I was dreaming. Then I almost slapped myself. There was no way I could be turning into one of those silly girls, fawning over some guy. As hot as Nathan was, no way was I going to let myself become obsessed again.

If Tonya were there, she'd be laughing her ass off at me. Tonya. The lies she told me over the phone popped back in to my mind. She could be sick. It was possible. I pulled out my cell and opened up the contact list, searching for Mrs. Robinson. When I located her, I pressed send and listened as it connected and started ringing.

"Hello?"

"Hi, Mrs. Robinson. It's Phoebe. I was wondering if Tonya was feeling any better?"

"Better? She's fine. Or, at least, she was when she left for school this morning. Did she leave sick?"

"No. Well, just at the end of the day she mentioned not feeling well." Yes, I lied. What else could I do? "I guess she hasn't made it home yet. I'll try her cell."

I said bye and hung up. Guilt and indignation warred

inside me. I'd lied to Tonya's grandma and doubted Tonya. But, damn it, she'd lied to me again.

So, if she hadn't been at school, and she wasn't at home sick, then where was she? And, more important, why had she lied to me?

* * *

The next day at school, I slid up to Tonya as she grabbed her things for class from her locker.

"Where were you yesterday?" I asked.

"What do you mean? I was sick."

"Tonya? Please, give me some credit. I'm not an idiot."

"What makes you think I was lying?" She paused and looked at me.

I hadn't mentioned the whole hearing voices thing to her yet, but it seemed like the perfect time. Especially considering the fact that I'd already told Nathan. If she found out I'd told him first, she'd probably kill me.

"Well, you know how I told you about not having a gift, like Lily and Chloe?"

"Yeah. You were supposed to tell the truth or something." This would have been so much easier if she'd at least pretended to be interested.

"A truth teller."

"Whatever. So, what, you can't lie anymore?"

"No." I rolled my eyes. "I can tell when someone's lying to me."

"How?" She looked sideways at me.

"I get cramps—"

"Come on, Phoebs. Isn't that a little Buffy?" She slammed her locker shut, and we started walking to class.

"Ha. Seriously. And then there's like a voice in my head that calls the person a liar."

"How can you be sure they really are lying?"

I tried to gauge her reaction, but her eyes were averted. She seemed to find everything and everyone around us fascinating.

"The first time it happened was right before Christmas break when I called you a liar. You even admitted that you'd lied. Remember? You told me you were going to see your mom, but, really, you were meeting up with Trevor. It happened again after the accident, and then yesterday when you told me you were sick."

She stopped abruptly and turned to face me.

"So, what? I don't have any privacy anymore? Great. Chloe was always running around telling me what I was going to do, and now that she's finally stopped, you're going to need to know everything I do or think?"

"That's not what this is about, Tonya. I don't need to know everything, but give me some credit and don't lie to my face about things anymore. Tell me to mind my own business, whatever, but don't lie. I, apparently, get enough of that without my best friend doing it, too."

I stomped away, letting my feet pound the frustration from me. Part of me had thought—okay, hoped—that she would think me having a gift was cool. I totally hadn't expected her to turn on me again. Well, screw her. I had enough crap in my life without her dumping on me.

The door to Mr. Arnold's class swung open as I walked through. I found my seat in front of Nathan's empty one and slumped in to the chair, tossing my binder on top. I started to stew, thinking about what a crappy-assed gift I had. I laid my arms on my desk and then rested my head on them. The darkness in that small space was nice, tempting me in to a little catnap.

My ear twitched as a tingling sensation passed through it. I rubbed at it, only for it to happen again and again. Swatting my hand at the fly I figured it must be, I jerked my head up and twisted around, coming face to face with Nathan's grinning face. His pencil stuck out toward me.

"Stop it," I snapped.

"Whoa. Who pissed in your cornflakes?" The pencil lowered.

"No one. I just ... never mind." I sighed and turned around. No way did I want to get in to a discussion about Tonya. Especially since she'd be walking through the door any minute. Gossiping about your best friend, even with your boyfriend, was never allowed.

"Is this a test?" he asked.

I glanced over my shoulder, lifting my eyebrows. "A test?"

"Yeah. One of those 'if he really cares, he'll keep asking' tests that I'm bound to fail because if I do keep asking, it'll turn into a 'can't he tell I don't want to talk about it' test."

I cracked a smile. "No. It's not a test. I just had a crappy morning, and I don't want to talk about it."

"'Kay." He sat back a little before a sly smile curled his lips, and he leaned closer to me. "Hey. You want to go make out at lunch?"

"What?" I glanced around to see if anyone had heard, but everyone was engaged in their own conversations. Well, except Chloe, who was giving me a knowing smile.

"Just kidding." He smiled, and I felt my grin grow to match. "Unless you want to."

I snorted and looked back at the front of the class. Mr. Arnold got his things ready to start, and Tonya was finally making her way to her desk. I wasn't going to get a chance to talk to her before class. I hoped she'd be a bit ... I didn't even know what I hoped. Just not angry.

An hour later, I caught up with her in the hall. I grabbed her arm lightly, and she flinched away, but she paused and acknowledged me with a scathing look.

"Tonya, I'm sorry. I didn't try to use my gift. It just happened. I have no control over it, and it's actually turning out to be a pain in the ass."

I thought of all the useless little lies I'd been picking up on. Bianca liking Karin's new haircut. Karin going to another study group. Chloe needing money from Dad for a new bra. Well, that last one wasn't completely useless, because Dad had immediately turned red and pulled out his wallet.

"Whatever," she said. "Try not to use it on me. Seriously, girl, I need some privacy."

"I promise I'll try. Just... If you don't want me to know something, tell me to butt out, 'kay?" I said, and she gave me a half smile.

I so wanted to ask her where she'd been, but there was something different between us. Best friends didn't have to tell each other everything—God knew there was a crap load of stuff I hadn't told her—but I'd never known that she was deliberately hiding things from me before. It was a bit unnerving.

"I was with Trevor," she said, answering the question I'd been dying to ask again.

"What? You ditched school for your boyfriend?" We reached my locker, and I jammed my trig notebook inside and pulled out my English one.

"As if you wouldn't have done it if Nathan had asked."

"Besides the point. Nathan is, well, Nathan." I swear I tried not to sigh.

"Yeah, well, I happen to think Trevor is a lot more worthy

of school skipping than Nathan."

"So, what did you guys do?"

"He took me back to his place." Her cheeks darkened, and she gave me that kind of 'you know' look.

"You had sex with him?" I whispered. Not exactly a deadly sin, but not something I thought Tonya would want advertised.

"Yeah." The blush deepened.

"And?" I asked after I was able to pull myself out of my shell shock.

"It was, I don't know, good, I guess. I mean, it hurt a bit and then it was just kind of over. The second time was better, though."

"Over as in..."

"Two minutes? Maybe three."

We both laughed. Not exactly the sexy romance novel stuff we'd read about.

"Wow. Wow." I kept repeating it, unable to believe what Tonya was telling me.

"I know," she said, and, when our giggles drew a few eyes, we tried to control ourselves.

"Please tell me you used a condom," I said, practicality finally winning out over lurid curiosity; although, maybe it was part of it.

"Duh. Trust me, growing up as an accident, I'm not going to repeat my mother's mistakes."

Okay. I was a tad jealous. Out of the two of us, I'd always thought I'd be first. Of course, those daydreams had always involved Nathan, and, until a few weeks ago, he'd pretty much made those dreams more of a fantasy than a possibility. But after hearing how Tonya had described the experience, I wondered if she regretted doing it. Tonya wasn't known for her long-term relationships.

"Ready?" Nathan asked just as his arm seemed to drop out of nowhere and over my shoulder.

"What? Oh, yeah."

Tonya and I looked at each other and burst out laughing.

"What'd I miss?" He cocked an eyebrow at us.

"Nothing," I answered with another giggle.

"Come on. You can tell me."

"Trust me, you don't want to know. I'll catch you later," I said, then waved bye to Tonya.

Luckily, Nathan managed to distract me through my boring classes, and those he wasn't in were interesting enough to let me make it through the rest of the day. That night, as I sat at my computer desk, was entirely different.

I wished I'd had the guts to ask Tonya more. Dad had given my sisters and me the speech when we were twelve, so I knew about sex. Although it was more than he probably knew thanks to playground talk. But this was different. Until a few weeks ago, sex hadn't been a top priority for me. Now, though, Nathan was a good enough kisser to make me think of jumping his bones every time our lips touched.

Part of me wanted to do it. To have the experience and that thrill, but, at the same time, Nanna's ancient lesson of why buy the cow when the milk is free was engrained in my brain. Tonya had found it pretty easy to give in. Would I be the same? It was stupid to even worry about it. Nathan and I hadn't even been out on a real date yet, but I wondered how I would know if I was ready.

I shut down my computer and decided to go to the one person who might be able to help me.

I gave a light courtesy knock on Lily's door before walking in.

"Hey," I said, flopping on to her bed. I grabbed a book off her nightstand and fanned the pages a few times before throwing it on the floor.

She sat in her computer chair, her short legs crossed on the seat, and when she spun around to face me, I was suddenly filled with embarrassment.

"What's up?" she asked.

"Can't I just come and spend some time with my favorite sister?"

"You? Without an ulterior motive?" She leaned down from her chair and picked up the book, putting it back on the nightstand in the exact position it had been in before I'd touched it.

"Whatever. You've been spending too much time with Chloe. You're starting to get her snarky attitude."

"Hmm ... I could have sworn she just told me the same thing, only it was you I was around too much. So, why are you here?"

I loved that Lily said it with love and humor. From Chloe, those words would have sliced through me.

"When did you know you were ready to have sex with Dylan?" I blurted it out in a mad rush.

"What?" Her entire face flushed a bright red, and I wished I could have asked Chloe. Lily was one of those extra sweet people, the next Mother Teresa, which made talking sex with her even weirder.

"How did you know you were ready?"

"I didn't. I mean—we're not..." Every freckle on her face seemed to be glowing.

"You're not having sex?" My eyebrows shot up in surprise. "Why not? I mean, you guys have been dating, like, forever."

"I'm not ready."

"How do you know?"

"I don't know. We've talked about it, and I know he wants to, but..." Spinning back to her computer, she shrugged a shoulder and let her voice trail off.

"But?"

"It's not something I want to talk about, okay?" Her voice trembled.

"Is everything okay with you?" I asked.

Guilt filled me as I realized that was one question I'd probably never bothered asking her before. Lily was the solid one. The one who was constantly calm and there for me when I needed to feel better.

"Yeah. I'm fine," she answered.

"Are you sure? You sound kind of sad."

"I'm sure. I just need to get this paper done."

Wow. A brush off from Lily. Well, there's a first time for everything.

"Sure. I'll leave you to it."

I left her room, and ran in to Chloe just outside the door. She had a huge grin on her face.

"Shut up," I said before a word even passed through her lips, and shoved past her in to my room.

"Did you really believe Lily would be having sex? She's probably never even had a dirty thought cross her mind in her entire life."

"So, I guess I should have asked you?"

"I could have at least told you it's gonna be a long while before you need to worry about that."

I slammed the door on her smug face. God. I hated having a sister who knew more about my future sex life than I did.

CHAPTER 7

THE ONLY THING BETTER than a Friday was a Saturday, and this time, it wasn't just because there was no school. Nathan and I were going to have our first real date. He worked at the gas station until six, so we'd decided to skip dinner and just catch a movie.

The doorbell rang at just after seven, and I raced to answer it.

"Wow. You look hot," he said when I opened the door, wearing my new skinny jeans and a black top.

He looked gorgeous as usual, his hair still damp and smelling absolutely delicious. I couldn't decide if I wanted to sniff him or run my hands through his hair. Instead, I practically shoved him out the door before my dad could do some crazy interrogation.

When we arrived, the theater was packed. There wasn't a whole lot of entertainment for anyone under twenty-one in Beachgrove on a Saturday night. I talked to a couple of girls from school standing behind us in line while Nathan used the automated ticket booth.

"Ready?" he said, turning from the machine. I nodded and said bye to the girls. He slid his hand around mine. "I still can't believe you want to see this movie."

"Why? Because I'm a girl?"

"Maybe."

"Well, maybe I just realize the benefits of a scary movie."

"And what would that be?"

"I can scream and snuggle up to you." I gave a sassy smile, and, tugging his hand, pulled him toward the concession. "Come on. I'm dying for some popcorn."

"How do you do that?" he asked when we'd gotten in the long line.

"What?"

"Flirt like crazy and then just walk away."

"Well, you said you wanted to do the chasing, so I can't make it too easy for you." I stood up on tiptoes and leaned in, but stopped an inch away from him. I waited, hoping he'd close the distance.

"You're right. I did say that." He smiled and stepped around me. "The line's moving."

My face scrunched in an angry-but-trying-not-to-laugh way. He was playing with me, and I liked it. Much better than my vain pursuit of him the past couple of years.

We ended up getting seats in the middle of the theater. Nathan tried for the back row, but it was filled with some other people from school. The movie was as scary as I expected. Halfway through, I had my knees pulled up to my chest with one hand covering my eyes.

"Stupid bitch! Get out of the house!" I whispered frantically.

I leaned closer to Nathan and closed my eyes. No longer providing a shield, my hands moved to cover my ears. Why I always wanted to go to those movies was beyond me. It was like I was asking to get the crap scared out of me then get angry when it did.

"Sure you want to watch the rest?" Nathan asked, a huge grin on his face.

"Yes. Shh."

I shifted a bit closer to him, letting myself relax as the tension in the movie lessened. My hands dropped to the armrests, and I brushed one against Nathan's hand. My fingers itched to prolong the contact, but I refused to give in to temptation, knowing if I did, I would start losing our game.

About five minutes passed before I felt his hand again. He trailed his fingers along my arm so lightly that I would have missed it if I hadn't seen him move. Once I knew what he was doing, though, it set off a race of shivers across my entire body. I kept still, knowing he was playing, maybe testing me to see if I would wait for him to make his move.

Finally, his hand slid over mine, linking our fingers together. The next time I had to cover my eyes, his hand helped block my view. Occasionally, he'd squeeze my hand and set my stomach to swirling, but in between those times, I just felt happy. Lame word to describe it, but it seemed better than content or comfortable, which I definitely wasn't.

We sat through the credits. Not something I normally did, but Nathan made no move to get up. Once we were alone, he lifted my hand and kissed the back of it. I looked up at him and sucked in a sharp breath. In the dim light, his gray eyes resembled a piece of late Nanna brought from England when she immigrated.

He let go of my hand to cup my face, then pressed his lips to mine. The background music faded until all I could hear was our breathing. In and out. A rhythm that picked up pace with each cycle. It was almost hypnotic, lulling me deeper in to the kiss.

The sudden flare of lights pulled us apart just in time to avoid the humiliation of discovery. Dylan ambled around the corner and up the stairs with his broom, his hand wrapped in a soft cast, and I giggled. Getting caught making out in the movie theater by my sister's boyfriend was not how I imagined ending our night.

"Hey, man," Nathan said, nodding to Dylan. Dylan ignored the greeting and gave me a nasty look. He was still pissed at me for making him walk home. Well, tough, because I was still pissed at him for, well, for being him.

"Come on. Let's go before we get banned from this place or something." Nathan stood and tugged me up from my seat.

"Or something?"

"Yeah, like they call my dad." We walked down the stairs and through the dark hall to the lobby.

"They wouldn't do that," I said doubtfully.

"Wanna bet? Maybe if I were just some other kid in town, but the sheriff's kid? I get ragged on by everyone."

"Seriously?"

I'd never thought what it would be like having a cop for a parent. Maybe it was similar to having a lawyer for a dad. The nagging about being a model citizen and our rights and responsibilities, blah, blah, blah.

"I already got in trouble over the fight," he said.

"Which fight?"

"Uh. Hello? The one between you and Vivian."

"What?! Why would you get in trouble for that? You stayed completely out of it," I said.

"Yeah, well, apparently, it got back to my dad that you guys were fighting over me."

So much for avoiding utter humiliation. "Oh my God. Please tell me your dad won't be calling mine."

"Nah. I think you're safe. According to my dad, I was the one at fault for playing two girls at once."

"Were you? Playing two girls at once?" I tried to make the question sound light, but the stillness that came over him told me I hadn't quite succeeded.

"Phoebe, I swear I wasn't trying to do anything like that. My thing with Vivian was over a long time ago. I just didn't know how to get loose of her. Writing that note was an act of desperation."

I laughed as I remembered his expression when I'd grabbed the note. There was no way I ever wanted to forget it.

We wove our way through the crowd toward the arcade games. I wasn't much for video games, but I did love the claw machines. The only one working was filled with stuffed animals on one side and a candy bin on the other. I loved that, no matter what, you came out a winner, because if you didn't get a toy, it gave you chance after chance to get a piece of candy.

"Let's play this one," I said, choosing to ignore his 'are you crazy' look.

I pulled a dollar from my purse and fed it to the machine. Music and lights roared to live. I grabbed the stick and directed the claw over a *Stewie* doll jammed in to the corner. I jumped up and down, yelling encouraging words when it pulled *Stewie* from the pile, only to groan as it slipped from the claw's grasp inches from the hole. I did manage to grab a piece of candy on my first try, and tossed it in my purse. It was one of those toffees that stuck to your teeth forever. No way was I going to eat it on a date.

"Amateur," Nathan said, bumping me out of the way with his hip. He stuck in his dollar and positioned the claw, grabbing the stuffed doll that I'd lost. This time, though, *Stewie* hung in and fell in to the bin. Nathan reached in and pulled the stuffed doll out.

"Wow. Just what I always wanted." He cuddled the toy

like a little girl, smiling gloatingly at me.

"You're a cheat. No way would you have won that if I hadn't pulled him from the corner."

A loud, angry voice coming from the corner of the lobby broke in to our conversation, and both of us glanced in that direction. I started to dismiss it until I spotted a familiar face at the center of it.

Tonya stood with her back pressed against the wall, Trevor's face only inches from hers. Neither of them looked happy, and I was tempted to go over, but I knew she'd be pissed. Was it really my place to get in to their business?

"You wanna go over?" Nathan asked.

"I don't think so. It looks like they're arguing."

I kept watching them. Everything about Tonya's posture seemed off. Arms crossed over her chest, her head dipped down, trying to evade Trevor as he thrust his face toward hers. Maybe I should have gone over, but even as the thought entered my mind, the two of them moved toward the door.

"You okay?" Nathan's voice eventually penetrated the fog in my head.

"Yeah. Sorry. It was just weird to see Tonya like that. I've never known her to take crap from anyone. Usually, she's one of those in your face fighters."

"We can catch up to them if you want."

"Nah. I'm sure she's alright. Besides, you promised me some ice cream."

"Didn't you just polish off a huge ass bucket of popcorn?"

"What can I say? You make me so hungry." I wiggled my brows. He threw an arm around my shoulder while keeping his grip on the *Stewie* doll with the other.

An hour later, I was on the front porch, savoring the fact that I hadn't foregone the ice cream as he gave me a chocolate flavored kiss goodnight. Even without the lingering taste of chocolate, he would have been delicious. How Chloe could be so sure that sex was not in my near future was beyond me.

"Chloe must be wrong," I said, pulling back just an inch.

"About what?" His words made me realize I was talking aloud.

"Oh. Nothing important," I said, sure that I blushed at even the idea of telling him my thoughts.

"Some kind of psychic stuff, huh?"

"Yeah."

The porch light flicked on, totally dousing the mood. Nathan stepped back, and we both instinctively looked toward the door. Heat filled my cheeks when I found my dad standing in the doorway.

"Hey, Mr. Matlin."

"Nathan." Dad nodded. "It's getting a bit late."

"Yes, sir. I'll talk to you later, Phoebs. Night."

"Night," I said, giving a half-wave as he headed to his car. Dad disappeared from the door, but I waited until Nathan backed out of the drive before going inside. Dad sat on the couch, his feet propped up on the old sewing footstool his mom had left Lily when she died.

"Thanks, Dad."

I tried to control the sarcasm, but it was hard. Having him watch over my shoulder was not the way I'd pictured ending my first date with Nathan.

"You're welcome." His grin told me he understood all too well the frustration I felt. "Next time, tell Nathan there's no necking on the porch."

"Dad!"

"Phoebe, there are some things I need to know and others

that I don't. As long as you're safe and happy, I don't need to see things like that." His smile faded. "You'll always be my little girl."

"No way do you do this to Lily."

"Not now, but, trust me, Dylan went through the same thing Nathan's going to."

* * *

I didn't hear from Nathan the next day, but I knew he was working, so I hadn't expected it. Tonya was MIA as well, and that was totally not like her. I tried calling her cell, but she'd turned it off, and I gave up after a couple of tries, not wanting to seem stalkerish.

The absence of both of them did give me more time to contemplate the way Tonya had acted the night before. She'd looked so meek. It reminded me of how she acted every time she went to visit her mom. Maybe her mom was back out, and she was just acting out in fear. Each time Shondra got out of jail, Tonya was in a constant state of upheaval with her mom threatening to take her to L.A. or San Diego.

I'd talk to her on Monday, I decided.

* * *

Monday morning, the hallways were jam packed as I shouldered my way through the throngs to get in to the chemistry lab. Tonya was already at our table, and I plunked down in the chair next to her.

"Hey. I tried calling you yesterday," I said, pulling out my experiment notes.

"Trevor took me to the San Diego Zoo."

"Sweet. I haven't been there in years."

"It was awesome. He kept making these silly faces at the otters. It was so cute. He's amazing. He said it was his favorite place to go, and that since I'm so special to him, he wanted to share it with me." Her eyes got a dreamy look in them.

My romantic gag reflex wasn't as strong as it was before my date with Nathan, but Trevor was going down a pretty sappy road.

"Wow. Sounds perfect," I forced myself to say, struggling to keep the edge of mockery out of my voice. No reason to piss her off.

"He is. Phoebs, I'm in love." She sighed, and my eyes rolled. "Don't give me that look. I'm serious this time. Trevor's not one of these high school boys that I can boss around. He's strong and smart. I feel like a little dumb girl sometimes when he's talking about the courses he's going to be signing up for."

Feeling dumb wasn't what I would go for in a relationship, but I could get what she was saying about bossing guys around. Nathan had been bossing me around a bit, and it was kind of sexy, but I doubted I'd let it go on too long. I liked being in control a bit too much. Besides, I did have a mind of my own.

We began setting up our experiment. Luckily, it was a simple lab all the chemistry teachers did at the beginning of the year because Tonya kept going on and on about Trevor. From what it seemed, he'd either been with her, talking to her, or texting her every waking minute. A little creepy, but she seemed overjoyed by the attention.

"What did you do this weekend?" she asked when she eventually ran out of Trevor stories.

"Nathan and I went to the movies."

"Please tell me he took you to that horror movie you wanted to see, because there's no way in hell I'm going to that with you," she said.

"Yeah. And, trust me, there are benefits to watching a scary movie on a date."

"Gross. No details. I know you and just what you would do in the dark with Nathan. You start drooling every time you even think of him, which is pretty much all the time now."

"Ha-ha. Anyway, it was nice to go see a decent movie for once. Not those cheesy romances you always drag me to. We saw you and Trevor afterward." I tried to fit the last bit in casually, wondering if—okay, hoping—she would tell me what they'd been arguing about.

"Oh. I didn't see you." She averted her gaze back to Lily's notes from last semester. Any interest in her voice was completely gone. I took it as her way of telling me to leave the subject alone.

"Let's get started," I said.

We pulled on our aprons, and I wished I'd been fast enough to get one of the few lab coats. I hated to ruin good clothing by spilling the science crap on me. Thank god we hadn't worked with anything dangerous yet. I was hoping, by next year, they'd have purchased more coats; otherwise, I was dropping all of my science classes.

Tonya tied my apron behind my back as I switched on a Bunsen burner and moved to the first step in our procedure. I flipped through my notes, struggling to decipher my writing, finally giving up and going to the copy of Lily's notes she'd done for her class. Lucky for Tonya and me, Lily hadn't decided to take physics instead. We would have been screwed without her. Although, I suppose we could have asked Karin for help, but, in Tonya's words, she'd rather eat her own crap than ask Karin for help again.

"First, we turn on the burner. Done," I said, and pointed to it. "Then... Hey; grab another beaker."

Tonya reached across the table to grab the breaker, her sleeve barely missing the flame.

"Watch it," I said, shoving her arm away from the little blue flame. "Roll up your sleeves before you set yourself on fire."

"You know I'm already too hot," she joked, and pushed up her sleeves before getting back to work. "So, next, we're supposed to use the tongs and put the beaker over the flame."

Tonya lifted the beaker, putting it in place. I watched her hand steady it, but something further up her arm drew my eye. Her smooth brown skin was marred by five round marks. Deep, angry bruises—the exact imprints that would be left if someone had grabbed her. Grabbed her hard.

"What the hell happened to you?" I blurted the question out, letting my fingers skim the marks.

"Nothing." She pulled her sleeve down. I didn't need the cramps to tell me she was lying.

"It looks like someone grabbed you. Did Trevor do that?" I grabbed her wrist with one hand while the other shoved the shirt up to completely expose the purple marks.

"It's nothing." She tugged against my hold.

"That's not nothing. Did he do this?"

She yanked her arm away, and I let go easily, not wanting to hurt her anymore. Was that why she had flinched when I'd grabbed her arm earlier?

"Drop it, Phoebe." Her tone was flat, and she refused to meet my gaze.

"How can you tell me to drop it? If he did that..." I couldn't believe she would tell me to do that. That wasn't the kind of thing I could just forget seeing.

"You promised you wouldn't push."

"This is totally different, Tonya. He hurt you." I thought of

125

the seemingly endless praise she had been giving him, and nearly puked with the next painful contraction of my stomach.

"My mom came home, okay? So, drop it." She snatched her pencil off the table and started writing in her notebook.

I didn't want to drop it. Mainly because, even if the voice weren't ringing through my head, it still wouldn't feel right. Shondra wasn't the greatest mom in the world, but in the ten years I'd been friends with Tonya, her mom had never laid a finger on her. Her gran wouldn't have allowed it. She was strict, but no one hit her babies.

My hand trembled as I forced myself through the next few steps of the procedure. I wanted to shake some sense in to Tonya. I wanted her to let me help.

"Stop it," Tonya said, not even looking up from our notes.

"Stop what?"

"You're trying to figure out how to get around your promise to back off." She held up a hand when I started to defend myself. "If you don't want to be left to do the rest of this experiment alone, then I suggest you keep your questions to yourself."

My mouth opened and closed like a fish until I gave up. "Do you want me to find Lily?"

"No." She gave a small smile, accepting my peace offering. "I'd rather not have anyone else see. You know, in case Mom got in trouble or something."

A bitter taste coated my mouth. In all the years I'd craved a gift, been angry at my mom and then my sisters for having what I didn't, I'd never dreamed there'd be a day that I'd wish I could believe a lie.

I felt sick. The image of Tonya's arm kept flashing through my mind. Part of me wanted to keep pushing her, to say I knew she was lying, but another part knew she'd been serious about me backing off. If I questioned her more, she'd shut me out. Then I'd never find out what happened. So, instead, I kept quiet.

I didn't see her for the rest of the day after chemistry class. I wasn't sure I wanted to see her—at least until I knew what I would say.

After my last class, I found Nathan waiting at my locker, hands shoved in to his pockets, leaning against the one next to mine. I went around him, giving him a slight smile. He rolled around, so he was propped up by his shoulder and watched me dig around for my things.

"What was up with you today?" he asked. "And don't say nothing, 'cause you were bitchy to everyone, including Lily."

Nathan wasn't the first person I would have thought of talking to about Tonya, but there wasn't anyone else I trusted enough. Lily, maybe, but she might say something to Dylan. Then it'd be all over the school. And Chloe just had a big mouth. Last time I told her a secret, I ended up with tampons hanging off my locker. Sixth grade had been pure hell after that.

Maybe Nathan was the person I was supposed to tell. What was the point of having a boyfriend if you couldn't talk to him? Well, besides the fun stuff.

"Tonya had bruises on her arm this morning." I put my books in, for once, taking the time to organize my stuff.

"So? Maybe they were from the accident. She banged herself up pretty good then. My dad said that the truck was totaled. They were lucky to walk away from it."

"That was over a week ago. And these weren't accident bruises." I slammed my locker shut and finally looked at him. Even now, those deep blue-purple marks stayed with me.

"They were made by someone grabbing her arm."

"Who do you think did it?" He took my hand, and we walked down the hall to the exit.

"She said her mom did."

"And you don't believe her?"

I thought of everything I knew about Shondra James. "Shondra's been in and out of jail all Tonya's life. Every time she gets out, she makes all these promises to Tonya. She's gonna change. She's not gonna hook up with any guys. Stuff like that. After a few weeks, she's back on drugs again and threatens to take Tonya away. I don't think she's been out of jail longer than eight months straight in Tonya's entire life."

"So it's possible Tonya's telling the truth?"

"No. And not just 'cause some voice told me. Her mom never laid a hand on her before, and when one of her boyfriends hit Tonya, she booted him. That's probably the only time Shondra's ever put Tonya first." I shook my head.

"So if it wasn't her mom, then who?"

"Trevor."

"Her boyfriend? You asked her?" His right eyebrow raised in question.

"Yeah, and she wouldn't answer. Just avoided saying anything."

"So, naturally, you think he did it."

I knew he wasn't trying to be sarcastic, but the words got my back up. I yanked my hand from his.

"I didn't imagine those bruises, I didn't imagine her practically begging me to back off, and I didn't imagine her lying about her mom doing it."

"That's not what I meant. It's just ... before you start accusing him and demanding answers, maybe you should check him out or something." He grabbed my hand again, pulling me a bit closer to him. "Maybe he did it, but there was a perfectly valid reason, like she was about to be hit by a car, so he grabbed her or something, and she didn't think you'd believe her."

I shrugged a shoulder. Crap. I hated logic.

"So how am I supposed to check him out?"

"We could ask my dad to do a background check. He's got access to that kind of stuff."

"I don't think that would help." I shook my head. "Besides, Tonya would freak if she knew I'd done that."

"Well, what if you hired a private detective to watch him."

I rolled my eyes. "Yeah, because I've got a money tree growing in my closet. That's why all my clothes are on the floor."

"Okay, okay. I'm just trying to help."

"I know," I said, and bumped his hip with mine.

We stopped next to my car, and I fished the keys from my backpack. I opened the door and leaned in to start the engine. I sat in the driver's seat and let my legs hang out the door. Nathan stood in front of me. He rested his arms on the car frame and ducked his head down to mine.

"I don't think this is something you can help with," I said. Then a random idea popped in to my head. "Actually, maybe you can help."

"Am I going to like this? It's not going to be like that Science Fair project you tricked me in to helping you with last year, is it?" Nathan asked.

"No. Besides, that was only a disaster because you decided to bring Vivian along." I stopped him with a raised hand when he started to defend himself. "Anyway, back to Tonya. You can help me by going on a double date."

"Double date?"

"You don't sound too excited."

"Those are kind of middle school, don't ya think?"

"That's beside the point. If we go on a double date with them, then I can catch him in a lie."

"So, say you're right and he is hurting Tonya. How are you going to get him to lie about it? It's not as if you can just ask him. Even I know Tonya would spaz."

"Well, maybe he'll lie about something else. I don't know. Stop asking me questions. This is a good idea. I know it. Now, are you going to help me or not?"

"Do you think I would have spent the last five minutes listening to you if I wasn't willing to help?"

"Whatever," I said, swinging my legs inside the car.

He bent down and brushed a quick kiss across my lips.

"I'll call you after work and let you know my schedule. I think I'm gonna have to work part of the weekend. Hey. Don't take off yet."

I waited as he ran to his car, grabbed something from inside, and then came back, hiding whatever he had behind his back.

"For you," he said, and revealed the surprise. It was the stuffed *Stewie*. "I forgot to give him to you the other night."

He gave me one more kiss then took off before I could even say thanks. After jogging to his car, he waved over his shoulder and climbed in. He was sweeter than I'd thought. I wondered for a moment if he'd done things like that for Vivian, but pushed it from my head as quickly as it came. Dwelling on the time he dated her wasn't going to change anything.

I called Tonya once I was home. It was hard to pretend that I believed her, and even harder to say that I wanted to get to know Trevor. How do you face someone you think is beating up their girlfriend? I must not have been very convincing, because Tonya didn't seem to believe me.

"Are you serious?" she asked after I brought up the double date idea.

"Yeah. Didn't we always talk about how, one day, we'd be going on dates together; even have a double wedding?"

"Uh. I think we were about ten when we agreed to that," Tonya said.

"Fine. We'll skip the double wedding and just do the date. Come on. It'll be fun."

"What about today? I know what you were thinking. That Trevor..." The accusation went unvoiced, but it was there between us. A living entity that was still growing in my mind. I didn't want it to take away this chance.

"I won't bring it up. Promise. I talked to Nathan—"

"You told Nathan? What the hell, Phoebs!"

"I know, but he made me realize I should get to know Trevor before I..."

"Judge him? Phoebe, I swear everything is great. I have everything under control. Trevor is so good to me. Better than I deserve."

"Well, you deserve the best." Tonya had enough crap happening in her life, thanks to her mom. She didn't need Trevor adding any more.

"You'll love him once you get to know him."

"Sure."

Yeah right. If he was anything like he was on New Year's, then I highly doubted it.

I buried any negative thoughts about him, so I could get my plan in to action. By the end of the call, Tonya and I had everything arranged. Despite my ulterior motives, it was fun setting it up, pretending we were ten again. That Ken and his twin brother, Kenny, weren't going to be our dates just made us giggle even harder.

When I went to bed, I prayed. I didn't talk to God very often, but, this time, I prayed that I was wrong about Trevor.

CHAPTER 8

"HE'S DOING EVERYTHING WRONG," I said, shoving my hands deep in to my jacket pockets.

"Wrong, according to you," Nathan said as we waited for Tonya and Trevor to park his truck. "Maybe this is the real Trevor, and Tonya was telling you the truth about the bruises."

"Oh. Shut up," I said, unwilling to admit that he might be right. I'd planned everything about this double date perfectly, or, at least, to the best of my abilities. Maybe I should have asked Chloe what was going to happen, so at least I wouldn't have been so unprepared.

"What did you expect? That he'd be foaming at the mouth?" Nathan smiled and raised a brow.

"No, but this is nothing like he was at Nadine's party. He could barely string two civilized words together." I hated when things didn't work according to my plans.

"And I guess he did beat the crap out of Dylan," Nathan pointed out.

"I'm not going to hold that against him. Most of the time, Dylan deserves it." I disregarded the fact Dylan was one of Nathan's friends.

"I'll admit Dylan's been an ass lately, but he's gotta still have some good qualities if Lily's dating him. Obviously, Trevor does, too. Otherwise, Tonya would have dropped him faster than she did that guy Derek last year."

I shuddered at the mention of that drug dealing creep. He'd convinced Tonya he wasn't dealing until she caught him selling to her mom.

Turning back to the truck, I watched as Tonya and Trevor got out of the vehicle and started toward us. Tonya was as enamored as she'd been the day of the party. I'd even caught her practicing a signature with his last name during one of our classes.

Tonight, though, dinner had been a disaster to my plan. Trevor had done everything my Dad said a guy should. He held the door, complimented Tonya, and completely fawned over her. Each time he spoke, I wanted to puke with the sugary sweetness of it, yet Tonya was lapping it up.

Nathan tried to distract me while we ate, but even the feel of his hand sliding up under my skirt wasn't enough. I simply swatted him away, although I was giving serious consideration to letting him get away with it in the theater.

We were heading in to the movie theater, and I was about to lose any chance of catching Trevor in a lie. I watched them walk closer, wondering how to adjust the failed plan. Nathan turned and stepped in front of me, blocking my line of vision. I glanced up at him.

"Phoebe, can you just relax? I know what you're trying to do, but it's kind of boring for me. Especially now that he's proven you were wrong about him. So unless you want to have a date with me, I'm gonna leave."

"What?!"

For a moment, I thought he was joking, but the serious face he wore, so unlike the Nathan I knew, told me just how fed up he was.

"I played these friggin' games with Vivian, and I don't really—"

"I'm nothing like Vivian." Could there be a better insult?

He sighed. "I didn't mean it that way. I'd just rather know that you're here with me because you want to be with me, and that you're not using me. Can't you just accept that you might be wrong about this guy?"

Just great. A guilt trip to go along with everything I was already worried about. But he looked serious, and not the least bit manipulative. After waiting so long to be with him, was I willing to risk him walking away because I had a sudden obsession with unmasking my best friend's boyfriend, who might not be fake at all?

"You're right," I said. He looked doubtful, so I stood up on my tiptoes and, wrapping my arms around his neck, kissed him lightly. "We can ditch them and go make out in the back of the theater."

"Girl, you dragged us all on this date. We're going to the bitter end so that you learn your lesson." Tonya's voice came from behind Nathan, and I looked over his shoulder to see her and Trevor staring.

"My lesson?"

Had she figured out I'd been trying to get dirt on Trevor?

"That the things we thought were cool seven years ago are actually lame."

If my laugh was louder and longer than the others, it came from the relief that she was totally unaware of my plotting. We started walking to the entrance, and I had to make a final decision. Either I continued to doubt Trevor, or I could trust that Tonya knew what she was doing. By the time we hit the doors, I decided I would go with Tonya. Not because of anything Trevor did, but with the knowledge that she'd be pissed if I admitted I didn't believe in her.

Both Trevor and Nathan groaned when Tonya reminded

them about the romantic comedy we were going to see. Nathan even shot me a dirty look. He knew that if it hadn't been a double, we'd have been going to see the new action flick. The romantic comedy had been Tonya's price for this date, and we were all paying for it.

After getting our tickets, we joined the endless line at the concession. Nathan headed to the restroom, and Tonya followed a moment later. I smiled at Trevor, trying my best to look friendly. When he smiled back, it was hard not to be taken in. He was gorgeous, with a kind of *Corbin Bleu* thing going on. It was even harder to picture him hurting Tonya.

"So," I said for the sake of filling the dead air between us, "you're going to UCSD in the fall?"

"Yeah, but I'm not sure what for anymore."

I clearly remembered him saying law before. A lie. Was he covering his tracks? *Stop it, Phoebe.*

"What were you going to do?"

"Law, but my dad is pushing me to become an accountant."

"Your dad wants you to be an accountant rather than a lawyer? My dad would be doing the happy dance until he died if I said I wanted to be a lawyer."

It had been an idea that I'd contemplated a year ago, for about a minute, before realizing that law school was super competitive and you had to have kick ass grades to make it in. Dad thought I was capable. I thought I didn't want to spend the next ten years of my life in school.

"Both my parents are accountants, and they want me to be part of the family business. I know it doesn't sound that exciting, but I guess I wouldn't mind it. Math was always my strong subject. Besides, it will mean a lot less student loans than law school."

"Have your parents met Tonya yet?"

"Yeah. They love her. I keep trying to get her to introduce me to her grandma, but she freaks at the idea."

"Mrs. Robinson can be pretty scary. None of the guys Tonya has dated ever lasted past the first meeting."

We made it up to the counter, and I bought a pack of *Junior Mints* for Nathan. Trevor bought a soda and a giant tub of popcorn, loaded with the cheddar powder Tonya was obsessed with.

We moved over to the side and chatted about school a bit more, but when Nathan came back, I lapsed in to silence, letting my mind run through what I'd learned about Trevor. What I was seeing didn't mesh with anything I'd seen before. At the party, he'd been rude and shown his violent side when he'd fought Dylan. This was an entirely different Trevor. He was obviously educated and wanted to be a boring accountant. He sounded exactly like what Tonya's gran wanted for her.

Nothing he said was lies. So, why was my gut telling me he was still wrong?

Tonya came rushing up, her eyes wide, and grabbed my arm to pull me to the side.

"Oh my God. You'll never guess who's here." She paused. I didn't bother asking since, a heartbeat later, she told me. "Vivian and her posse."

"Great." My gaze flicked over Tonya's shoulder, but I didn't see Vivian. "Hopefully, she's going to a different movie. Or, better yet, maybe she's leaving."

"Uh. No such luck. She's heading this way."

I turned, and, sure enough, there was Vivian flanked by four friends, smiling at Nathan. She came up to us, her eyes completely focused on him. Double date night just got far worse than I'd anticipated.

"Nathan, can I talk to you? Alone?"

"Um ... I'm on a date." His hands twitched in a lame gesture to me as I moved to his side.

"Don't you think you're taking this a bit too far?" she asked, giving him a look of pity.

"Taking what too far?"

"This whole pretend to break up. I know you were frustrated, and I'll change, okay? I'll let you make some of the decisions." Was she really that oblivious to his red face or the awkwardness we all emanated as she stood there telling him he should get back together with her? Apparently, because she kept going. "You can even take me to that new horror movie."

"Gee. Thanks, but Phoebe and I already went to see it."

She faltered, her eyes flashing over to me. "Puh-leaze. Are you really expecting me to believe that you'd rather date a Matlin freak than me?"

"I could have sworn he wrote you a note to let you know," I said. Maybe it was a bit catty to get involved, but, hey, she was insulting me.

And just as quickly as the words came from my mouth, I was covered with diet coke. Vivian's empty cup hit my chest, and the sticky, sweet liquid flowed down my face.

I jumped her. It was one of those instinctual, uncontrollable things. I grabbed her hair and yanked as hard as I could. She screamed, but whatever satisfaction I would have felt stalled when Nathan grabbed me around the waist and pulled me off her.

Vivian scrambled back, and I lunged against Nathan's hold.

"That's what you get for poaching," she said then took off

with her sidekicks as I managed to get one arm free from Nathan's hold.

"That's right. Run!" I called after her, my courage buoyed by the sight of her quickly disappearing back. I stopped struggling against Nathan's hold and wiped my free hand across my face, flicking some of the soda off to the side. The adrenaline rushing through me caused my entire body to shake. Even my fingers trembled, and I curled them in, but it didn't help.

"That is one crazy bitch," Trevor said as we all watched Vivian and her group huddle on the other side of the lobby. He nudged Nathan with his elbow. "You really hooked up with her?"

"Please don't go there right now," I said before Nathan could answer, and then took a deep breath, sucking in a drip of soda that clung to my lower lip. I looked down at my dress. "Crap. Chloe's going to kill me."

"Chloe?" Nathan asked, letting me go.

"It's her dress. I borrowed it." Running my hands down the front, I tried to brush off the liquid before it stained the fabric. I glanced up when I heard a snort. Tonya and Nathan both had their eyebrows arched high. "Okay. So maybe she doesn't know I borrowed it, but if it was that special to her, then she should have checked out my future."

"Checked out your future?" Trevor asked, reminding me of his presence.

"Oh, you know, the magic eight ball thing." I gave a curt smile and looked back at Nathan. "Do you mind if we go? I don't want to sit around soaking wet and sticky."

"Yeah. Sure."

"I'll call you tomorrow," I said to Tonya, then turned to Nathan. "Let me hit the restroom first."

Ten minutes later, my face was soda and makeup free, and water spots covered my chest. I held my jacket in front of me, trying to hide the evidence of Vivian's attack. Nathan was leaning on the wall next to the women's room door. Standing beside him was Dylan, decked out in his work clothes and wearing a new black name tag with 'assistant manager' etched in white.

"Hey," I said, nodding at Dylan. "What's up?"

"He's our personal escort," Nathan said as Dylan shifted uncomfortably from one foot to the other.

"What?"

Was there anything else to add to my utter humiliation? I wanted to kick Nathan when a chuckle burst from him.

"Apparently, throwing a smack down is enough to get you kicked out."

"What about Vivian? She started it." It felt like déjà vu.

"She's already gone. We refunded your tickets, and you guys can come back another night, but..." Dylan shrugged.

"Whatever. We were leaving anyway."

I started walking, letting them follow. I couldn't believe that, for the second time, Vivian had managed to attack me, yet I was the one getting in trouble. Where's the justice? I should get Dad to sue her or something, but that would require admitting that I hit her back. That would be the first thing Dad asked. *'Did you walk away? Two wrongs don't make a right.'*

I shoved the exit door open so hard it slammed in to the outer wall then stomped toward the parking lot.

"Hey, hey. Wait up!" Nathan jogged to catch up with me, and I stopped to watch him.

"I'm getting sick of her crap. And I keep getting in trouble."

"You're not in trouble, Phoebs." He threw an arm over my shoulder, hugging me to his side.

"You don't think this is going to get back to my dad? Are you kidding me? I'm so dead when he finds out."

"It's not like you started it. Besides, he can't kill you if Chloe gets to you first." He lifted his hand and let a finger flick over an exposed soda spot.

"Gee. You really know how to cheer me up."

"I try." He dropped a quick kiss on the tip of my nose. "Come on. Let's go. You're getting a little sticky."

We got in the car, and I turned the stereo on, letting the music fill the comfortable silence. When we pulled up to the house, only Lily's light was on. Chloe probably had a date with her flavor of the month, and Dad must have been working late. Not an uncommon event, even for a Saturday. I unlocked the front door, and Nathan trailed me inside.

"Did you want to try and go back? We could make the late showing," I said, looking over my shoulder as we went down the hall. He gave a shrug, which I wasn't sure how to take. "Or we could just watch a movie here. Dad's finally got us hooked up with an online subscription."

"That sounds good. I don't think Dylan would let us back in anyway."

"Yeah. Having my sister's boyfriend working at the theater should give me some perks, but with Dylan, I think we'll be lucky if he ever lets us go back. And even then he'll only do it to keep Lily happy."

"You know, he's not all that bad," Nathan said, and I remembered that they were pretty good friends. Or, at least, they had been until Dylan entered his asshole phase a few months back.

We went down the stairs, and when we reached the

bottom, I pointed through the doorway to our left. "TV's in there. I'm gonna go change."

"Need any help?" he asked, eyebrows wiggling up and down.

"Ha-ha. I don't think so."

"Just checking. I'm highly trained in zippers."

"I'm pretty sure I can handle it."

I rolled my eyes and gave him a shove in the direction of the rec room, then went to my room, making sure the door shut behind me. I pulled the dress off and flung it across my bed then tugged on a fresh pair of jeans and a shirt. I took a glance in the mirror, wondering if I should bother with makeup, but a lipstick note distorted my image.

Wash it now, or I will kill you! C

A growl escaped my throat, and I wished for the millionth time that my private life was actually private. I snatched the dress from my bed and went down to the laundry room. The washing machine lid stood open, a pre-poured amount of detergent sitting on the edge. Obviously, Chloe wasn't going to take any excuse for it not being cleaned. I dumped everything in and joined Nathan.

He was searching through the DVDs stacked on a floating wall shelf. Normally, Lily or Chloe kept the discs organized, but, sometimes, they surrendered to my chaos until it drove them nuts.

"I couldn't figure out how the TV worked, so I thought we'd go old school. Any preference?" he asked.

"Zombies," I said, sidling up to him. I pulled out a case, flashing him the cover.

"What's that?"

"Just the best television show ever made! I can't believe you've never heard of it."

I stuck the DVD in while Nathan sat down on the couch. When I turned back around, I hesitated, wondering where to sit. It would have been so much easier at the movie theater, but here... Was I supposed to sit right beside him? Leave a bit of space?

I chickened out. "Can you get the lights?" I asked.

I waited until he stood up and made it to the switch before I dove for the couch. I curled my legs up to my chest and gave a little smile, proud of my sneaky avoidance of...well, whatever it was I was avoiding.

Nathan sat down right next to me, pressing against my side, and draped an arm behind me, along the back of the couch. It was a heady experience being alone and so close to him, and I loved how warm he was. I kept waiting for him to make another move, because necking on the couch was a heck of a lot easier than in the movie theater, but the move didn't come. By the start of the second episode, his arm was still across my shoulders, and I had given up any pretense of being cool. Each ear was semi-plugged with a finger, and my eyes were squinted. The show wasn't as scary as maybe a zombie movie would be, but knowing when everything would happen made it even tenser.

The scary part passed, and I relaxed enough to drop my hands, letting one rest on my knee. I snuggled a bit closer, hoping that he'd take a hint and move in for a kiss, but he didn't. Giving up, I leaned back and focused on the serious dialogue the characters were having.

"Did you hear something?" Nathan asked, glancing behind us.

"Ha-ha."

"I'm serious. Listen." He grabbed the remote and paused the show. "There."

A rustling sound came from the laundry room. Images of flesh eating zombies filled my mind until I forced logic to tame them.

"It's just the washing machine. I had to put Chloe's dress in."

A huge thump followed my words.

"That was not the washing machine," Nathan said, one eyebrow cocked.

"Lily? Is that you? Chloe?" I called, staring back down the hallway. No answer came.

More rustling and banging. My heart picked up its pace, and my entire body was suddenly tense, with a deep shiver running through me. God. I hated zombies almost as much as I loved them.

"Aww. Are you scared?" Nathan asked, all sugary sweet. "Want me to go look? You *are* just a girl."

He was deliberately provoking me, but I grabbed on to the bait anyway. "No. I'll do it."

I got off the couch and went to the hallway, flicking on every light as I went. The noises from the laundry room kept coming, getting louder the closer I got. No light shone from under the door.

"Lil? Chloe? Are you in there?" I asked when I reached the closed door.

Everything got real quiet. I leaned in close to the door, trying to listen. I thought I could hear heavy breathing, but it must have been my own. I twisted the knob and started to pull it open, only to have it swing out full force and a body come surging toward me. I screamed, threw up my hands, and did a half run, half stumble back toward Nathan.

It was the laughing that stopped me. Nathan's and Chloe's. Nathan was in the entrance to the rec room, and Chloe was just outside the laundry room. I swatted at Nathan's arm, making contact with a satisfying smack.

"Hey!" he said, rubbing the spot I'd hit. "I didn't do anything."

"No, but you're laughing, and you're closer." On that, I marched back to Chloe and gave her a whack on her back, succeeding despite her evasion attempts. "You're so dead."

Chloe held up the still stained garment I'd borrowed. "Not as dead as you."

CHAPTER 9

ANY HOPE I HAD of forgetting my soda shower disappeared Monday morning. Everyone at school knew, and many had no problem bringing it up either through repetitive questions or lame jokes. Yet another downfall of living in a small town.

"You're going to take her down, right?" Tonya asked as we headed to bio. I just rolled my eyes in response. "Phoebs, you can take her. I know you can."

"Sure, and I'd end up spending the next year and a half living in my room, grounded." I gave a massive yawn, and again wondered why I hadn't tried to avoid scheduling a class first thing in the morning. Next year, I had to figure out how to get a spare for first period.

"You're no fun." She briefly pouted then it was back to how she and Trevor spent the rest of the weekend. She droned on for a few minutes, then stopped mid-sentence to look at me. "Oh. When you come over tonight, I slept over at your place on Saturday and then spent Sunday with you."

"Okay." I drew the word out as the thought floated around my head. I didn't like the idea of the lie. Especially considering it was so she could spend the night with Trevor. "I take it you haven't told your gran about Trevor yet?"

"Ugh. You know what she's like. I don't want her to scare him off." She flipped her braids back over her shoulder and gave a secret smile. "Besides, things are getting good."

"Good? Things?"

Her eyebrows wiggled up and down. "Yeah. You know ... things."

"Oh my God! I don't need to know any more!" I nudged her with my shoulder. Even as I said it, though, I wanted to know more. It was that juicy kind of gossip that I just couldn't turn away from.

"Please," Tonya said, rolling her eyes. "You know you want to hear all the nasty details."

"Nasty details?" Nathan came up on the other side of me as we reached the lab. Tonya and I burst in to giggles. "You know, if you guys keep doing this every time I come up, I'm going to think you're talking about me."

"It's not about you." I chuckled.

"Yet." Tonya gave me a huge smile as she strutted in to class.

"I think I'm better off not knowing." Nathan shook his head and wrapped an arm around my shoulder. "Want to pair up for lab today?"

"Sure. I don't think I can handle more of Tonya's details right now."

"Nate!" Both of us turned to see Andy flying down the hall and come to a stop a couple feet away. "Hey, man. I wanted to catch you before the shit hits it."

"Hits what?" Nathan asked.

"Viv and a few of her friends are spreading it that you guys are back on, and that if she sees Phoebe with you again, she's not going to hold back."

"Great. Just what I need." I slipped from under Nathan's arm and stomped in to class.

"Man, think I can sign up for bio today? I can't wait to see this ho-down."

"I heard that, Andy," I called back to him.

Nathan mumbled something and hung back at the door, talking some more. I found an empty lab table and dumped my stuff on the floor.

"Hey. I thought we were lab partners?" Tonya said from the table behind.

"I'm going with Nathan. I can't focus on anything with you getting all raunchy on me." I ignored the surprised snort from a guy across the aisle from us. "Besides, according to Andy, Vivian is going to beat me up if she sees me with Nathan again."

"So, what? You're provoking her?"

"You really think she's going to do anything? Need I remind you that she was the one who ran from the theater?" I couldn't even believe Vivian thought simply telling everyone Nathan was dating her would make him do it. Was she truly that stupid?

"Tell me you're going to beat her scrawny ass." Tonya practically bounced with glee at the idea.

"No. I'm just going to do what my gift apparently calls on me to do. Call her out as the liar she is."

"Boring," Tonya sighed.

"Yeah, well, I like my freedom, and any hint of violence will bring the wrath of Dad down on me."

Nathan walked over and threw his stuff under the table with mine, although he took the time to fix the chaos that had erupted from my binder.

"You sure you still want to be my partner?" he asked, pulling on his lab coat.

"Yes. And how come you have a lab coat instead of an apron?" I slipped the white apron over my head and then tied it behind me.

"Uh. Cause it was on the supply list."

"There was a supply list?" I glanced over at where Chloe stood near the front of the class. Lab coat. "How did I miss that?"

"Maybe because you were late the first day of class." Right. Another way Vivian had screwed me over.

Mr. Arnold hadn't arrived yet, so I still had a chance to pull something off to shut Vivian up for good. An idea started to form, and I turned to Tonya, who was putting on her matching apron. "Get your cell out. We're going to show everyone that Vivian is a liar and that she's too chicken shit to follow through."

"Interesting. I think this might be as good as kicking her ass." Tonya rubbed her hands together gleefully, then pulled out her cell.

"Do I even want to know?" Nathan asked.

"Probably not. Just go with me on it, okay?"

Vivian strolled in, that smug look coating her face. Her little posse floated behind her, their eyes pinned on me.

"Oh, Vivian!" I called, motioning her over.

It seemed to give her pause, but she came like a lamb to slaughter. When she stopped in front of me, it felt as though everyone was watching us. I may not have been anybody important around school, just one of the Matlin freaks, but Vivian was one of those disgusting girls, who was only popular because of some inexplicable reason.

"I think there's been a bit of a communication problem," I said, giving her a sympathetic look. Nathan stood silently beside me, and over Vivian's head, I could see Tonya holding her cell, capturing every second. "It seems that you're under the impression that Nathan is still dating you and that you're going to kick my ass. Well, just so you know, you're wrong."

I smiled and flipped her the middle finger, then turned to

Nathan and gave him a lingering kiss on his startled lips. It was all so junior high, straight out of some teenybopper movie, but it gave me a rush of adrenaline, knowing that I'd finally got Vivian. After a year of torment, watching her date Nathan, having her constantly shove it in my face, I was finally vindicated. When I glanced back at Vivian, she looked furious enough to hit me, but she didn't. Maybe she realized that there'd be no way of escaping after the first attack. Not with her posse blocking her only escape route.

"What?" I asked, posturing up just a bit. "Aren't you going to hit me? Beat me up?"

She glared at me, and I swore I could see her vibrating with anger and humiliation. She had no problem with a sneak attack that would give her an advantage, but this was one she was likely to lose. I smiled as she spun on her heel, pushed through her friends, and marched for the door.

"Oh. And don't worry, Vivian. By lunch, everyone in school will know you're too chicken shit to do anything," Tonya called, holding up her cell when Vivian looked back over her shoulder.

Vivian pushed the door open and shoved past Mr. Arnold, who was attempting to come through. He watched her leave then turned back to the class. He scanned the room until his gaze settled on Nathan and me.

"Is there a problem?" he asked.

"No, sir," Nathan and I said, glancing at each other. The rest of the class flew by with no Vivian. When the bell rang, Tonya took great pleasure in telling me she'd already sent out her directorial debut.

"I think I want to be a director," Tonya said. "I could seriously get used to this power."

"Power?"

"Yeah. I mean, did you see Tonya's face when she knew I'd recorded everything. Can't you just see some snobby actress being pissed with the shot I took? I could bring Hollywood down."

"That sounds more like an Owen plan," I said, shaking my head.

"Ouch. Okay. So maybe I just want to make a shitload of money without starving myself to be some stick actress." She tossed her hair and pranced down the hall.

Tonya's little video didn't quite make it to everyone in the school, but it only took one person showing it to Vivian to break her. It was actually a bit sad watching her sob dramatically in to her friend's shoulder in the cafeteria. She must have really believed Nathan would drop me just because she said so. Oh, the stupidity. And that was where my sympathy ended.

She milked it for a few days, then seemed to finally accept reality. I could only hope it stuck, because there was something nice about not having to watch my back constantly, even if it did mean I had to listen to Tonya go on and on about missing the drama of it all.

I still didn't trust Trevor. Not that I said anything else to Tonya about it. Nathan, on the other hand, patiently listened to me vent my frustrations about not having any evidence to back up my theories.

In the three weeks after the movie date, the four of us had hung out a few times, although nothing even remotely resembling a double date, and, each time, Trevor had been perfect. Tonya wasn't hiding anything from me, and Trevor never stepped wrong. It was like the guy I'd met on New Year's was an entirely different person—an evil twin or something.

"Maybe she was telling the truth," Nathan said, interrupting my most recent rant after school one day.

"She wasn't. I know it." I glanced at him. He sat on the couch while I paced the rec room. Tonya and Trevor had just left, and despite my repeated attempts to catch him on anything, Trevor had been completely honest, and it drove me nuts. And knowing that Nathan didn't totally believe me only made things worse. "I didn't imagine those bruises, Nathan."

"That's not what I'm saying." He sighed and got to his feet, grabbing his jacket from the back of the couch.

"You're leaving? I thought you were staying for dinner?"

"Yeah, well, I don't feel like listening to you talk about another guy for the next hour."

He bounded up the stairs, and I debated whether to follow him. My shoulders slumped. He was right. I always harped on about Trevor, but I couldn't shake the feelings I had. The guy was a certifiable creep, and he was dating my best friend. But this was Nathan, and he was walking away from me.

"Nathan, wait!" I called, propelling myself up the stairs after him. I managed to catch him just as he opened the door.

"I'm sorry. Please don't go. I promise not to say another word about you-know-who." I reached for his hand and pulled him away from the door. "Stay. Please?"

"You promise?" he asked, arching a brow.

"Promise." I tugged him back to the basement. "Besides, my dad isn't gonna be home for another thirty minutes."

Suddenly, I wasn't pulling him. He was nudging me along. It was nice knowing that with a few words, I could get him to do anything I wanted. I'd thought about us going further, but, according to Chloe, I had a bit of a wait before sex was in the picture, though she wouldn't give me the specifics. I wanted to resent her for knowing before me, but I kind of liked not having the pressure of should I or shouldn't I.

He followed me in to my room and shut the door behind him. I flopped on to the bed, waiting for him to join me. When he didn't, I flipped on to my back to look at him.

"What's wrong?"

"Your room. It's..."

"Clean?"

"Yeah. What happened? Are you sick or something?" He sat next to me and reached a hand for my forehead.

"Ha-ha." I grabbed his hand and pulled him down beside me. "Lily happened. I borrowed her notes for Calculus, and she needed them back, so she started looking, and voila! Clean room."

"You are truly devious. You know that, right?"

"Hey. I never said she had to find them. I would have looked." I tried for an innocent look.

"Yeah, but she probably needed them this year."

Any comeback I had was stopped by his lips. I pressed closer, deepening the kiss, letting any thoughts of Lily and Trevor drift away. Being with Nathan always felt so right. I never felt uncomfortable with being me. Not even my family made me feel that way. Dad tried to be accepting, but he looked at me the same way Nanna did, with the expectation that I be more like Mom. Chloe wanted me to be more like her, and Lily, well, she might be the only one who could accept me for me. She wanted me to be happy. All the time. Not me, at all.

Thoughts of my family drifted away as the feel of Nathan, the taste of him, consumed me. Somehow, I ended up lying on top of him, his hands roaming across my back and down to my hips, pulling me against him. He tasted like chocolate and mint. He'd been snacking on the candies in the kitchen when I wasn't looking.

My shirt crept up, and his fingers followed. I lifted slightly to help him get closer until the cloth bunched under my chin. We pulled apart, and my shirt came off, along with his. I took a moment to look at him. I'd been right about the working out at the gym. He was definitely on his way to a six-pack.

He reached behind me for the clasp of my bra, but stopped when his watch beeped. It was five o'clock, and my dad would be home soon. Ever since Nathan started coming over, Dad had come up with a no boys in the bedroom rule. I thought it was unfair since Lily had been dating Dylan for almost four years, and the rule never surfaced for them.

I rolled off Nathan and lay on my stomach, my face turned to watch him. Standing, he pulled his shirt back on and then adjusted his jeans, bringing a smile to my face. I loved knowing that he was so affected by me. He grabbed my shirt from the floor and tossed it over my back.

"Let's go before I get banned from your house."

I pushed off the bed and tugged the shirt on. He opened my bedroom door, and I trailed him down the hall. We reached the top of the stairs just as Dad walked in to the house, making me wonder if he was picking up on some of Chloe's gift.

"Mr. Matlin," Nathan said, nodding. His reddened cheeks were probably only confirming my dad's suspicions.

"Nathan, nice to see you upstairs."

I rolled my eyes and pulled Nathan in to the kitchen. Dad hung up his coat before joining us. It took a moment to register his empty hands.

"I thought you were picking up fried chicken from that new place downtown?"

"Nanna called and said she was feeling lonely, so I invited her over. You know how she is with fried foods. Lily is going to pick up sushi."

Nathan gagged, and I looked over to see him swallowing repeatedly.

"Maybe I should head home," he said, ending with another gag.

"Too late," Chloe said, coming in to the kitchen. She hopped up on the counter, ignoring the look Dad gave her. "Don't worry, Nathan. I already told Lily to pick up enough for you."

His face paled, and I swore a hint of green tinged his cheeks.

"Yes, Nathan. Please stay," Dad said then turned to me. "Nanna said she was looking forward to meeting the boy Phoebe has been fighting over. Which has me a bit curious as well."

"Dad—"

"Save it for now," he said, cutting me off. "Once will be enough for this story. Nathan, no need to look so green. Lily only gets enough sushi for the girls. She'll pick up some cooked food for us."

"Dad! You spoil all the fun." Chloe slid off the counter and went to the door, opening it as Nanna reached the porch. She came in, giving Chloe a kiss on the cheek.

"Chloe, dear, you look so lovely in that dress. I'm so glad Phoebe didn't ruin it."

So that was how it was going to be. I took in a deep, calming breath and gave her a hug. The exchange felt a bit stiff, and I wasn't sure which one of us still held the grudge. Okay, it was probably me, but Nanna was pretty stubborn, too.

"Nanna, this is Nathan."

I let go of her and motioned to Nathan across the room.

"Well, you're certainly an improvement over the last boy Phoebe went out with." She reached out her hand to shake his. He came toward us, extending his hand. I surged forward and grabbed his hand before Nanna could get a grasp. She chuckled behind me.

"No need to make it easy for her," I said under my breath when he gave me a curious look. I gave Nanna a tight smile. "We'll go lay the table."

"Nice to meet you, ma'am." Nathan gave a slight nod over his shoulder as we entered the dining room. "What was that about?"

I glanced through the doorway to make sure no one was listening, but the three of them had wandered in to the kitchen.

"Nanna can see things you've done, but she either needs to touch you or something belonging to you to do it."

"Ah. So you were saving me. Shouldn't I be worried that my jacket is hanging off a chair in the kitchen?"

I shrugged a shoulder. "She'll do it anyway, but it's better if you're not there to see her reaction. It's why Dylan never comes over when he knows she's here."

"What did she do to him?"

"Nothing. They were fine for a while, and then about six months ago, she stared at him real hard, but it totally freaked him out. I thought it was because he and Lily started, you know ... but it must have been something else."

"Is there anyone in your family I'm safe around?"

"My dad and Lily." I saw him give me a skeptical look. "Okay. Lily."

I handed some place mats to Nathan, and while he laid

them on the table, I pulled the plates and silverware from the china cabinet. We were setting the last of the cutlery when Lily arrived with dinner. She placed the carryout bag at the head of the table. Nathan, eyeing the bag with disgust, shuffled to the side until he was at the opposite end as the food.

"Don't worry, Nathan. I ordered some teriyaki beef for you and Dad."

"I believe it's the smell that's bothering him. Or, at least, it was the last time he was around sushi," Nanna said as she took a seat.

I groaned as I put the last of the utensils on the table then sat down next to the chair Nathan hovered behind. Lily casually made her way behind me, and I watched as her hand darted out to touch his back. She was done in a second, moving to the empty seat beside me.

"You're looking a bit better, Nathan," Chloe commented when he finally sat. She opened the food containers and started passing them around.

"Actually, I am." He took the carton of sushi from me, giving it a tentative whiff.

"Lily only settled your stomach. She didn't change your taste." I snatched the container from him and scooped out another salmon roll.

"She what?"

"I'm sorry, Nathan. I can't stand the sight of people gagging or getting sick." Lily handed him the teriyaki beef with an apologetic smile.

"No. That's okay. I guess I just thought..."

"What?" I asked.

"That I'd feel something, you know, when she was doing it."

Chloe gave a snorting laugh, followed by a cough as she choked on a bite of food.

"Chloe, that's enough." Dad took the teriyaki beef from Nathan and shoveled a heap on to his plate.

The conversation ended as we all started eating. I slowly chewed my food, watching Nanna. She'd been quiet. Too quiet. I kept waiting for her to pounce on me about Vivian, or, at the least, going to Mom's grave again. She glanced up at me, a knowing smile on her face.

"So, Nathan, how long have you known Phoebe?" Nanna speared a small piece of tempura with her fork.

"Um, a couple years."

"I'm surprised it's taken this long for the two of you to start dating."

"Uh. Yeah. Well..." Nathan faltered and glanced at me for help.

"Do we really have to play this game?" I asked her. "Nathan was dating Vivian. Then he decided not to date her anymore."

"Is this the girl you've been fighting with?" Dad looked from Nanna to me.

"I haven't been fighting her. She attacked me twice."

"And you walked away?" He wore that look that said he already knew I didn't.

"This is so unfair! I only defended myself." Everyone was staring at me, with expressions ranging from amusement to concern to disappointment. "Okay. So I may have hit her back the first time. But I didn't touch her the second time."

"Then why didn't you tell me about this?"

Because I had tried to hit her. Not that I was going to admit that to Dad.

"I just wanted to forget about it."

"Maybe I should go," Nathan said.

"No! We can go eat downstairs."

Holding my plate, I started to stand.

"Sit down, young lady," Dad said. "We'll put this to rest. For now. But if I hear about any more fighting, there will be consequences."

Chloe and Lily tried to fill the room with a semblance of normal conversation, chatting away about school and friends, though I noticed Lily didn't bring up Dylan. Nanna must have picked up on it, too, because she reached over and touched Lily's hand, following it up with a long stare. Lily didn't meet her gaze, which only added to my suspicions over the last few weeks that something was going on with her and Dylan.

While Chloe and I cleaned up after dinner, Nanna made small talk with Nathan. It seemed innocent enough, and Lily and Dad were there to make sure that she didn't go too far. Although, I'm not sure why she even bothered. She'd already grabbed one of his hairs from the sleeve of his shirt under the pretext of brushing it off, but I saw her slip it in to her pocket. Now she'd be able to check up on him whenever she wanted. When I went back in to the dining room, Nathan looked up at me, an expression of pure relief shining there.

"Ready to watch our movie?" I asked.

"Yes," he said, practically jumping up. His chair teetered on its back legs, and he grasped it before it fell backward in to the china cabinet. "Nice meeting you, ma'am."

"Oh. I'm sure I'll see you again."

I hated the cheeky little smile she gave. Hopefully, the implications of her comment would go straight over Nathan's head. Having him realize that my grandma could use the strand of his hair to check up on him was not the best way for me to enjoy having a boyfriend.

Lily giggled as I snagged Nathan's arm and got him away from Nanna before she could freak him out even more than she already had.

"Is your grandma always so strange?" he asked once we were safely downstairs.

"Yeah. Though she fits in pretty well with the rest of my family."

"You included?"

"Ha ha."

He sat on the sofa and flicked on the television, scrolling through the menu until finding the movie we planned to watch. I threw a bag of popcorn in to the microwave Dad had finally allowed us to put downstairs. When I ran up to get us a couple of sodas, I hoped Nanna would be gone, but luck was never on my side. She sat at the table with Dad, sipping a coffee.

"He's a good boy," Nanna said. Thinking she was talking to me, I looked at her from around the fridge door, but she was staring at Dad. I knew she was referring to Nathan. At least she wasn't revealing any of his dirty laundry.

Dad coughed and stood up, holding his coffee mug with both hands. "I've got to make a quick call for work. I'll be right back." He snuck a peek at me, and I rolled my eyes.

"Nanna, if you have something to say..." I let my voice trail off. Confrontation with Nanna hadn't been working well for me lately.

"He's right, you know," she said, finally turning her gaze on me.

"Dad?"

"Nathan. You spend more time talking about Tonya and her boyfriend than you do ... well, enjoying him."

Was Nanna actually telling me I should be getting it on

with my boyfriend?! Thank god Dad wasn't around.

"Your gift is still new, Phoebe. And you lack control."

"So, you're saying I should just forget about the fact that Trevor is a jerk and might be hurting my best friend?"

"No. I'm not saying that, but do you trust your gift? Absolutely? Can you say the voice you heard was the truth beyond any doubt?"

She sipped her coffee, and I noticed the slight tremble in her hand. She was getting old.

"Of all my grandchildren and great-grandchildren, I worry about you the most. Your gift has come to you so late, and you have no experience controlling it. You hear the voice and blurt it out, not stopping to think if you have influenced it with your own ideas and desires."

"So this voice is all in my head? I'm just making it up?"

"No, dear. But you need to listen with your heart as well as your head. I meant it when I told your father that Nathan was a good boy. But you are consumed by the certainty of what is happening with Tonya to the exclusion of everything and everyone else around you."

The sound of machine guns rose from the basement, reminding me that Nathan was waiting for me. I didn't say anything to Nanna as I left. Mainly because I didn't know what to say.

When I got back down to the rec room, blood and gore filled the screen as zombies took over a town. I snuggled in next to Nathan, stealing some of the popcorn he'd dumped in to a bowl while I'd been talking to Nanna.

I thought back to the day Chloe had tested my gift. How I hadn't caught lie after lie, until the very last. But that one lie had been the only one she truly hadn't wanted me to know. Everything else had been ... what? Lies? Fibs? Nonessential untruths?

I glanced at Nathan. I'd heard him lie about why he'd broken up with Vivian. He'd claimed it had nothing to do with me, yet the voice had called him out. Had it been my wishful thinking that had me hearing the voice? I wasn't sure I wanted to know if I'd been wrong about that. And without asking, there was no way to know for sure.

Nanna did have a point about one other thing, though. I had been ignoring Nathan, and he was fed up with it. Maybe on the verge of being fed up with me.

"I'm sorry," I said. He looked down at me, his eyes questioning. "You were right about me obsessing. No more suspicions. No more plotting. Tonya says he didn't do anything. He seems like a great guy. From now on, you're the only guy I'll think about. I'm done obsessing."

"What? I'm not worthy of obsessing over?" He cracked a smile, and some of my guilt lifted.

"Oh. I don't know. If I did, then that wouldn't be much work for you, now would it?"

I ran my hand up under his shirt, loving the way the muscles contracted. Creaking from upstairs reminded me that Dad was home, and, lately, he'd been prone to spontaneous runs down the stairs. I withdrew my hand and gave him a sassy smile.

"You don't play nice. You know that?" he said, shifting to get comfortable.

"Hey. You were the one that said you wanted to do the chasing."

CHAPTER 10

"I NEED YOU TO cover for me," Tonya said, sliding up to me while I emptied the mountain of trash from my locker. The plastic bag I held was nearly full, but I still had a pile to go.

"When? Where? And most importantly, why?"

"Trevor is taking me to the Triple Feature on Saturday, and I need you to tell Gran that I'm going with you."

Almost six months of dating and she still wouldn't tell Gran about Trevor. Why not? I quashed the thought as soon as it came to me. For the past four weeks, I'd been good at not thinking anything about Trevor, even the couple of times we'd all hung out together.

I pulled my mind away from Trevor and on to the Triple Feature. It was Beachgrove Cinema's attempt at cashing in on what had once been my most hated day of the year. Prom. From six o'clock on Saturday evening until three in the morning, the drive-in theater just outside of town was converted into a rom-com haven, with three romantic-comedies playing non-stop all night.

Beachgrove High sponsored the Triple Feature as the major prom fundraiser, staffing it with volunteers and parent chaperones. It was the one time of year the town suspended curfew and was usually the highlight of the year for anyone fifteen to eighteen since there wasn't anywhere else to go.

Under the guise of fundraising and covering costs, the school and theater managed to get away with charging a hundred bucks a ticket. I hated to think what they would be charging for drinks and food at the concession. In a less affluent community, the place would probably have been dead, but Beachgrove was one of those places where my dad's law firm income placed us in the lower bracket.

Dad said the whole thing was a lawsuit waiting to happen. One kid gets hurt after normal curfew, and the school and drive-in would be shelling out big bucks. Not that that deterred me or any other high school student from wanting to go. This was going to be my first year, and if he was so convinced about it ending someday, I didn't want to miss my chance.

"So? Will you?" Tonya asked.

"Sorry. Nathan already asked me to go with him. Dad said no at first. Some lame excuse about it being too late for me to be out with my boyfriend. Not that he minded when he told Lily she could go with Dylan. So, I convinced Lily to let us make it into a group thing with Owen, Karin, and Bianca. Dad couldn't say no to that."

"And you didn't invite me?!"

"I figured you would have plans with Trevor. You guys are together practically every minute you're not at home or school. Besides, Dylan and Trevor didn't exactly hit it off last time, and I figured it was better they didn't meet up again."

"Whatever. Besides, that doesn't matter. I just need you to get me out the door. Please?"

"When are you going to tell Gran about him?" I asked.

"Soon. She's still so wrapped up in dealing with Mom since she got out. Even though Mom's still in San Diego, she's been calling and asking to come home, and you know how Gran hates not letting her come. Come on. You still owe me for that double date."

"Hey. You were the one who first mentioned that double dating stuff."

"Yeah; back when we were ten. Come on, please?" she said, her lips in a pout.

"I don't know. I already feel bad about lying to your gran all the other times. Maybe you guys can just come with us. Then it won't be a lie."

"When did you turn into some goody-two-shoes?" She huffed and leaned her back against the neighboring locker. "Fine. I was going to pay for your ticket, but now you're on your own."

"Gee. Thanks. Dylan already picked up our tickets for us. He gets them at a discount since he's the all important assistant manager at the cinema, so we only had to pay fifty bucks a ticket."

She perked up. "Can he get any more? Trevor was bitching about the price."

"No. He reached his limit. Sorry," I said, trying to hide my satisfaction. If Trevor wanted to be with Tonya, he could pay full price. I may have promised Nathan I wouldn't obsess over Trevor anymore, but that didn't mean it wasn't always in the back of my mind.

The voice hadn't popped up again, at least not with Trevor and Tonya, but my gut still clenched anytime he was around. Nanna said I had no control of my gift, but, personally, I thought that was all the more reason to believe it. Each day, I caught more and more people in lies, which occasionally still freaked me out, but at least I had the brains to keep it to myself. Well, except for the time Owen lied about not crushing on someone. That time, I had to tell Tonya, and maybe I mentioned it to Bianca and Nathan.

We headed to Mr. Arnold's class, and I kept an eye out for

Nathan. Usually, he met me at my locker, but I hadn't seen him yet.

Karin caught us just before the warning bell, which was strange since I rarely saw her during school. She was on the advanced track, and most of her classes were at the senior level or college credit. She always stuck out in our group of friends, and she only hung out with us because of Owen. Which, if they paired up, would be even weirder. Thank God Owen wasn't interested.

"Hey," she said, gasping for breath. "Bianca and I are planning on going to Town Center tomorrow morning if you want to join us. Kind of a girls' day thing before heading to the drive-in."

"Sounds spiffy," Tonya said. I nudged her with my elbow. Sometimes, she could be so rude. Especially to Karin, who was totally unaware of the high level of sarcasm Tonya used with her.

"Okaaay." Karin gave Tonya an annoyed look and then turned to me. "Bianca's driving, so we'll pick you up at about ten." She walked off and gave a little wave.

"You're such a bitch to her," I said, slapping Tonya's arm lightly.

"I can't help it. She's one of those perfect, snotty types. I don't know why we always have to include her."

"Because she's our friend, and she's the only reason we didn't flunk History last year."

"Okay, so she's not that bad, but there's just something about her that pushes my buttons. Guess I'll come over to your place tomorrow morning since she's obviously not going to pick me up."

Tonya opened the classroom door, and we went in. I expected to see Nathan in his usual seat behind mine, but he wasn't there. Maybe he was sick. I contemplated texting him, but it would take me too long. It would have been pointless anyway since he walked in a few minutes later, followed by Vivian.

He winked at me while Vivian just smiled. It was her smile that set off every suspicious bone in my body. Completely disregarding Mr. Arnold as he began his lecture, I turned in my seat to look at Nathan.

"Where were you?" I whispered.

"Vivian trapped me at my locker." He focused on pulling his binder out of his backpack.

"And?" There had to be more to it than that. Vivian's smile said there was more to it. His avoidance said there was more to it.

"Nothing." He checked to see if I'd bought it. "Okay. She asked me if I could help her and her mom move some stuff this weekend."

"This weekend? I seriously hope you told her no."

"I told her I was busy."

"So why was she smiling?"

"How should I know?" He looked thoroughly confused.

I huffed and swiveled back to Mr. Arnold. I knew Nathan wasn't lying, but, still, just knowing Vivian was up to her scheming ways again made me mad. And that Nathan was so passively undisturbed only pissed me off more. Didn't he care that Vivian was most likely trying to break us up?

A few minutes later, I felt a tap on my shoulder and glanced back to see Nathan holding out a folded note. It was nothing like the intricate fold of the note he and Vivian had been passing months ago, but my stomach still clenched in fear that the message would be the same.

I slowly unfolded it and tried to make out Nathan's

horrible chicken scratch.

I know what you're thinking. Forget about Vivian. Know what I'm thinking about?

Quickly, I wrote back while Tonya peeked over to see what he'd written.

What?

I flicked the paper back at him, not bother with folding it. That kind of crap would have just annoyed me more. Less than a minute later, a soft brush of air swept across my neck, followed by the paper drifting over my shoulder. I snatched the paper and opened it.

You

The word was followed by an arrow to turn the page over. I flipped it over, aware of Tonya's rapt eyes on the note.

And your hot pink panties

I choked on my gasp while Tonya gave a loud laugh. My face flamed, and when Nathan coughed, I knew his would be, too. He obviously didn't realize Tonya would be able to see it.

"Is there a problem, Ms. Matlin?" Mr. Arnold asked from the board. Everyone in class followed his gaze and stared at me. Instinctively, I crumpled the paper and tried to shove it in my backpack.

"No. Sorry. I just choked on my gum." I sat up straight in my seat, and when he turned to answer a question from someone else, I glanced over at Vivian. She was watching me, some of the glee in her face diminished. I gave her a wicked grin, gleefully watching her frustration build.

Mr. Arnold coughed and surveyed the room, so I picked up my pencil and pretended to copy the notes he'd written on the board; I'd just scan Lily's from last semester. Instead, I drew a cartoon of Vivian pulling out her hair while her eyes melted. Maybe a bit childish, but it made me feel a bit better.

Nathan's fingers trailed along my neck, and I wished I hadn't pulled my hair back in to a ponytail. I swatted at his hand and shot him a nasty look over my shoulder. Just because I wasn't taking notes, or giving a hundred percent attention to the teacher, didn't mean he could totally distract me. I needed to be able to get something out of the class. That he just blew a kiss back caused my stomach to clench. Not the painful cramps of a liar, but with the exhilarating knowledge that I loved playing his game.

* * *

The rest of the day flew by with Nathan managing to make me completely forget about Vivian. I just wish he'd been with us the next day to help me forget about Trevor.

It was impossible to relax and concentrate on shopping with Tonya's cell phone continually ringing or buzzing. I glared at her as she smiled over another text from Trevor and waited impatiently in front of her, barely resisting the toe-tapping I so wanted to do. Whatever annoyance I projected apparently wasn't enough, because Tonya started typing away, and I finally gave up on her and wandered away.

I had a new top to find, and it was already one, which meant I had three hours before I had to start getting ready for the Triple Feature. Tonya had been my best hope of finding a cute top since she had some funky radar that practically threw the best clothing at her. She already had four bags dangling from her arm, and she hadn't even been looking to buy anything. Bianca would help, but she had some Goth cheerleader thing going on, and I wasn't sure I wanted anything she was feeling. And there was no way I'd follow Karin's fashion advice. Her clothes were just plain fugly. Not cheap. Just outside the realm of normal taste.

Shuffling through the nearest rack, I pulled out a multicolored halter-top. Killer style, but it looked like the designer had vomited the colors on to the fabric. I hung it back up and moved on to the next rack.

"Hey. Why'd you leave me back there?" Tonya asked as she reached around me to pull off a black top. It had a standing half-inch collar and short ruffles along the buttons that went from the neck to the slight empire waist. It was the best thing I'd seen all morning. Tonya passed it to me. "Here. Try this one."

"How do you do that?" I asked, taking the hanger and heading for the change rooms.

"Do what?"

"Find the best clothes without even looking."

"It's instinct, I guess. God didn't give just your family gifts."

"What did he want?" I asked as we waited for one of the staff to come and open a room for me.

"God?"

"Trevor."

"Oh. He just wanted to know what time the first movie starts."

Somehow, Tonya had suckered me in to her plan to deceive Gran. I still felt a bit uneasy about it, but when Nathan guessed that my reluctance was due more to having it out for Trevor, I'd been forced in to it.

Tonya's phone beeped again, and I groaned. "Just ignore it," I said. "He's going to see you in a few hours anyway."

She shot me an 'are-you-crazy' look and flipped open her cell. I went in to the change room and pulled on the shirt. It was cute, damn it. Just once, I wanted to find the good stuff, even if I just passed it off to her. I redressed and slung the top over my arm, leaving the hanger on the floor of the small room.

Bianca sat on a love seat directly across from the change area while Tonya was talking on her cell. Bianca and I shared a look. Trevor was turning into a pest, and he wasn't even in town yet.

"You find anything?" she asked, and I held up my shirt in response. "Cute. A bit tame, but cute."

"Come on," I said. "Help me find some earrings."

We wandered over to the jewelry racks near the cashier, and I let the shiny baubles distract me from Trevor. For a minute at least. Then Tonya giggled, and I wanted to puke.

"You really don't like this guy, do you?" Bianca asked me. She held up a pair of giant hoops to her ear.

"No way am I going anywhere with you in those. And I'm trying to like him. He seems perfect. At least everyone says he is." Everyone but me.

"He seemed okay the one time I met him," Bianca said.

"Maybe I should be ragging on Nathan to call me more," I said. "Then again, it'd be kinda creepy to have him calling me every two minutes."

Bianca shushed me with a chuckle as Tonya pocketed her phone and scanned the store for us.

"What was it this time?" I asked, doing a horrible job of hiding my irritation. This was supposed to be about enjoying a shopping trip with my best friends, and, instead, I was battling Trevor for attention.

"He was just wondering what we were up to, and to double check what time he was meeting us."

"The last text you sent told him that."

"I think it's sweet that he keeps wanting to talk to her," Bianca said, smiling. She was enjoying stirring the pot.

"It's annoying."

"Ha!" Tonya nudged my shoulder, then said to Bianca, "I think Phoebe's jealous that Trevor cares enough about me to want to know what I'm doing."

"Jealous that my boyfriend doesn't border on stalkerish? Yeah. I don't think so." I could tell that pushed Tonya's buttons, and knew if I kept going, we'd end up in a massive fight. Not what I'd been aiming for. "Anyway, I'm getting the shirt, and from now on, you're picking out everything I buy."

"Hey. Don't I get to pick anything?" Bianca wrapped an arm around each of us. Tonya and I glanced down at Bianca's slightly bizarre ensemble, a tattered purple and black plaid mini skirt with a hot pink polo shirt, then looked at each other and laughed. Bianca looked at her outfit then back at us. "What?"

"Nothing," I said, giving a lame cough to cover my slight chuckle. "Hey. What happened to Karin?"

"She went next door to try to find something for tonight," Bianca explained.

Tonya made a gagging sound. "The only things there are penny loafers and golf shirts. I think I'd take your advice on clothing before I asked her."

I went over to the cashier and handed her the shirt to ring up. Tonya and Bianca kept browsing, but I was completely broke. I'd considered raiding Chloe's closet, but after the disaster with the dress, I figured it was better to play it safe. And with Lily being almost seven inches shorter, my options with her closet were pretty limited. After paying, I took my bag and headed over to the racks of skirts Bianca and Tonya were searching through.

"Oh my God! Look at this! It would go perfect with that purple top I bought last week." Tonya held up a dark purple mini-skirt for us to inspect. "I'm going to try it on. Here. Hold this." She thrust her purse and bags at me, then took off for the changing room.

"This is why I never like going shopping with you guys," Bianca said with a groan. "I'm starving, and we can't even get out of the first store we go in to."

"Hey. It's not me. I'm done. And I'm hungry, too." I glanced toward where Tonya had disappeared in to the tiny room. Tonya was a delayed shopper. If she tried on something she liked, it took forever for her to get it off. She'd probably spend the next ten minutes imagining it with every other top in her wardrobe before she came back out.

I knocked on the door to her change room. "Hey. We're going to go and find Karin, so we can grab a bite to eat before we all starve to death."

"Sure. Oh, hey, pass me my wallet." Her arm reached over the door, and I dug through her purse to pull out the red faux snakeskin wallet.

"Thank god," Bianca said as we left the store. "I think I'm going to die of starvation."

I barely contained a snort. Bianca was one of those naturally ultra-thin girls that never set foot in a gym, or tried a diet. Not that she was as bad as Karin with her fake complaints about not being able to gain weight, but, one day, I hoped karma would catch up with her, or both of them. Not that I wanted them fat, but, still, a little chunkier would make me feel better. I'm sure Dad would simply tell me that I should hit the gym like Chloe if I wanted that perfect size six, but, honestly, I was just too lazy. Size ten was working for me.

Tonya's cell phone rang just as we went in to the clothing store to get Karin. Both Bianca and I groaned then laughed at the absurdity of a guy calling fifteen times in the span of two hours.

"Are you gonna answer it?"

I pulled the cell from Tonya's purse and saw Trevor's name floating across the screen. Tonya would want me to answer it, even if it was just to say that she'd call him back. Before I could change my mind, I hit end and held it down until the phone powered off.

"Nope."

"You know she'll just call him back as soon as you tell her he called," Bianca said, her eyebrows raised.

"True. Or we could just not tell her he called. She won't even know her cell is off." I would have done the same even if it hadn't been Trevor calling. Really. "Besides, it would add on another ten minutes until we could get to the food court."

"You are so bad," Bianca said, an evil grin that matched mine spreading across her face. Her stomach gave a well-timed rumble. "I never heard her phone ring. It must have been covered by the grumbles of my stomach."

I shoved the turned off cell phone back in Tonya's purse and arranged her junk to make it hard to find. The less chance she had of coming across it, the less chance she had to think of its silence. For a brief moment, guilt assaulted me, then I thought of how annoying the calls had been, of the bruises on Tonya's arms, of the voice that rang through my head when he lied.

I wouldn't lie. If she asked, I'd admit he called, but, otherwise, I wasn't going to tell her. Not a lie. Just a simple, not so innocent, omission.

CHAPTER 11

NOT SO SIMPLE, REALLY. And I have to admit, it wasn't even close to innocent either. Not that I was about to admit that fact to Tonya as she stood at my front door four hours later.

"Did you turn off my cell when we were at the mall?" she demanded, holding the offending phone up as if presenting evidence.

"What?" That came out sounding so guilty.

"What the hell, Phoebe? Trevor called and left like fifteen messages. He thought something was wrong."

Nothing had been wrong. After I'd turned the thing off, the four of us had enjoyed a fun, Trevor-free lunch. I'd even forgotten about doing it until Tonya arrived totally pissed.

I considered lying, but despite my gift at reading other's lies, telling them wasn't a talent of mine, so I opted for some partial truths and possibly a bit of deflection.

"I'm sorry. I only turned it off because I wanted us all to spend some girl time together." The truth, minus my continued distrust of Trevor. Now for deflecting. "Can you help me get Lily dressed? She's totally flaking right now. Saying she's too tired. And if she doesn't go, Dad says I can't go, which means you won't have me as your cover."

"What?!" Tonya marched passed me, heading for the stairs and an unsuspecting Lily. "What's up with her lately anyway? She's a bit more freaky than normal."

"I don't know. She's been tired a lot." I knew the healings she did sometimes wiped her out, but this was more than normal. Then again, it could just be she was realizing what a prick Dylan was.

"Well, she's going tonight, because if you can't go, then I'll be royally screwed if Gran calls your dad." She stomped down the stairs, went straight to Lily's room, and gave one short knock on the door before flinging it open.

Lily practically jumped up from her bed where she'd been laying. "Tonya! You scared me." She gave a slight chuckle that didn't quite make it to her eyes.

"I can't believe you're trying to ditch this," Tonya said, crossing her arms over her chest. I couldn't see her face, but I was sure she gave Lily the evil eye.

"What are you talking about?" Lily asked, completely confused.

Okay, so maybe I'd lied a bit, but, hopefully, Lily would at least pretend to be mildly put out about going. Behind Tonya's back, I tried to do some kind of charades gesture that would get my point across to Lily, but I sucked at games. This whole mess of Tonya confronting Lily perfectly demonstrated how I sucked at lying even more.

"Phoebe said you were trying to bail tonight."

"Uh..." Lily hesitated, and I got in one more choking motion before Tonya twisted around as if sensing my frantic attempts to get Lily to cover for me. But it must have worked, because Lily said, "Oh yeah. I'm a bit tired."

"Come on. Please. I need Phoebe to cover for me, and since she's suddenly developed a conscience and doesn't want to lie to my gran, she has to go tonight."

"And I have to go because...?"

"You know Dad won't let me go with Nathan if you're not

going." I practically crossed my eyes, trying to signal Lily to keep going along with everything.

"Ah. Well, I suppose I could go." Not that she had been intending to bail, but there was a reluctance in her voice that made me wonder if she really wanted to.

"Thank you, thank you!"

Tonya did a little happy dance out of Lily's room, and we went down the hall to mine. Tonya sprawled across my bed while I sat at my desk. I fiddled with my iPod, then plugged it in to my desktop computer to charge. The computer was a relic, but, unlike Lily and Chloe, I wasn't going to save up for months just to buy a laptop that I wouldn't know how to use anyway. I was only marginally better at typing on a keyboard than texting with my cell.

"So, when is everyone coming over?" Tonya asked, grabbing a magazine from my nightstand.

"Pretty soon, I guess. We all agreed on five-thirty. God. It's gonna be a tight fit with all of us in the truck. When is Trevor getting here?"

"Oh. He's going to meet us there. That way, we can have our own space." She tried for a sly, sexy look, but failed miserably when we both started laughing.

"You better not have sex in there, 'cause if Karin finds out, you know she'll rat you out."

"God no! I don't even like it."

"What? Then why are you doing it with him?" I tried to imagine not liking sex with Nathan, but it was hard when I couldn't even say that I liked it, which kinda sucked.

"He's a good kisser, and I like, you know..." She gestured around her chest with her hands. "But I thought after the first time it would get better, or at least last a bit longer."

"Oh my God, Tonya. You're dating a minute man!" I burst

179

out laughing and tried to avoid the playful whacks Tonya was aiming at me.

"Shut up. You and Nathan aren't even doing it yet." Failing to reach me with her swinging arms, she threw a pillow at me. I caught the pillow and tossed it back at her. My distraction plan had succeeded. Now, I just had to hold her off until the others arrived.

"Who said we weren't?"

"Chloe. She also told Bianca you're gonna be waiting a while." This time, she laughed louder. It sucked having a friend who was also friends with your sister. Not that Bianca and Chloe hung out a lot, but, apparently, it was enough that Chloe was spilling about my love life to her, and Bianca, in turn, was sharing with Tonya.

"Whatever." Not my smoothest comeback, but anything less lame was interrupted by the doorbell. Hoping it was Nathan, I leapt out of the chair and ran up the steps, with Tonya following at a much slower pace.

My luck with answering the door hadn't changed. Instead of Nathan, I found Dylan. I opened the door, trying to put on my polite face. Not the easiest task since Dylan ranked pretty low in my books, just above Vivian and Trevor. But he had gotten us the tickets half price, and he'd agreed to let me turn his date with Lily into a group event, so I figured I needed to at least be polite. For a while.

"Hey. Lily's downstairs," I said, and he nodded.

I went to the top of the stairs and yelled down to let her know it was Dylan. She made a response that I took for 'be right up'. I went back in to the living room to find Dylan making himself at home, sitting in my dad's recliner, his feet propped up on the coffee table while flipping through the channels on the TV.

"So, thanks for the tickets." Awkward, but what else could I say? Dylan and I had had little to talk about when he was a nice guy. Now that he'd turned into an ass, there was even less.

"Yeah, well, Lily told me your dad wouldn't let either of you go unless it was a group thing, so it's not like I had a choice." He shot me a dirty look before focusing back on the television screen.

Interesting. Lily was lying to Dylan. My lips tipped into a small smile. My angelic little sister was being a bad girl, telling fibs to her boyfriend.

"Where is everyone?" Tonya pulled out her cell phone to check the time. "Trevor's going to get there before us and start worrying. Especially after the whole turning off the cell thing you did earlier."

A groan of disgust escaped before I could control it, and I avoided the sharp look she sent my way. I'd been doing such a good job of distracting her, and now Dylan had broken my flow, and she was right back at it.

"That creep isn't coming, is he?" Dylan said, sitting forward to glare first at me then Tonya. Dylan got a little less jerk-ish. If he didn't like Trevor, then how could I be wrong?

"He's not a creep," Tonya spit out. "He's my boyfriend, and, yes, he's coming. He's going to meet us there, so he doesn't have to look at your ugly face."

"Really?" Lily asked softly from the entry to the living room. "Can we please not fight tonight? I seriously don't have the energy to pick up the pieces."

"They're not gonna fight, Lils. And if they do, they can deal with it on their own." I sank on to the couch.

Then Dylan completely floored me. He tossed the remote on to the coffee table and stood up to look at Lily.

"You look real pretty, Lils," he said, and gave her such a sweet smile I could almost see the Dylan she must have loved. "I'll be good. Promise."

She smiled back, but it faded as he stepped closer to her. By the time he took hold of her hand, it was gone, replaced by a sad look that only lasted a moment before she was yawning.

"Sorry," she said, covering her mouth. "I haven't been sleeping very well."

Liar. She'd been sleeping almost twelve hours a day, sometimes more, for the past couple of months.

She pulled away from him and sat between Tonya and the armrest, leaving no room for Dylan to sit beside her.

The bell rang again. Bianca leaned on the button even after I opened the door. Owen was squished to the edge of the porch, trying to put as much space between him and Karin.

"Girl, took you long enough," Bianca said, finally removing her finger from the bell and letting the constant chime echo itself to silence. "Please tell me you're all ready."

"Yes. I guess we're just waiting on Nathan."

"He'll be here any minute. I caught a glimpse of him getting in his dad's truck as we passed his place."

Nathan was driving since he was the only one who could get a truck. It would be a tight fit for the ride to the theater, but, once there, he'd be able to reverse in to the spot then we'd all pile in to the back of the truck.

"Guys, Nathan's almost here," I called in to the living room.

I grabbed my shoes and sat on the small stool beside the door to slip them on. Dylan, Lily, and Tonya joined us at the door just as two vehicles pulled up. The first was Dad's silver minivan, which he parked in the driveway. Nathan's was the second, and he pulled his dad's truck up behind my *Sunfire* in front of the house.

"Hey, Mr. Matlin," Bianca said as Dad made his way up the porch.

He greeted everyone as they parted to let him through. Once inside, he dropped his briefcase on the floor beside me.

"What time are you expecting to be home?" he asked, looking at Lily.

I rolled my eyes at his back. God forbid I give him an honest answer.

"The last show should be done by two, so probably around two-thirty. I'll call if it's going to be later," Lily answered.

"I know you will," he said, and this time, he caught my rolling eyes when he turned to me suddenly and said, "No more fighting."

"Sure. Whatever."

I wasn't sure what I'd done to earn his distrust, but, so far, he'd refused to allow me on a solo date with Nathan after curfew, even after giving Lily permission, and now he was expecting me to lie about how late we'd be out. Deep inside, I knew it wasn't me he didn't trust, but Nathan. Dylan had been around for years and had proven himself over and over, even if I thought that trust was sorely misplaced. And, well, there was the fact that Lily was an angel.

"I'm serious, Phoebe." He glanced over at my friends, who all seemed to be finding something interesting on their shoes or in the sky. "I'm trusting you."

I nearly rolled my eyes again, but knew if I did, I probably wouldn't make it out of the house for at least a month. Instead, I gave a tight smile and followed Lily and the others out to the truck.

Everyone piled in. Good thing Trevor was meeting us

there, because even with Dylan and Lily going in his car, and the extra large cab, we were sandwiched in. Owen had managed to maneuver his way in to sitting between Tonya and Bianca while Karin sat up front with Nathan and me.

Bianca kept us entertained during the twenty-minute drive with comments about the mall and Dylan's out-of-date Bieber hair. I even managed to relax a bit, because Tonya seemed to have let the whole cell phone thing go.

When we pulled up to the theater, Trevor's new truck was idling just outside the ticket plaza, and he followed us through the gate. Nathan handed over our tickets, and then reversed in to a spot beside Dylan's car. We poured out of the vehicle, and I took a deep breath, stretching my arms, glad that I had opted to bring my—well, Lily's—black cardigan.

The drive-in theater was one of the few old relics left in town. It had been built over forty years ago and still featured the plug-in radio set that hung on the window. Nathan propped it up on the side of the truck and cranked the volume up, filling the space around us with the sound of Elvis. Every time I went to the theater, the same songs played, and probably had since they'd opened.

Nathan and Owen hopped in to the bed of the truck to spread out a blanket and arrange the few pillows Lily pulled from Dylan's trunk. I turned to talk to Tonya, but she was already standing over by Trevor. She grasped his arm and dragged him over. Both were smiling. There was no way either of them could be truly mad at me. I felt a bit smug, knowing my quest to have a Trevor-free shopping day and then my distraction technique had worked so well.

Nathan reached out a hand to me, and I grasped it, letting him pull me up and on to the truck bed. It was already six, and, despite the lack of complete darkness, the first movie would be starting soon. We snuggled down on a pillow together in the middle of the truck bed, our backs pressed against the cab, and covered our legs with a blanket. It wasn't cold out, but I wasn't going to pass up a chance to cuddle with him.

Owen and Bianca spread out on their stomachs in front of us, propping their chins up on their hands. Tonya and Trevor sat inside his vehicle, hopefully behaving because Karin kept glancing their way from her position beside me. Lily and Dylan were still inside his car. I glanced around Nathan and could see Lily pressed against her door, with Dylan hidden on his side by the angle I looked from.

Seeing that distance between them reminded me of the assumption Dylan had made that our dad had been objecting to both Lily and I going on single dates to the Triple Feature. Not just me. Something was definitely going on with Lily, but I had no clue how to ask her about it. She was so quiet, and even though she was my favorite sister, I always found it easier to talk to Chloe. Maybe because she never shut up, and I got some major satisfaction by interrupting her.

"You okay?" Nathan asked, tightening his arm around me.

"Yeah," I said, and smiled up at him. "Perfect."

He titled his head down and lightly pressed his lips to mine. I leaned in to him.

"Hey," Bianca said, causing us to break apart and look at her. She'd twisted around to glare at us. "No macking on each other in front of the unattached."

"Unattached?" Nathan asked.

"Yeah. Us without a life mate. Us singles," she clarified when he continued to draw a blank.

I laughed at her terminology, and risked a peek at Karin.

She was sitting with her eyes glaring daggers at the back of Owen's head. I looked away before she could catch me staring. She didn't want to be one of the unattached, but since getting in the car, Owen had been doing his best to flirt with Bianca—something that was almost painful to watch. He definitely lacked finesse. Bianca had called before they arrived and told me she was going to take pity on him and play along with his attempt to shake Karin loose.

Karin wasn't exactly one of my close friends. She was more of a tag along, but I still felt bad knowing Owen didn't like her.

"I'm gonna go grab a drink. Wanna come with?" I asked Karin.

She looked a little startled by my suggestion.

"Sure."

"Can you grab me a Coke, too?" Nathan pulled out a ten and held it out to me.

I shook my head, and said, "I'll buy the drinks, and you can buy the food after the first movie."

Karin and I slipped down from the edge of the truck and headed for the concession stand. We didn't talk at first. Maybe because we rarely spoke without Bianca or Owen around. Finally, I couldn't stand the silence.

"So, you have plans for Spring Break?" I asked once we were in line.

She didn't say anything for a moment, and when she did, it wasn't to answer my question.

"Owen doesn't like me, does he? As more than a friend, I mean."

Wow. Okay. How does a person respond to that? I wasn't the dream crusher Tonya was. I couldn't just tell her flat out, but, then again, Owen would probably stop talking to me if he found out that I had encouraged her.

"Um ... I don't know. Owen and I don't talk about things like that." I avoided eye contact by focusing on the length of the line in front of us.

"It's okay. I figured out I'm not his type."

"His type?"

Owen had a type? I tried to picture him with any kind of girl and couldn't. He always struck me as more of a loner type. He hadn't been dating anyone recently, though I'd heard him mention an ex-girlfriend.

"Yeah. He always seems to date really feminine girls. Super sweet and in to fashion and all that."

I was speechless. Not only did Owen date, but he, apparently, had a type, and it was nothing like I would have guessed. A hippie, tree-hugging girl, yeah. Fashion plate, no way.

"How do you know this?" I asked when my shock wore off.

"Well, he dated Nadine over the summer, and that was after he hooked up with that foreign exchange student from England last year."

"Owen dated Jeanette? And Nadine? How did I not know this? How did Chloe not tell me?"

"It was probably due to the complete absorption you had with your devastation over Nathan and Vivian dating."

"I just can't believe it." A mental picture formed, and I cringed at the image of Owen and Nadine kissing. That was just plain wrong. Owen was...Owen. Weird Owen who we could tease and was oblivious to half the jokes we made about him.

The line moved, and we went with it automatically. Chloe was handing sodas and tubs of popcorn to the people in front of us. She smiled and acted natural, but I could see her attempting to avoid physical contact with the people.

Lily was much better at hiding her reactions when she was using her abilities. Chloe, on the other hand, froze and stared off in to space. The school nurse in elementary school had told Dad that he should get Chloe checked out for some type of seizure. She'd brought it up again and again, until, one day, Chloe told her that her husband was going to start sleeping with a coworker. Two months later, she was separated and never brought up the possible seizures again.

The couple ahead of us left, and we approached Chloe. She was decked out in a white shirt with a pair of red lips painted in the center—the official logo of the school's prom fundraiser. Just one more reason I was glad I wasn't possessed by the same drive to achieve as Chloe. Spending a weekend working to raise money for a dance I wasn't even planning on going to sounded even worse than staying at home.

She pulled a *Coke* and *Sprite* from off the soda fountain and passed them to me, along with my exact change all before I could even say a word.

"Why didn't you ever mention Owen and Nadine dating?" I asked while I pretended to survey the candy selection.

"Nadine and who?"

"Owen. Tall, skinny, long curly hair." I would've been surprised by her not knowing the name of one of my best friends if I didn't already know how self-focused she was. If they weren't her friends, they didn't exist.

"Oh. They dated?"

"How could you not know? Nadine is, like, your best friend."

She shrugged and flipped her hair back over her shoulder.

"Nadine and I didn't talk for, like, three months last summer. We had that fight about Andrew. Besides, she's got a new boyfriend practically every other week."

Karin ordered some popcorn, but when Chloe passed her the loaded bucket, she froze and stared right through me, dead-eyed. A moment later, she blinked and any enjoyment she'd been feeling before I'd come up was gone.

"You okay?" I asked her.

Karin gave us a curious look, completely unaware Chloe had had a vision.

"Yeah. I ... I'll talk to you when we get home tonight." She looked way too serious. I itched to drill her with questions, but the people behind me were getting antsy, slowly surging forward like a wave of zombies.

The first movie was right out of the 80's. Cheesy music, big hair, and ripped jeans. It was kind of weird to think that those could have been my parents, or at least my dad. My photos of Mom were right on. Her junior high graduation pictures demonstrated her vast skill with a pick and hairspray as her bangs stuck straight up a good four inches, only to curl forward at the top and fall like feathers around her face. But imagining Dad with a mullet or even a pair of ripped jeans with a patterned sweater was just plain wrong.

Nathan and I cuddled close, trying to ignore the fact that we weren't alone. Not the easiest thing to do with Karin sulking in the corner of the truck bed as Owen and Bianca playfully flirted to fend her off.

Owen and Nathan went off during the break between the first two movies, and the girls and I started to gossip about some of the people we could see from our vantage point. Couples making out or fighting. Bianca even spotted a guy from our Spanish class the previous semester picking his nose. We were discussing the various other bad habits the guy had when Lily popped up at the side of the truck. She stood up on her tiptoes and rested her arms along the side to peer over at us. Being so short must have really sucked.

"Where's Dylan?" Karin asked, glancing over at the empty car.

"The manager was having some computer problem. I guess since Dylan's used the new ones downtown, they asked him to help."

"Come sit," I said, and patted Nathan's empty spot beside me. She looked totally drained, and I felt terrible for practically forcing her to come. Even though she hadn't looked tired earlier, it seemed as if she were about ready to collapse. She almost fell as she climbed up, but managed to pull herself up and sit on Nathan's side of the body pillow we'd been sharing.

"Do you mind if I watch the next movie out here?" she asked, avoiding my gaze.

"Sure. You okay?"

I didn't play the protective older sister routine often, I usually left that to Chloe, but, sometimes, Lily would get that lost little girl look and I wanted to just curl my arms around her. I didn't give in very often. Mainly based on my theory that two minutes didn't make me wiser, stronger, or more daring. Chloe, however, claimed her five-minute head start on us made her much superior to us mentally, emotionally, and physically.

"Yeah. I'm alright. It's just that Dylan isn't feeling well, so it's a bit draining being with him right now."

"You know you don't have to heal him if you don't want to," I said.

"It's not really a choice when you're sitting half a foot

away."

"Well, you can chill with us, and Dylan can enjoy his pity party in the car alone." I swung an arm over her shoulders and squeezed it briefly, then scooted over a bit to give her some space, not wanting her to feel something inside of me that needed healing.

Owen and Nathan arrived with food, and although Nathan quirked an eyebrow at Lily sitting in his spot, he didn't say a word. Instead, he plopped himself on my other side and handed me a bucket of buttery popcorn.

"Hey. I thought you were getting me a hot dog?" I said, scrunching up my forehead and striving for an evil eye.

"Well, I figured you didn't need it since I'm already—"

I elbowed Nathan lightly. Guys could be such pervs.

"Please don't finish that," Bianca said over her shoulder. Nathan and Owen chuckled, and it occurred to me that Owen was probably more of a guy than I'd ever realized before.

The second movie was slightly better, if only fashion-wise. The plot was eerily similar to the first, and the acting sucked, but it had at least been filmed after I was born. Dylan reappeared shortly after it started and frowned at Lily, but kept his mouth shut. He watched the first part of the movie in his car, sulking, I would guess, and then finally joined us on the truck, ending up beside Owen since I had squished Lily against the edge. She needed a healing break.

When the next intermission came, I decided to try and get Tonya to join us. It wasn't so much that I wanted her to be with us, as I didn't want her to be with Trevor. Nathan gave me a knowing look as I scooted over the edge and hopped to the ground. Walking around to Trevor's truck, I knocked on Tonya's window, glad to see that they weren't making out.

"What's up?" Tonya asked once her window had rolled

down completely. She avoided looking at me, but I could see her eyes rimmed with red and faint tear tracks on her cheek. Getting Tonya to join us suddenly felt a lot more vital.

"I was wondering if I could talk to you. It's important."

I watched her glance at Trevor, who scowled and made some remark under his breath. It pissed me off, and, suddenly, my mouth was running.

"Is that a problem, Trevor?" I snapped.

"Phoebs, don't start," Tonya said.

"What? He can be a prick, and I shouldn't call him on it?"

Trevor leaned over, his arm extended with his finger jutting toward me. "Listen, bitch. I'm sick of taking your crap. You think I'm stupid or something? I know you turned off Tonya's phone, and you're always talking smack about me behind my back."

The car and Tonya between us fed my courage.

"Yeah; I turned her phone off. You were practically stalking her. I got sick of hearing how you can't let her do anything without you." My voice had risen, and I could feel the stillness of my friends behind me. "Now, if you don't mind, I'd like to talk to my friend."

I stepped back, feeling pretty smug, even if my legs were shaking. The self-satisfaction fled instantly, though, when Trevor suddenly got out of the vehicle and came around to the side where I stood. Instinct propelled me backward until I ran in to a human wall that smelled of Nathan.

"Back off, Trevor," Nathan said.

I glanced at him, and although he looked calm, I could feel how tense he was. Owen and Dylan stood slightly off to our left while Bianca, Karin, and Lily knelt in the back of the truck, watching with widened eyes.

"Tell your bitch to shut the hell up then and mind her own

damn business."

He took another step closer. Tonya quickly got out of the truck and placed a hand on his arm. He shrugged her off the first time, but the second time she reached for him, he turned and cuffed her on the chin, causing her fall back against the truck and cry out in pain.

Every bit of me froze in astonishment and horror. Had he really just hit my best friend right in front of me? In front of all of us? I waited for some reaction from Tonya, but there was no shock or anger. Just a subtle shifting away; a cowering. Even as I went to make my move, Nathan was pushing me behind him and going for Trevor.

Everything happened so fast. Nathan swung his fist and connected with Trevor's face. Trevor stumbled back, colliding with Tonya, and fell when she shifted out of his way. We all just stood there, none of us having any idea of what to say or do.

"Get the hell out of here," Nathan said.

"You can't kick me out." Trevor spat out a stream of red tinted spit and pushed himself up to his feet.

"No, but I can," Dylan said.

He probably couldn't, yet he spoke with an authority that convinced Trevor.

"Tonya, get in. We're leaving." Trevor went around to his side of his truck and finally looked at her. She was still standing there, her hand cradling her chin and tears streaming down her face. "Now!" he yelled.

"Screw you," I snarled, and curled Tonya in to a hug. "Come on. Let's go to the restroom."

Tonya hesitated, her eyes shifting from me to Trevor, then back again.

"Tee, it'll just get worse if you go with him," I said.

"I just want to go home," she whispered, keeping her head down.

Trevor didn't say another word. Just got in his truck and pulled out of his spot, flipping us off as he drove away, maneuvering his way between the parked vehicles.

"Everybody is staring," Tonya said softly, and I shot them all a look over her head. They took the hint and scattered.

Lily hovered just behind Tonya, her hands twitching at her sides. I gave her a slight nod, and she lifted her hand to Tonya's back, touching her so gently I wondered if she really felt Lily at all until she spoke.

"Thanks, Lils." Tonya pulled away from me and smiled over her shoulder at Lily, who made her way to Dylan's car. Her immediate pain was gone, but considering the red swelling forming on her jaw, she was going to be feeling it later.

We got in to the vehicle, and Nathan pulled out silently, trying not to hit any of the parked vehicles. He knew if he scratched the truck, he was a dead man.

Tonya didn't say anything on the drive home, and I wasn't sure what to say. 'I told you so' was on the tip of my tongue, but I knew uttering those words would turn me into a horrible person. We pulled up to her house ten minutes later, and I finally opened my mouth to speak.

"Don't," Tonya said, her voice quivering just a bit. "I'll call you tomorrow."

She climbed from the truck, and Nathan and I watched, not pulling away until she was safely inside with the door locked behind her.

Once she was gone, emotions flooded me. Anguish at what Tonya had suffered. Horror that I had witnessed something like that. Anger that suffocated me. I had let this happen. I knew that Trevor was a liar, that he had hurt Tonya in the past, but I hadn't listened to my gift. I'd let Tonya, Nanna, and Nathan convince me I was wrong and that he wasn't so bad.

Tonya had been guided by love and fear. Nanna had never met the guy, and, honestly, she hadn't told me I was wrong about him; just to not rely entirely upon my gift. Nathan, though, he had seen the bruises. He had met Trevor. And he had been the one to blackmail me in to giving Trevor a chance. A chance to beat up my friend.

"Jesus. I can't believe that happened," he said, flexing the hand he'd punched Trevor with.

"Really? Because I could have sworn that I told you what an ass the guy was."

The truck lurched, and Nathan stared at me in shock. There was no way he could have missed my fury.

"What is that supposed to mean?" he asked, pulling over to the side of the road.

"It means I knew that he'd hurt Tonya, and you kept telling me I was wrong." I gazed out the side window, not wanting to look at him. Guilt was eating at my heart, creating a pain so intense that I could barely focus.

"I didn't say you were wrong, Phoebs. I told you to give him a chance and get to know him before you passed your all mighty judgment."

"No. You blackmailed me," I said, brushing off the hand he rested on my arm. My stomach twisted with guilt, quickly churning it into righteous anger. "You told me you would break up with me if I didn't stop trying to convince people about what he really was like. He never would have had a chance to hurt her again if I hadn't given in to you."

"You really think that's what I meant? That I didn't care if he was hurting her?"

"Obviously not."

"I can't fricking believe this!" His palm slammed the top of the steering wheel. "You're blaming me for not knowing the guy was abusive?"

"You knew! I told you what he'd done. I told you—" I turned to face him, crossing my arms over my chest.

"You told me some voice in your head called him a liar. That the same voice in your head called Tonya a liar when she covered up some bruises. You know what my dad would do if one of his officers told him some voice in their head was telling them things? He'd have them in to the department shrink before they could even blink."

"So you don't believe that I have this gift?"

"No. Yes. Jesus, Phoebe. I don't know. This is seriously crazy shit."

Crazy. He thought I was crazy. My heart broke. It squeezed tightly for just a moment then exploded into a shower of confetti, the delicate pieces leaving a horrible hollow ache where my heart should have been. Maybe that was why I'd always tried to keep the teasing between us; tried to make things into some game. Because underneath everything, and behind the sweet kisses, I knew that he didn't really accept me. That he thought I was crazy.

My silence must have registered with him, because he sighed deeply and put the truck back in gear. We drove the rest of the way back to my house without a word. When he pulled up, I jumped from the vehicle and practically ran for the door. I knew he was following, but I didn't look back.

"Phoebe, I'm sorry. I shouldn't have said that. I don't think you're crazy. I just can't accept things like that without proof. Even you said that you couldn't be sure what had happened to cause those bruises."

"I was sure until you planted doubts in my head. You let this happen, Nathan. You. And I don't think I can forgive that." My eyes flicked over him, and then quickly away. I shoved the key in to the lock and opened the door, letting the soft glow of the foyer lamp meld with that of the porch light.

"So, what now? That's it? We're done?"

"I need some time." My voice cracked, and I hated myself for showing a hint of weakness.

"Time. Sure. Whatever. Time for you to decide whether or not I caused Trevor to hit Tonya. Time to figure out if maybe you should have spent some of your efforts convincing Tonya about him instead of me." He paused, and I knew he wanted me to give some kind of protest, but I couldn't. This was his fault. Eventually, he gave up waiting. "Fine. I'm outta here."

I watched the tail lights of the truck disappear down the road and was still standing there ten minutes later when the lights from Dylan's car flashed across me as he pulled in to the driveway. I didn't move until Lily began walking purposefully toward me. Then I ran. I couldn't let Lily make this better. I needed to feel the hurt. I needed to remember why I shouldn't want to call Nathan already.

My room was cold and empty. Even curling up under the covers didn't help. I squeezed my eyes shut, willing them to hold in the tears that wanted so badly to fall. I'd gone to bed angry; furious with Nathan and Trevor. But, in the light of the morning, I just felt alone.

I stayed huddled in bed until a soft knock at my door propelled me from my cushy haven. Lily called through, but I didn't answer her. I knew she wanted to help, but I wasn't ready for it. At my desk, I sifted through a pile of papers, searching for something, anything, that would take my mind off Nathan.

My phone was tucked under Lily's notes that I'd borrowed. I flipped it over and over in the palm of my hand before pressing the screen. I started as it lit up, and my fingers twitched.

Nathan's name and number popped up on the screen. It had been less than twelve hours since I broke up with him, but I already wanted to hear his voice. I'd never thought I'd be so weak or needy. My thumb drifted over the send button, but, at the last moment, I scrolled to the next name and kept going until Tonya's name appeared.

Talking to Nathan right then wouldn't do any good. I was still too angry. Tonya was really the one I needed to speak with, but I dreaded that conversation. What would I say? 'Sorry your boyfriend punched you' or 'sorry I pissed Trevor off so much that he punched you instead of me' didn't seem quite right. 'Sorry I was right' sounded even worse.

A knock at my door gave me stalling time, and I gratefully dropped the cell on to my desk.

"Come in," I said, swirling my chair around.

"Hey." Chloe peeked around the door. "Just wanted to see how you were feeling."

"Like crap. You may as well come in." I spun my chair in circles as she sat on the bed. "Did you know?"

"A bit. I only had glimpses, and they didn't fit together too well."

"But you knew about Tonya and Trevor? And about Nathan and me?" I tried to sound blasé, but didn't quite manage.

"Yes." The word came softly, yet still it pierced my chest.

"How could you not have told me?" My feet dropped to

the ground and halted the nauseating spins.

"Phoebe, you know my visions are the future. They can't be changed."

"That's crap! Not everything you've predicted lately has happened, and you know it."

"Well, obviously, I was right this time. What should I have done instead? Huh? Told you and ruined the entire night for you, while you waited for Trevor to pounce? What would the point have been?"

"I don't know, but Tonya is hurt, and you could have done something to prevent it." I crossed my arms over my chest and gave her the evil eye.

"You know what, Phoebe? You blame Nathan and me, and I know you're going to dump on Nanna, but what about you? And Trevor? Or even Tonya?" She mimicked my pose.

"Tonya didn't ask to be hit!" I snapped back. "I tried to warn her, but everyone else said I was being silly."

"I didn't say she asked for it." She rolled her eyes. "But she knew what he was like, and she stayed with him anyway. Maybe you should find out why."

"God. I hate it when you get all smug and self-righteous." My lips curled on one side in a sneer.

"That's not what I'm trying to do, Phoebs."

"Whatever." I twisted away from her and snatched up a pair of jeans from the floor. "Now, if you don't mind, I'm busy trying to decide what clothes to wash."

She gave me a brief glare and then left. I tried to shove aside her words about my shifting blame. Blame didn't matter nearly as much as Tonya.

Instead of calling, I fumbled through a text, asking Tonya if she'd like to get some coffee. A minute later, I got my one-word answer. *Yes.* I grabbed my jacket and headed upstairs, purposely stomping down the hall and bumping Chloe's door open. It was childish, but I felt a smidge of satisfaction that she'd have to get up and close it again.

Driving toward Tonya's place, my stomach churned the entire way. The words I wanted to say jumbled in my mind with everything I knew I probably should say. Fury kept me from forming the proper ones, and it made me sick to think that when I saw her, everything could come out wrong. That I wouldn't be able to keep some of it in.

Tonya was sitting on the front steps, arms wrapped around her legs and chin resting on her knees. When she saw me pull up, she leapt up and jogged over. The curtains in the living room parted, and Mrs. Robinson's face appeared. I gave a small wave, and she nodded. No friendly greeting, though. She probably knew about how I'd covered for Tonya. Great. No more homemade cookies for me.

Tonya climbed in the passenger side, giving me the small smile her gran withheld.

"Hey," I said, ignoring the fact that I was being totally lame. My hands twisted on the steering wheel as she tugged on her seatbelt. It was hard not to stare at the bruising.

"Hey. Thanks for coming to get me. I don't think Gran would have let me leave by myself." Her eyes rolled with annoyance.

"I take it she knows?"

"Yeah. She was still up when I got home. She flipped when she saw..." She let the sentence trail off, gesturing to the massive purple and red bruise along the left side of her jaw. Even with her darker complexion and multiple layers of make-up, it was impossible to miss. Lily's quick healing after it happened had only relieved the immediate pain. "I can't believe she didn't ground me."

An uncomfortable silence settled between us, and I flipped on the radio. I drove toward the town center instinctively, weaving between lanes and generally driving like my dad never wanted to know, but before we hit the parking lot, I reconsidered. There were a lot of people there. People we knew. People who would wonder and question what had happened to Tonya's face. Would she want all of them to see her now?

"Want to hit up the new coffee shop by the park?" I tried to sound like it was based solely on my desire to go there. Not to avoid people. "Lily said they have the best iced mocha latte."

"Sure. Gran bought some muffins there the other day, and they were pretty good." She grit her teeth, or was that a smile? It was hard to tell with each of us avoiding looking at the other.

The stilted, unimportant words continued to flow between us, but neither of us seemed able to stop pretending that everything was back to normal. The words carried us in to the cafe and out to the park with our drinks. It wasn't until we sat on a wrought-iron bench overlooking the small pond that we gave up on the meaningless blather. We had no more empty words to keep the meaningless blather going.

The water rippled with the slight breeze, pushing it closer to shore, lapping against the rocks. Lily and I had once tried to swim there, but after braving the rocks, we took one look at the brownish-green water with its real live bugs and headed for the indoor pool instead. Trevor was like that water—great to look at from a distance, but up close, it was better to just walk away.

"Say it," Tonya said after a minute of silence.

"Say what?" I glanced at her. There were so many things I

wanted to say, that I needed to say, but what was she expecting?

"I told you so." She stared straight ahead, and I could see the glistening of tears in the corner of her eyes.

"That's not what I wanted to say."

"Phoebs," she said, disbelief arching her eyebrows. "It's true. You warned me, and I didn't listen. It's my own fault."

A tear trickled down her cheek, and I wrapped my arms around her. "It is not your fault, Tonya. Trevor made a choice to hit you. He's the one to blame."

"I know that. I do. But..."

"There are no buts. He did this to you. You didn't force him to punch you." I gave her a squeeze, wanting to push out any idea she had that she might somehow justify what happened.

"No, but I guess I just figured ... I stayed with him. That time you saw the bruises on my arm was the first time it happened. He didn't mean to hurt me."

I pulled away and knelt in front of her, forcing her to look at me.

"He did mean to, Tonya. That's what guys like him do. They convince you that it'll never happen again. That they didn't mean to do it, or that it was somehow your fault. There is absolutely no way you are to blame. At all."

Her breath hitched and came out in a sob. "I just thought that he wouldn't do it again. And then you stopped bugging me about it, and everyone seemed to like him. Even you."

The indignation I had felt the night before resurfaced. Nathan and Nanna had forced me in to giving Trevor a chance, to see him as a good person, and that was why Tonya had kept dating him.

Okay, so maybe they didn't force me, but if they had just

supported me, even a little, this never would have happened. I should have listened to my gift, if I hadn't let them convince me to doubt myself, Tonya would never have been hurt. They were just as guilty as Trevor.

"And it's not like he was like that all the time. He was always so sweet."

"Not always."

"No, but he really seemed to love me. I mean, he always wanted to be with me and take care of me. You saw how nice he could be."

"That doesn't mean he's not an abusive prick," I pointed out. "What did Gran say?"

"She cried at first, and then she got all pissed. I think if Trevor had been anywhere around, she'd have killed him."

"And?" I asked when she stopped talking. There was no way Gran would have left it at that.

"No internet for six months, which includes on my phone, tablet, or any other device that could possibly connect me to the world. She already cut down the data plans to limited texts. And I have to start seeing my therapist again." She sighed and gave another eye roll.

"Good."

"Yeah, well, I can handle the therapist. She's not all that bad, and she did help with my mommy and daddy issues, but no internet? How can I go that long without tweeting? I'll be completely out of the loop on everything."

"Hey. I manage fine," I said.

She gave a sobbing chuckle. "Yeah, because I'm constantly filling you in. I may as well commit social suicide if I have to depend on you. Maybe I'll make nice with Chloe." We both laughed at the idea of her befriending Chloe. "Well, it's either her or Bianca, and Bianca always posts the weirdest crap."

The light laugh felt good, smothering the awkwardness between us.

"Are you really okay?" I asked, sliding back on to the bench.

"Yeah. I wish things had ended up different, you know, but I'm glad it's done." She shrugged, and her lips tilted into a sheepish smile. "I kept thinking it would never happen again. That, each time, that was it. I didn't even realize how sick I felt every time I was with him, wondering if he was going to snap, until this morning when I realized it was done. I'm never going to see him again."

She noisily sucked at the last of her latte, and I let her words fill me with relief. But, even then, there was a niggling feeling in my stomach that the words were simply that. Words. She wasn't lying, but she wasn't speaking the truth either. It sounded more rehearsed as if she'd had to convince herself of their truth.

"What about pressing charges?" I asked. "You know my dad would help—"

"No!" Her head shook violently. I'd already risked our friendship too many times to push this issue as well. She ran her hands along her cheeks, wincing when she touched the bluish-purple flesh. "I just want to put it behind me."

"Do you wanna talk about it?" I offered, but I knew that wasn't the greatest idea. I was best known for my verbal vomit, and that wasn't going to help Tonya. But she needed to know that I was there for her.

"I'm going to be spilling my guts to the shrink every Thursday until I'm eighteen, so I think I'll pass. Besides, you already missed your opportunity to gloat, so starting now, this whole Trevor mess is off limits."

Putting Trevor in the past was more than fine. Now I just

had to remember to put Nathan there, too.

CHAPTER 12

NATHAN WAS BEHIND ME. It was where I'd been thinking and praying of putting him for the past thirty-odd hours. Him literally sitting behind me, his soft puffs of breath fanning across my neck, was not how I'd envisioned it. It was only twenty minutes in to class, and I'd already had to fend off his trailing fingers along my shoulder, the whispers of my name, and even a note he'd eventually slid around me to place on my desk.

I hadn't even opened the note. I'd simply ignored it. But the problem with ignoring it was that, ten minutes later, it was still sitting in front of me, tempting me to take a peek. My pencil tapped spastically on my desk in one hand, while my other hand fiddled with the zipper of my hoodie, barely containing the urge to reach for the folded paper.

Something flicked against my head, and I flinched in surprise, reaching up to rub the spot hit. A small, pink pencil tip eraser dropped from my hair on to the floor, and I glanced over my shoulder. Tonya was staring at me with one of her 'what's your problem' looks, gesturing toward Nathan.

I shrugged my shoulder and turned back to Mr. Arnold. He was writing some formula on the board, and I stopped my furious tapping to copy it down. Not that it made any sense to me at the moment, but it was better than obsessing over Nathan.

I hadn't told Tonya about breaking up with Nathan. It

wasn't that I was hiding it. I just didn't know how to tell her without bringing up the whole Trevor thing, and I'd promised not to bring him up again.

When class ended, I was ready to scream. Nathan had seemed determined to annoy me for the entire hour. I wasn't sure what purpose he had in mind, but he was definitely pissing me off. I shoved my notes in to my binder and snapped it shut.

"Phoebe," Nathan's hand skimmed my arm, "what's wrong?"

"Seriously?" I glanced up at him before letting my eyes flicker over Tonya, who was standing behind him, listening in.

"You're still mad?" His eyebrows soared in surprise.

"Uh, yeah."

"I can't believe you're still angry. I thought you just needed a breather or something. Look. I get that you're upset, but it's not like I knew what would happen." He gave me one of his sexy smiles and moved close enough that I could smell the soap he'd used that morning. "I'm sorry, okay? Why don't I come over after school, and we'll talk."

"I don't have anything left to say to you." I scooped the note from my desk and tossed it on to his. Walking away, I felt both Nathan and Tonya watching me. But my double escape was short lived. I barely made it to my locker when Tonya caught up to me.

"What the freaking hell was that?" she asked.

"What was what?" Maybe dumb would work for me this time.

"Come on, Phoebs. What was up with giving Nathan the cold shoulder? For a second, I thought I was looking at Vivian. Did he cop a feel or something a bit too much for your virgin sensibilities?"

"Ha ha. No," I said, choosing to ignore the Vivian insult. I tossed my stuff inside my locker and grabbed my next set of books. A quick peek at her told me I was wasting my time by hoping that she would drop it. I slammed the locker shut. "Fine. I broke up with him Saturday night."

"What?! Why?"

"Because...just because. All right? I don't want to talk about it. Now, if you don't mind, I have to get to class." I tried to walk away again, but she blocked my path, practically squishing me up against my locker.

"No way are you not explaining that. We are so ditching next period. Now, spill." She placed her hands on her hips and waited.

"He's why I stopped bugging you about Trevor." I avoided her look, knowing she probably didn't even want to hear his name. "I knew something was wrong with the guy. I knew that you were covering for him, but Nathan convinced me to give him a chance. Actually, he blackmailed me and said that if I didn't stop being suspicious of Trevor, then he wouldn't go out with me anymore."

"And?"

"And what?"

"And what does that have to do with what Trevor did?" she asked, complete confusion evident on her face.

"Because if he hadn't done that, I would have caught him in a lie ... or something."

"You can't blame Nathan for something Trevor did. As messed up as I am right now with all this crap, even I know that. So, what's the real reason?"

Nathan was the reason. He was why Tonya had still been with Trevor. Why Trevor had had the chance to hurt her.

That was what I'd told Nathan. That was the real reason, wasn't it? But Tonya made it sound so completely illogical, and, honestly, I think I knew she was right, but, still, I couldn't let it go. I swallowed hard and closed my eyes, trying to think of how I'd felt Saturday night.

Vindicated.

It was an odd way to feel after what happened to Tonya, but it had felt like I finally had proof that I was right. Proof that my gift was real. Proof that I wasn't broken.

"Come on. Let's go outside," Tonya said.

If we were going to ditch class, I didn't want to lug around all my crap. Turning back to my locker, I opened it up and put my books back inside then added Tonya's stuff as well. She stepped back, giving me a bit of space, and I took a deep breath, trying to stay calm. Getting angry—or worse, crying—wouldn't help me escape Tonya.

We walked to the exit, not speaking until we sat at a picnic table outside the cafeteria. Even then I stalled, picking at the peeling brown paint covering the table. It was a bit breezy, and I wished I'd worn more than just my hoodie.

"Okay. So quit stalling and explain how any of this shit is Nathan's fault," Tonya said, sitting across from me.

"My sisters have had their gifts forever. I mean, right from conception kind of thing. Chloe and Lily always used to talk about feeling Mom or even having seen her. I had nothing. I was always the one without a gift."

"Nothing new, Phoebe. Remember me telling you this is the whole mommy issue you've had since we met?"

"Whatever. You only say that because you've got some serious issues with your mom." At least that was what her therapist said, and, apparently, it was what the shrink had said about me, too, when Tonya had blabbed my life story once. "Besides, this isn't about my mom."

"Yeah, well, you haven't gotten to the part where Nathan is to blame for … you know."

"The point is that when my gift started working, I was so happy. I was finally going to be normal, or at least normal in my family, but Nathan made me doubt that. He made me feel like I couldn't trust my gift or myself. That's why I'm not ready to forgive him."

Tonya was quite for a moment, then said, "Damn. if I could psychoana-whatever myself like you, I wouldn't be suffering for two hours every week."

The slight change in conversation was like a lifeline that I readily grasped on to. "Two hours? I thought you were only going once a week."

"Yeah, well, Gran decided that in addition to the shrink, I need to go to a counseling group, too. I'm kissing my Saturdays goodbye."

"That sucks. Well, that it's on Saturday, I mean. Not that... Anyway, maybe we both need a break from boys." Maybe I needed a break from letting Nathan make me doubt myself.

"Ha. Speak for yourself. I plan to move on to the next hot thing. Did you see that new guy? I think his name is Mike or Mickey. Something like that." She flicked a piece of paint I had peeled from the table in to the breeze.

"Mickey? Are you honestly saying that you would go out with a guy named after a cartoon mouse?"

"Hey. The guy is hot, and he's got a serious bad boy thing going on with a tattoo and buzz cut. I can't believe you haven't noticed him. I'm pretty sure I saw him heading in to your civics class on Friday."

"Huh. Well, if his name's Mickey then he's all yours." Besides, it wasn't as if I was totally over Nathan … or even a little over him yet.

"Well, if you're really done with Nathan, maybe I'll go for him." She smiled. I knew she was joking, but, still, my gut twisted.

"If you want to die anytime soon."

"So, why did you break up with him again?" she asked.

"Fine. So he might not be directly at fault, but if he hadn't convinced me to stop distrusting Trevor, maybe you would have finally listened to me. You even said that was one of the reasons you gave him another chance."

"Girl, you could twist the words of a saint just to prove your point."

As the wind picked up, clouds drifted in front of the sun and my arms broke out in goosebumps, causing me to shiver. "Come on. Let's get back inside before Mother Nature decides to dump rain on us as well."

We ran back to the school as gusts of wind blew in more storm clouds from the coast. The halls were deserted, so Tonya and I sank to the floor in front of her locker. We spent the rest of the class period flipping through a *Cosmo* magazine and debating when a person's butt crossed the line in to fat ass territory.

After the bell rang, Tonya and I headed to my locker to grab her books. I'd just handed them to her when I spotted Nathan walking down the hall toward me. I tensed, expecting another confrontation. Or, at least, some response from him. Maybe even just an acknowledgment that I was still important to him. After all, I'd broken up with him. His eyes settled on me before darting away to look at the person walking beside him.

Vivian.

Vivian. And I wanted to punch her face in, even more

than when she'd soaked me at the theater. She was smiling. First it was up at Nathan and then at me. I knew she'd been waiting. I just hadn't expected Nathan to go back to her. He said he didn't double back in the dating department, so why was he with her?

I slammed my locker shut. Vivian didn't know how lucky she was. If Dad hadn't drilled me about the importance of not starting a fight, and if I wasn't a bit freaked at the idea of being in an all-out fight, I'd have popped her in the face so quick she wouldn't have even seen it coming.

* * *

Later that afternoon, I was lying on my bed listening to music, trying to block out the lingering image of Nathan and Vivian together when Chloe opened the door. I pulled out my earphones and glared at her.

"Nice of you to just barge in," I said, sweeping strands of hair from my face.

"I didn't barge in. I knocked, and then took your silence for permission to come in." She leaned against the doorframe. "Nathan is upstairs."

"Tell him I'm not home." I seethed. How dare he come here after he'd been hanging with Vivian all day?

"Too late. He knows you're here."

"Then tell him I'm washing my hair, or better yet, tell him I don't want to talk to his cheating face."

"Not cheating if you're not dating. Besides, I don't think he was banging Vivian in the halls between classes, Phoebs."

"I don't want to talk to him." My aggravation with Chloe nearly beat the anger I felt toward Nathan.

"Tell him yourself." She disappeared from my door before I could argue anymore. Then just as quickly as she left, Nathan took her place, and my heart sank to the very depths of my stomach.

"Can we talk?"

God. His eyes had pure puppy begging power.

"What do you want me to say?" I asked, sitting up cross-legged.

"I just want to know that this is going to ... I don't know... get fixed."

"It can't be fixed." I pulled up a mental picture of Tonya the day after the assault, and it helped the bitterness I needed to feel flare to life. "It's not broken. It's just done. We're done."

"Oh, come on. I'm sorry. It's not like I knew Trevor was gonna do something like that."

"But I knew!" I jabbed myself in the chest. "And when I told you, you talked me out of it. You convinced me to give him a chance. God. You blackmailed me in to it."

"I never forced you, or blackmailed you in to anything, Phoebe." He pushed away from the doorframe and stepped in to my room.

"No. You just threatened to stop dating me if I didn't give him a chance."

"That's not what I said. I was just sick of constantly listening to you talk about the guy. I asked you to think about me when we were together, instead of Trevor. I felt like you didn't even know I was there half the time," Nathan argued. "I never said you had to like him, or that you had to stop warning Tonya about him. But I was dating you, and guys don't like their girlfriends obsessing over other guys."

"You made me doubt myself, Nathan! I waited years for my gift, and when it finally happened, you made me think I didn't understand it. That I couldn't trust it or myself."

"Phoebs, I didn't mean to make you doubt your gift. I was

frustrated with constantly listening to you go on about it."

"Yeah, because it made me such a horrible person to worry about my friend being hurt."

"I didn't say that," he sighed. "It's just that you had no real proof that anything was actually happening."

"Maybe I didn't have proof, but I knew it."

"Because of your gift?"

"Yes!" I yelled. "But that wasn't enough for you! Because you don't believe I have a gift."

"Whoa! That's what this is about? You think I don't believe you have this gift? Because I do believe you. I never thought you were making things up."

Stay mad. Even if he wasn't wrong, he wasn't right either. "What does it matter now anyway? You and Vivian picked up right where you left off."

He rolled his eyes. "I'm not dating Vivian again. Especially considering I'm still with you. She asked about borrowing my notes from last Friday. That's all."

"Sure. And I just imagined that she's been stalking you for weeks. I just imagined the gloating smile she gave me in the hall today when you were walking with her."

"I don't really care what Vivian did."

"Well, neither do I, because we're not dating anymore. She's welcome to you." I folded my arms across my chest and glared at him.

He looked hurt. As hurt as I was at the idea of him being with someone else, especially with Vivian, but I couldn't forget how he'd manipulated me.

"You don't mean that, Phoebe, and you'll regret saying it." He took a small step back.

"I don't think so." I already did, but pride kept me from admitting that. Instead, I flung myself back on the bed and jabbed my headphones back on. No music flowed out, but he didn't know that, and I didn't want to look for the iPod in the tangled sheets.

"Call me when you're ready to talk." He spun around and left. I heard his stomping feet on the stairs and then moving across the living room. The door slammed. He was gone.

I vibrated with anger and the urge to cry hysterically. I wanted to call him right then and apologize, beg him to come back, but I wouldn't. He'd been the one in the wrong. Not me. He was the one that needed to keep apologizing until I was ready to forgive him.

"You okay?" Chloe asked as she came in to my room.

"No, obviously." I yanked out the ear buds and levered myself up on my elbows. "Nathan is mad at me! As if this is all my fault. I know that Vivian is trying to get back with him. God. She's such a skank. And he'll probably just go along with it. How can he be so stupid?"

"Can I tell you something?" she asked.

"Chloe, I'd really appreciate it if you kept my future to yourself. I'm so not in the mood for your gloating."

She arched her eyebrows in a way that told me I was about to hear what she had to say regardless of whether I wanted to or not.

"Nathan made a choice, just like you did." She pointed a finger at me. "Maybe he wasn't one hundred percent right, but neither were you. Something is coming. Something real bad, Phoebs, and you're going to realize just how much of a bitch you're being to Nathan. He's not perfect, but he's a hell of a lot better than Trevor or even Dylan."

"I'm not being a bitch. You're acting as if I shouldn't be mad. How would you like your boyfriend convincing you that you're wrong to believe in yourself? Oh, that's right. You don't have a boyfriend."

It was a petty thing to bring up, but I felt like being petty. With Lily, I had to watch my words, but Chloe could take it. I never had to worry about hurting her feelings. Then again, I don't think she had any.

"Oh. Get over yourself." She rolled her eyes. "I didn't say you shouldn't be angry. Hell. I can't believe you even let Nathan talk you in to doubting yourself. But that's the thing, Phoebs. In the end, it was your choice." She spun on her heel and left the room. Just before she vanished down the hall, she turned back. "Nanna's coming over this weekend. The two of you will have an interesting conversation."

I threw my pillow at her, but she was gone before it even left my hand. Not that it would have hit her, or even come close. Instead, it slammed in to my laptop and caused a glass jar full of pencils, pens, popsicle sticks, and some random crap to spill on to the floor.

Great. Nanna. Just what I didn't need—something else to worry about for the next four and a half days.

* * *

Four days to prep for Nanna was not enough time. A year wouldn't be long enough. That Saturday, I'd made plans with Tonya for an afternoon of shopping and then a sleepover at her place, but Nanna, damn her, changed her plans without telling anyone and showed up while I was still asleep.

I'd pulled myself out of bed just after ten, and there she was in the kitchen, making breakfast. I should have realized by the glorious smell of sausage and eggs, but I wandered in, completely oblivious to the hell that awaited me.

"I see you finally managed to pull yourself out of bed," she said over her shoulder.

Knowing I'd be shit of out luck with breakfast if I pissed

her off, I bit my tongue hard to keep back a snarky response. My chair scraped along the floor as I sat at the table and tried to muster a welcoming smile.

"Where is everyone?" I asked as she placed two plates of food on the table and then sat down opposite me. I picked up my fork and dug in while she sat silently, staring at me.

"Your father took Chloe to a doctor's appointment, and Lily is out avoiding you." She started eating, keeping her eyes on me.

"Avoiding me?" A fork full of food hovered in the air before my mouth as I finally met Nanna's gaze.

"Yes; avoiding you. How anyone can stand to be around you right now is beyond me, but poor Lily has to feel all of your self-pity and misery."

"Well, I didn't ask her to." Okay. So that was a lame comeback, considering Lily couldn't help it. "And it's not self-pity. I have a right to be angry at Nathan."

"And at me?" She laid her knife and fork down and leaned forward.

"Yes." I'd wanted to avoid this, but Nanna was a pusher, and she always knew just which of my buttons to press. "The only reason Tonya kept dating Trevor was because I stopped bugging her about him. And the only reason I stopped was because you and Nathan convinced me I shouldn't trust my gift. So, yeah, I am mad at you."

"It amazes me sometimes how much you're like your mother." She resumed eating as if she'd made an innocent observation, instead of something that was bound to get my back up.

"Really? You're going to go there again?" Thank god Dad wasn't there, or else I'd be so dead for talking to Nanna like that. I stood and pushed my chair back. It rocked on two legs a moment before tumbling to the ground.

"You're overly sensitive like she was." Nana speared another piece of sausage. "She was always jumping to conclusions and being completely impulsive."

"So you think because I act on my gift, I'm wrong? You're the one that kept pressing me about it. That I should be careful trusting it. That I didn't understand it or how to use it. So, I trusted you. And you told me to give Trevor a chance." I bristled. "I would hope my mom was smart enough to realize you're the one that was wrong. Then again, she was too stupid to tell anyone she was going to die, right? Maybe that's why you didn't want me to believe in my ability and to trust you instead. Because then you'd have to face the fact that your own daughter didn't trust you."

The words weren't even out of my mouth before I wanted to swallow them whole.

"Well, you told me, didn't you?" Nanna was whiter than I'd ever seen her before.

The words were hateful, and I hadn't meant them. But that was the problem with verbal diarrhea. Once you spew it, it's impossible to take back. And it was impossible to erase the sickening look on Nanna's face, which matched the feeling in the pit of my stomach.

CHAPTER 13

'THINGS GET EASIER' HAD officially become my most hated saying. Who the hell says that anyway? Because after two weeks of not talking to Nathan, nothing about it was easier. In fact, it was getting harder not to speak to him. To not want to run my hands along his arms or through his hair. And it was even harder watching him be all buddy-buddy with Vivian.

I tried to remember how I'd ever handled them dating, and it only made me realize how much I missed being with him. There was no way I could go back to the casual flirting I'd forced myself to do before; we'd gone past that.

Nathan had said he would be waiting when I was ready to talk. I was ready. Time had shown me how much of an idiot I was. I'd tried to stay angry at him, but if Tonya didn't think he was to blame, then how could I? And I knew she was right. Nathan wasn't to blame. Being with him had been amazing, but there was still a part of me that didn't want him back. Did I really want to be with someone who had the power to make me question myself so absolutely that I would leave my friend in a position to be hurt?

A hand waved in front of my face. I jerked back, turning to look at the owner. Tonya was giving me a look like I'd gone crazy.

"What?" I asked.

"Exactly what I was going to ask. Last period is over, and

you've been staring at your locker for a full five minutes, completely ignoring everything I said."

"That's not true. I was listening."

"Oh, really?" She wore a skeptical look.

"Sure. There was the thing about a purple hooker shirt and something about moving to Nebraska." I flushed as she death-stared me. No way would I let her walk around in a purple hooker shirt. "Okay. I wasn't really listening."

"Girl, you are in a major funk." She twisted her arm through mine and dragged me down the hall, away from where I could stare at Nathan's locker.

"I'm not in a funk." I absently rubbed my abdomen as a twinge of monthly cramps hit.

"Oh, please. You're moping practically every minute of the day. I'm so glad I don't live with you, girl. I would totally consider shooting you if I had to deal with you all day and night."

"Gee. Thanks."

"You know I love you, but seriously, girl, you need to get back with Nathan and get yourself some action, because I'm living through you vivaciously."

"Vicariously. And why? I thought you were going to go for the new Mickey Mouse guy."

She shrugged a shoulder and made a noise under her breath. "He's too brainy for me. Besides, Gran said no dating until she talks to my therapist."

"Well, I don't think Nathan and I are going to happen."

"What are you talking about, girl? You know you're still hot for him, and unless he's chopped his hair off since first period, he's still cute."

"Yeah, right, cute—like being attached to Vivian's hip every time I see him." Even as I said it, I caught sight of the two of them heading out the side exit to the parking lot.

"I told you. You should have taken that bitch out when you had the chance. You would have been defending your territory, but now," she snorted, "you'd just look jealous and pathetic."

"Wow. You really know how to make me feel good about myself, don't you?"

"That's what friends are for." She laughed and tugged at my arm, dragging me toward the library.

I helped her find a few websites for a research paper she was doing for her economics class, and then logged on to my *Twitter* account. It had been nearly a month since I'd been on, and I scrolled down the page, trying to make sense of the tweets that popped up. I didn't follow many people, mainly because I didn't know how to find them, but Nathan, Bianca, Chloe, and Karin were there. I tried not to read Nathan's because I was not a sucker for punishment. I reached the bottom of the screen, the list of tweets automatically expanded, and Trevor's screen name flashed across the screen.

My eyes flickered over to Tonya, but she was engrossed in whatever was on the page she was reading. I looked at Trevor's tweet.

hookin up wit ma gurl 2nite

I wanted to vomit. The prick had managed to find another girl to suck in to his sick world. I wanted to scourer his profile for a clue as to who she was and try to warn her, or even tweet something about what he'd done. But every tweet I'd ever posted had actually been done by either Tonya or Bianca, and I knew if I did tweet anything, Tonya would find out. I closed out of the internet, struggling to control my disgust for Trevor as I waited for Tonya to finish.

"Are you coming over tonight?" I asked as we headed through the parking lot toward my car fifteen minutes later.

"Can't," she said. We tossed our backpacks in the back seat and climbed in to the front.

My stomach clenched, and I let out a hiss of air. God. I hated cramps. I waited a moment for the pain to pass and then started the car.

"I can't believe Gran is so strict all of a sudden," I said. "She seemed okay at first, but she won't even let you out except for school. What about the movies tomorrow?"

"Probably not. What are you guys going to see?" she asked.

"Some Greek God movie. Owen and Bianca have been raving about it, so now Karin wants to see it, too."

Tonya launched in to her typical anti-Karin monolog, and I pretended to listen. What I was really doing was thinking about Nathan. It was his type of movie. I could call, and invite him to come with. As a friend. Or I could ask Owen to call. He'd do that. He still owed me for covering for him in seventh grade when he lied to Mr. Stevens about his homework being stolen.

"You're off in Nathan-dream-zone again."

Tonya's loud comment pulled me back to reality.

"What? No. I'm listening. Karin's so stuck up, blah, blah, blah." Thankfully, we'd pulled up to Tonya's house. "Are you a prisoner all weekend?"

"Don't know yet," she said, sliding out of the car. She grabbed her bag from the back and then slammed the door closed. "I'll text you tomorrow."

"Call!" I yelled after her.

She turned around and kept walking backward to the door.

"Call Nathan!"

I rolled the window up and drove off. By the time I got home, I'd decided. I would call Nathan.

Maybe.

Maybe was where I stalled.

* * *

Three hours later, I was wrestling my cell from Bianca, who thought it would be hilarious to call him for me. I wished I'd never told her about possibly getting Owen to call him.

"I will never drive you anywhere ever again!" I yelled, twisting around her curled up body and attempting to snatch the phone from her.

"Okay, okay! But I am calling Tonya. Maybe she'll talk some sense in to you."

We stopped fighting, and I watched carefully as she pulled up Tonya with one push of a button.

"How did you get her number to come up so fast?" I always had to scroll through the list.

"She programmed your numbers in for you." She said it like it should mean something, and I stared in confusion. "She put herself as number one. She got hold of my phone once and redid everything. Somehow, my home phone number disappeared, and I ended up stranded at the mall when I couldn't remember it. Thankfully, she left Karin on as number eight."

We waited as the phone rang, but Tonya didn't pick up. Instead, it clicked to her voice mail, and Bianca left a quick message then hung up.

"There. You called," I said, and grabbed the phone. "Now, if you don't mind, I want to go watch TV."

We went in to the den and found Lily and Dylan already

huddled on the sofa. Lily looked like she was about to fall asleep, and Dylan was flipping channels, his feet propped on the coffee table. I tossed my phone, so it hit his feet, hoping he'd take a hint. He didn't.

"Can you switch it to the on-demand screen?" I asked, glancing at him as I filled a glass of soda from the side counter.

"Uh. I'm watching this," he said, continuing to channel-surf.

"Hey, Lils. We were gonna order a movie. Do you want to watch?"

I stepped near her and watched as her hands twitched. I was a horrible person. She'd been fighting the past few weeks to respect my wishes about not 'healing' me. I felt terrible about causing her discomfort on purpose, but Dylan was a douche-bag, and there was no way I was going to get in a power struggle with him in my own home.

"No. You go ahead. We'll go upstairs." She struggled to get up, and guilt consumed me. I was truly despicable. She wobbled, and I went to grab her, but stopped short when I realized what would happen then. Luckily, Dylan caught her.

"Maybe you should lie down," he said, genuine concern softening his voice. I might not have liked Dylan, but it was obvious he loved Lily.

Lily pulled away from his hold. "I'm okay. But maybe I'll take a nap."

Dylan followed her to her room, and a few minutes later, left without a word to Bianca or me. Usually, I felt required to see guests out, but not Dylan.

I settled on to the couch they had vacated and searched for a movie, nixing a few Bianca wanted to see. Mainly because they were the artsy ones I had no interest in. We finally compromised on a *Ben Stiller* flick. Once the opening credits started, I went to check on Lily.

The knock on her door went unanswered, so I gently opened it and peeked my head in. She was lying on her stomach, her eyes open and gazing at me.

"You need anything?" I asked, not moving any closer.

She smiled and rolled on to her back, and then propped herself up against the headboard.

"You can come in, Phoebs." She laughed at my doubtful expression. "I'm serious. It's fine."

I moved in closer, but took a seat in her computer chair. It seemed safer than her bed.

"You feel different today," she said, her eyes narrowing.

"Different good? Or different bad?" I spun the chair around, loving that I didn't have to lift my feet over piles of clothing. Maybe there was a benefit to having a tidy room.

"Different good. Did you talk to Nathan?"

"Ugh! Why does everything have to be about Nathan?"

"Maybe because you've been obsessing over him."

"I haven't been obsessing. Maybe a little fixated, but not obsessed."

"So you haven't talked to him, but you've made a decision." Sometimes, Lily made me wonder if she had Chloe and Nanna's gifts for seeing the future and the past.

"I guess. Yeah, but now I don't know what to say to him."

"Why? Because you may not always be right, but you're never wrong?"

"Exactly. I mean, maybe I shouldn't have blamed him, but, still, it makes me uncomfortable to think about how easily he managed to get me to doubt myself."

"He didn't get you to do anything, Phoebe. You did that all on your own." Her words were so close to what Chloe had said, but it sounded much more reasonable coming from Lily.

"I know, but it's easier to be mad at him. I mean, it's not like I can give myself the silent treatment or anything."

"True," she said with a soft laugh that quickly transformed into a massive yawn.

"I'll let you get some rest. You sure you're okay?" I asked as I rose from the chair.

"I'm sure. Just a little tired."

I closed the door behind me and went back to the den. Bianca was on her cell, and I collapsed beside her. She said bye to whoever she was talking to and hung up. I waited a moment for her to say who it was, but she shoved a handful of popcorn in her mouth.

"Who was that?" I finally asked.

"Tonya." She popped another handful of popcorn in.

"And?"

"She's busy doing something with her grandma."

"She didn't want to talk to me?"

"Nope. I guess I'm her new BFF now. Besides, it sounded like they were out somewhere."

It was a bit of a surprise that not only didn't she ask to talk to me, but that she'd actually called Bianca instead of me. Then again, it was nice to not be harassed one more time about calling Nathan. I was going to talk to him. I just needed to find a way to do it without having to apologize. Not an easy task, considering the things I'd said.

* * *

I tried calling Nathan the next morning, but he didn't answer, and I wasn't sure what to think about that. He could have been working, or just busy. Or he could have been laughing hysterically with Vivian at his side at the sight of my name finally flashing across the screen of his phone. I ended up leaving a stalker message of heavy breathing while I frantically tried to think of what to say until I hung up, thoroughly mortified at the magnitude of my patheticness.

Tonya was my next call, but she brushed me off with a lame excuse about being with Gran and hung up before I could tell her what a horrible idea it had been to call Nathan. Between her therapist and Gran, we'd barely had any time to talk outside of school. That she wasn't able to go to the movies with the rest of us later brought on my pity party full force.

"Do you know anyone in San Diego?" Chloe asked, coming up behind me as I sat at the kitchen table eating jalapeño flavored potato chips for lunch.

"I don't think so. Why?"

"I just had this weird vision of you there outside an apartment building."

"How do you know it was San Diego?"

"I got a glimpse of a street sign, and it was definitely not Beachgrove." She sat down across from me and stole one of the chips. "God. These are horrible. You're not eating just those for lunch, are you? You need to seriously start watching what you eat, or you're going to end up..."

"Fat?"

"No."

Good to know.

"Dead?"

"No."

Also good to know.

"So?"

She rolled her eyes and swiped a second chip. "Just very unhealthy. There's some leftover avocado you can have."

"Uh. No thanks." Just the thought of eating that stuff made

me gag. She sat there staring at me. "What do you want?"

"You should know that Nathan is going to the movies tonight with friends. He'll want to talk to you." Despite her complaints, she took another chip. "So, if you've realized you were wrong to blame him, have you realized the same about Nanna?"

My head tilting down, I glared at her from under my brows. "Don't push it."

She held up a hand in resignation. "Fine. I just think—"

"Shut it, Chloe."

"Fine."

I grabbed my bowl of chips and went in to the living room to finish eating in peace and quiet, but sitting quietly and alone on the sofa didn't mean I actually felt any peace.

Nanna was like a hangnail I couldn't clip. Constantly poking me, rubbing me the wrong way, but if I just ripped her out, it would hurt a hell of a lot more. And Nanna was forever pushing my Mom Button. For a while, I'd thought I'd gotten the whole mommy issue out of my system, but after the fight I'd had with Nanna, I knew it was still there. And I finally realized why.

Chloe and Lily had always understood what was happening the day we were born. Chloe had seen it while Lily had felt our mother's every emotion. But I had only a sick feeling to remember.

I surged off the couch and marched in to the kitchen. The bowl of chips flew from my hand in to the sink. I stood for a moment, watching it circle the silver space before tipping over and spilling the greasy snack.

"I'm going for a drive," I stated, though not to tell Chloe. No. It had been more of a command from my brain to my body, just in case it decided to rebel and go back to the chips.

Chloe didn't respond, other than to raise an eyebrow in ... something. Probably not curiosity, because she most likely already knew where I was going, even if I wasn't entirely sure of it myself.

* * *

Thirty minutes after walking out the front door, I was standing in front of my mom's grave. There wasn't much; just a small headstone with her name followed by the date of her birth and then death. It had been almost two years since I'd been there. The trees had grown, and there were more plot markers around. We used to come every month, flowers in hand, each of us waiting for our turn to say something. I never did. When my turn came, I would just stare at her name. Dad assumed I was talking silently. I wasn't. I had nothing to say to her.

"You lied to me." The words burst forth, catching me by surprise. I paused, maybe hoping that the supernatural would allow for a response. But nothing came. Mom wasn't here. It was just a place for us to hold on to her.

"How could you have lied to me?"

It had taken my gift finally working to understand why every time I thought of Mom, I had felt nauseous. My memory of my mother had been of her lying to me.

"Is that what you think she did?" Nanna stepped up beside me. Her appearance should have startled me, but it didn't. Somehow, part of me had known she would show up once I finally made it there. Maybe that was the reason I'd avoided coming.

"It's what I know," I answered.

"Because your gift tells you?"

My head snapped up, and I stared at her in amazement.

"Are you really trying to get me to question myself again?"

She sighed, kneeling to brush a bit of dirt from the engraving and pull the few weeds that had dared to creep above Mom. "It was a long time ago. Over seventeen years. That's a long time to hold a feeling."

"She lied to me. I know she did." My voice quivered, and I struggled to contain my rage. How could my mother have made her only words to me a lie?

"There's only one way to know for sure." She reached her hand up, asking for help to rise, seeking a memory I'd been too young to hold clear. I placed my hand in hers, wincing at the tight grip she took.

She froze midrise, her eyes focused on some point through my chest. Her hand tightened painfully on mine, and I knew this was the first time she had seen her daughter's last moments.

"What did she say?" I asked when her eyes fluttered and refocused, although they filled with tears. Seeing what had happened could not have been an easy thing, and I was glad I didn't have to see that part of my past.

"That she loved you." Her tears overflowed and wove a crooked path down her deeply wrinkled face. "And that she'd always be with you."

Neither of those brought the suffocating pain like I experienced while thinking about Mom.

"Then she spoke to your father and told him everything would be all right."

There it was. The lie. Mom knew that nothing would be okay. She died, and we weren't fine. I wasn't fine. On the surface, it may have looked like we were, but, underneath, there was the hollow part in all of us that could never be filled. Dad had done his best to be normal, but he had closed himself off, so his life consisted of work and us. My sisters had clung to Dad, and even now, they constantly checked up on him. And Mom's one lie had destroyed my ability to trust not only others but myself as well.

"She lied. The last words I heard her speak were a lie." Bitterness tinged my words, giving them a sharp edge that cut through my heart.

"You see your gift much like Chloe sees hers. Black and white. There's no space between for what could be or may have been." She sighed and smoothed her hand over my hair. "People lie for many reasons, Phoebe. Sometimes it is meant to deceive, or trick, or conceal, like how Tonya lied to you. But there are white lies, meant to spare someone's feelings."

"This was not a white lie, Nanna. She was dying, and instead of telling them what would be coming, instead of preparing Dad, she lied."

"No. It wasn't a white lie. But she wanted to protect you and your sisters and Michael. Maybe it wasn't the right thing to do, or even the best thing, but I know my daughter, and her every thought and concern would have been for the four of you."

"I've felt it every time I thought of her. The cramps. The nausea."

"She wouldn't have wanted you to feel that way. Your gift is unique, Phoebe. There's no way she would have known you would feel that way, or hold on to it for so long."

"That's why I stopped coming here. Being this close to her made it worse." I dropped to my knees and stared at the puffy white clouds pushing across the sky.

"And now?"

It was gone. There was no memory of what it had felt like to hear my mom lie. There was nothing but an aching hole. I didn't answer Nanna's question, and she eventually smiled and slowly lowered herself to sit beside me.

"When I questioned you about your gift, I didn't want you to stop trusting it. I wanted you to realize that the truth can have many layers, and lies are not always about deception."

I tilted my head to rest it on Nanna's shoulders, and, for the first time in years, I cried for my mom.

CHAPTER 14

"YOU CALLED HIM, RIGHT?" Bianca asked as soon as I found her at the cinema.

"I did."

"And what did he say?"

"He didn't answer." I flashed a sly smile as we got in to the concession line.

"But?" She gave me an expectant look.

"Chloe said he'd be here tonight and that we'd talk."

Initially, Chloe's vision had given me a lot of hope, but as I repeated it for Bianca, I started to realize that Chloe hadn't said anything about it going the way I wanted. And that could be pretty crappy. "I guess we'll see soon enough."

"There's Owen." She gestured to the ticket booth where Owen was waiting in line. "I think he walked here just to avoid getting a ride with Karin. He told her he wasn't sure he was coming, so she ditched us."

"Too bad Tonya isn't here. She'd love a Karin free night out," I said.

"You're lucky she isn't here. You know she'd be all over you about Nathan."

"Well, lucky me that her gran has put her back on lockdown." When Mrs. Robinson first found out about Trevor, I'd thought that I'd finally have Tonya back full time. No more bailing on us, but it was like nothing had changed. Instead of Trevor taking up her time, it was her gran.

"At least you're looking hot tonight." She fingered the long side braid Nanna had done for me as part of our bonding experience at Mom's grave—something I just didn't see happening again anytime.

"Are you implying that I usually look like crap?"

"Whatever. You know I would kill to have your hair. If my parents stopped being so fanatical about me having long hair, I might actually grow it out." She ran her hands through her short spiky hair, which had changed from purple to blue tipped sometime in the past week.

"You could always let them think you were conforming."

She looked at me like I was crazy. "Uh. You have met my parents, right? One small move in their direction and they'll have my entire life mapped out before I could take a single step back. I'll be finishing college before you're out of high school."

"Then I guess you'll simply have to suffer through your jealousy of my superior hair."

"Yeah, but your outfit balances it out."

"What do you mean?" I glanced down at my black shirt and skinny jeans. I thought I looked good.

"It's a bit...Chloe."

"Bitch!"

"Here," she said, and gripped one of the shoulders of my shirt, yanking it down. Luckily, the stretchy material didn't rip. It gripped the side of my arm in a now off-the-shoulder look then she took off her extra-long silver studded necklace and put it over my head. "Chloe so wouldn't wear this."

"Thanks."

"Owen!" Bianca called and waved her hand in the air to catch his eye. She spun back around, her eyes huge. "Nathan's here."

"Where?" I glanced in the direction she'd been facing, but I couldn't see him in the sea of moviegoers.

"Oh, uh, he was heading through the ticket line."

I raised a brow at her suddenly strange tone. "Do you think I should go find him?"

"No. I mean, didn't Chloe say he was going to come and talk to you? Besides, you don't have a great track record when you chase after him." She paid for her order, and I wished I had the spare cash to get something, but a full price movie ticket was the limit to my budget.

"You're right. You are." I nodded.

Owen joined us as we entered the concession line. I glanced around again, hoping to see Nathan. Usually, his height made him easily visible, but I couldn't see him anywhere.

"I just don't want to wait any longer," I said.

"Wait for what?" Owen asked.

"To talk to Nathan."

"That might not be the best idea right now," he answered, shifting from one foot to the other while managing to avoid looking at me.

"Why?" I looked from Owen to Bianca, wondering what was going on. Bianca was close-lipped, and I knew she wouldn't spill. So I turned back to Owen, knowing that, unlike Bianca, he wouldn't try to lie. "Why not?"

He quickly cracked. "Uh. Vivian's with him."

God. Couldn't that bitch just fall down and die or something? Maybe that seemed mean, but it was Vivian, and ever since Nathan and I broke up, she'd been hanging off him like a dog in heat.

Owen's comment put a pretty effective end to our conversation, and we made our way through the line. Andy ripped our tickets and pointed to the right. The theater was only half-full, and we got good seats right in the center of a row just up from the middle. I waited a few minutes before looking for Nathan, but it took me less than a minute to scan the place and find him against the back wall. He was standing at the end of the row, staring at me. He lifted his hand in a wave. Rather than returning it, I looked down his row and found Vivian talking to one of her little posse.

I swiveled around, fury building inside of me, pissed at Nathan and Vivian, but mostly at myself. He was with Vivian only because I'd pushed him away. If Tonya were here, she'd be wearing her smug face and urging me to take Vivian down. Instead, I was going to wallow in my self-pity.

"You okay?" Bianca asked as the first previews started.

I nodded in response and pulled out my cell phone. I didn't want to be super annoying and call Tonya, but I did want to tell her what was going on. It took me until the third preview to get a text message typed out, and then I asked Owen to turn it on to vibrate, so I didn't have to turn it off.

Focusing on the movie was almost impossible, and I did try. But I could feel Vivian's spiteful gloating behind me, making me squirm in my seat with frustration. Was she why Nathan hadn't called me back? Was this his way of telling me that he had chosen her? I twisted around and looked over my shoulder. He was hard to see, but in a few flashes of brighter screen time, I could make him out, and, thankfully, Vivian wasn't beside him. She was a few seats down. Two of Nathan's football friends separated them.

"You're being pretty obvious," Bianca whispered, causing me to turn back around.

"I'm going to the restroom," I said, ignoring her comment. I needed to get some air, and maybe I hoped Nathan was as aware of me as I was of him and would follow me.

The hall was nearly empty. Only a few staff members milled about with their rolling trash bins and brooms, wasting time until another movie ended. I paused for a moment, waiting to see if Nathan had followed me, but the door stayed closed, so I headed in to the restroom.

When I came out a few minutes later, he was there. Instantly, I felt nervous and jittery, unsure of what to say. It didn't help that he was wearing his hot date outfit—black jeans and a vintage *Green Day* shirt. He'd worn the same thing on our first date.

"Hey," I said, stopping in front of him.

"Hey. I got your message, but I was at work." He shoved his hands in his pockets and scuffed his sneaker along the carpet. "I was gonna call you back, but I figured I'd just see you here."

"Oh."

"But you didn't come over when I saw you inside."

"Inside. When you were with Vivian."

"Phoebe, I'm not dating Vivian. I already told you I wasn't interested in getting back with her. It was supposed to be just the guys from the team, but a couple of them invited their girlfriends, and, well, somehow, Vivian ended up coming. I didn't know until we got here."

I started to say something, but my pocket began to vibrate. Pulling it out, I saw Tonya's name flashing on the screen and pressed decline, sending her to voicemail, then I shoved it back in my pocket.

"I know. That you're not here with Vivian, I mean. I just didn't want to risk getting in to it with her again. My dad would totally flip if I ended up in another fight. And—" My cell started up again, cutting off my words. I yanked it back out. "It's Tonya. Just let me get rid of her, or she'll keep bugging me."

I flipped it open, but before I could even say hi, I could hear her crying.

"Tonya? What's wrong?"

"Phoebe. Oh god! I made a mistake. Can you come get me?"

"Where are you? What's going on?" Panic started to set in as her sobs pulsed through me.

"I—I just want to go home."

"Tonya, calm down. Where are you?"

"I'm—" Her words ended when the phone went dead.

"Holy shit. Holy shit." I fumbled around, trying to pull up her number until Bianca's demonstration from earlier came back to me. I jammed my finger on to the number one and held it until the line began to ring.

"What's going on?" Nathan asked as I waited for her to pick up.

"I don't know. She was hysterical, said she needed me to come get her, then the line went dead. Shit, shit, shit."

"Hello?" Tonya's voice quavered through the phone.

"Where are you? I'll come get you right now."

"Oh. I'm fine."

Liar.

"Tonya, where are you?" I swallowed past the bile that crept up my throat from my churning stomach.

"I'm sorry I called you. Gran and I had a fight."

Liar. My stomach cramped.

"Where are you?"

"Don't worry about me. I gotta go, okay? I'll call you later."

Again, the line went dead.

I called her back, waiting while it rang twice and then went to voicemail. I tried again, and it went directly to her mailbox. Her phone was off. And I started to panic. "Her phone's off. I don't know what to do. She said she had a fight with her gran and that she's fine, but I know she's lying. She wouldn't tell me where she was."

"Calm down and just take a moment to think. Where could she be?"

"I don't know! She was supposed to be home, but I know she's not!"

"Okay. So let's call there. I know you say she's lying, but let's just double check. Maybe she's there and wants to leave, or at least her gran might know where she is." He took the phone from me, and within seconds, he had it ringing. Someone must have answered because he started talking. "Hi. Can I speak to Tonya? Oh, okay. Do you know which one? Thank you."

"She's not there, is she?" I asked as he handed the phone back to me.

"Her grandma said she was with you at the movies. Where else would she go? If she's not with you or at home, then where?" He guided me over to a bench, and I sat down while he crouched in front of me. I could see his father, and his police officer training, in Nathan, taking charge, being the calm one, thinking logically. "Is there some place she wouldn't tell you about going?"

"Nowhere! I mean... Oh god. She wouldn't..." My lips couldn't form the horrible idea that came to mind.

"Wouldn't what?"

"Trevor." My stomach lurched at the idea of her going to see him.

"Okay. Let's call him. If she's there, we'll go get her."

241

"I don't have his number. I deleted everything about that ass wipe after what he did."

"I might still have it." Nathan pulled out his phone. "Yeah. Here. Do you want me to do it?"

"Yes. No. Wait! He might lie. If he lies to me, I'll know it."

"Phoebs, you gotta chill. If you're rude, he might hang up." He handed me the phone, and I took a deep breath then pressed the send button.

"Hello?" The sound of Trevor's voice drove a nasty chill down my spine.

"Hey, Trevor. This is Tonya's friend, Phoebe."

"What do you want?" His dislike of me was obvious, and I struggled to stay pleasant. Not the easiest thing to do when my skin crawled at even the sound of his name.

"I just got a strange call from Tonya, and wondered if you'd heard from her?"

"No."

Liar. A vicious cramp seized me, and I took another deep breath, willing it to pass.

"So she didn't come over to your place or anything?"

"No."

This time, when my stomach clenched, I gagged as a massive wave of nausea hit me.

"Okay. Thanks."

I hung up, threw the phone at Nathan, and then raced for the restroom. I barely made it to the toilet before emptying my stomach. Once the shaking stopped, I went to the sink and quickly rinsed my mouth out. Nathan was still waiting when I came out, and Bianca and Owen were with him.

"I went and grabbed them while you were..." He motioned to the restroom, and I nodded.

"She's there. At Trevor's," I said.

"You're sure?"

My instinctive response was to get angry with him for questioning me again, but it was instantly squashed by the sound of Tonya's scream echoing through my mind. He was right. I needed to be sure. My eyes closed, and I tried to think about Tonya the past few days. Her reluctance to give details about what she and Gran were doing. Her sudden lack of interest in the new Mickey guy. And then there was Trevor's tweet.

hookin up wit ma gurl 2nite

It was possible that instead of some unsuspecting girl, it had been Tonya. Who knew where she'd really been last night? The hollow pit in my stomach said she'd been with him. I was sure that was where she was now.

"Definitely. I have to go get her," I said.

"We can call the cops," Nathan suggested.

"And tell them what? That my friend says she's fine, but I know she's lying because some voice in my head is telling me she is?" I gave a humorless laugh. "I really don't want your dad to think I'm crazy."

"I'll drive then," Nathan said. "No way should you be going anywhere near that asshole alone."

"Do you want us to come with?" Bianca asked.

"There won't be room in the truck for all of us once we pick Tonya up," Nathan said.

"Owen and I can take my car, and we'll follow you."

"Fine. Let's go." I started moving to the door, and they all fell in line behind me. Once we were in the parking lot, reality started to sink in and I stopped abruptly. Nathan skidded past me, while Owen and Bianca nearly plowed in to me. "I don't remember how to get to his place."

"We used my dad's GPS the time we went there. He

practically never uses the thing, so it should still be stored. Come on." Nathan grabbed my hand and propelled me forward. Owen and Bianca veered off toward her car while Nathan and I continued straight. We climbed in to his dad's truck, and a minute later, we were heading for San Diego.

"Get the GPS from the glove box," Nathan said. I opened the compartment, grabbed the GPS, and pushed the power button. Once it had loaded itself, I handed it to Nathan. He waited until we stopped at a red light to search for Trevor's address. "Here it is."

I pulled out my cell and called Owen, knowing Bianca couldn't answer hers because she was driving. I gave him the address and the basic directions to get to Trevor's just in case we got separated.

Then the rush of adrenaline began to wane. I felt completely exhausted and consumed by the nausea Trevor had brought on with his lies. I leaned my head against the cool window and stared in to the blackness. Outside of town, there were no lights to illuminate the roadside.

How could she have gone to see Trevor? How could she have lied to me about it? I wanted to yell at her, scream at her for being an idiot. I prayed that she was okay, that the call had been some complete misunderstanding, and that she was actually at home, safe and sound.

Even without my gift, I knew I was lying to myself.

"I'm sorry."

I looked at Nathan, his words bringing me out of my thoughts.

"I shouldn't have blackmailed you in to giving Trevor a chance, and I shouldn't have brushed off your concerns." He sounded a bit stiff like he'd been practicing what to say and was trying to remember the exact wording.

"I'm sorry, too." My words were as stilted as his, although mine came from a reluctance to apologize. I hated doing that, but Nathan was worth it. "I shouldn't have blamed you for what Trevor did."

"But you were right about him."

"Yeah, but I wish I hadn't been." I sighed and shifted closer to him in my seat so I could place my hand on his thigh. He was warm like he always was, and it made me want to snuggle closer.

Talking made me realize how badly my breath smelled. To distract myself, I rummaged through my purse for some gum.

"What are you looking for?" Nathan asked.

"Some gum. My breath is kind of funky."

"Check the glove box. My mom is a fanatic about her teeth. She may have something."

I opened the glove box, found a pack, and pulled out a stick of nasty tasting dental gum. The repetitive chewing had a calming effect, though my knees didn't stop their jackrabbit thumping. The drive wasn't long, only about thirty minutes, but each minute felt like an eternity. Each one, a minute that Tonya could be in trouble. I tried calling her cell again, but there was still no answer.

"You okay?" Nathan asked.

"Yeah. I just hope Tonya is." I rubbed my hands down my face, then placed them on my knees and tried to still my bouncing legs. "I don't understand why she would go and see him. I would kill the guy if he'd done that to me."

"Who knows? Maybe she was just picking up some of her stuff."

I picked up the GPS and checked the arrival time. Four minutes. I put it back in the dashboard holder and glanced out the window. My gum popped in my mouth, and I blew an awkward bubble. It was the old person type of gum meant only for chewing. Not bubble blowing. I tried another bubble, but it snapped across my tongue. I looked at the GPS again. Two minutes. Bubble. Snap. One minute.

"There it is." I sat up in my seat. The area was familiar, and the GPS was announcing we'd arrived. I jumped out of the truck as soon as Nathan parked. He followed behind me, as I pushed the call button for Trevor's apartment. He didn't answer. I pressed it again and again, my finger bending painfully with the pressure I used. "Answer the fucking door, asshole."

"Maybe he's not home."

"He's here. I know it." I stepped back and looked up at his window. He was right above us on the second floor. The blinds were drawn, but backlit. He was up there. Bianca and Owen came up behind me, and Nathan explained Trevor wasn't answering. "Shh! Listen."

They all shut up, and we listened. Then I heard it. It was faint, but it was there. A cry and then something louder. Trevor yelling.

"I'm calling the cops," Owen said, and I tried to remember why I hadn't done that earlier.

I lunged back at the call button and did what I'd seen done on TV and the movies, pressing all the buttons, over and over again, hoping someone would just let us in. No one did. But one answered the call.

"Hello?" a man's voice said.

"Thank god! Can you let us in? We need to get in, please! My friend is hurt." I was crying. Trevor was getting louder. I could hear him yelling clearly now. What was scaring me was that I didn't hear Tonya.

"Is this about that couple fighting upstairs?" the man

asked.

"Yes. Please! We've called the police, but please let us in."

He didn't reply, but a moment later, there was a buzz and the door pulled open under Nathan's tugging hand.

"I'll wait for the cops," Owen called behind us, and caught the door before it closed. Even as he said it, I caught a flash of blue and red lights reflecting along the road with the corner of my eye.

I ran up the stairs with Nathan and Bianca right behind me. Trevor's door was behind the stairwell, and I thumped on it with the palm of my hand. I could hear Tonya now. She was crying. Whimpering.

"Trevor! Open up. I know Tonya's in there." I slammed my hand against the door when there was no response, and then pounded my fist on the door repeatedly.

"The cops are here," Bianca said from the foot of the stairs.

"Trevor, please, open the door," I begged, trying to sound a bit less angry and scared.

"Miss, move away from the door."

I glanced over my shoulder and saw two police officers behind me. Nathan wrapped a hand around my arm and tugged me back, giving the officers space to move.

"My friend is in there. I know she is. Please, help her."

"Miss, step back and let us do our job." The female officer glared at me, causing me to take that commanded step back.

"Phoebe, just be quiet," Nathan said. It sounded harsh, but I knew he was only trying to help. With his father being the sheriff, he knew what to do around working officers. "Let's wait downstairs."

"She didn't need to be rude," I said, my entire body shaking with fear and anger as we moved to the stairs.

"She wasn't. That's the way cops are when they're on duty. They need people to be a bit intimidated."

We walked back down to where Owen was waiting and collapsed on the bottom step. I wanted, needed, to know what was going on. I could hear them knock on the door and identifying themselves as police. It seemed like forever before there was the creak of the door opening.

Once the police had gone inside, it was impossible to hear anything. Then the sirens of an ambulance reached us, and my stomach dropped. Tonya must have been hurt.

When Nathan gripped my arm, I thought he was preparing to stop me from going back up, but he was just moving me out of the way so the paramedics could get through. They took the stairs two at a time.

"I should have called the cops as soon as she called me," I said, watching the paramedics disappear up the stairs.

"You didn't know what was going on." Nathan rubbed his arm along my arm. "Besides, what would you have said? That you thought Tonya was here, but couldn't prove it? That you thought she was hurt, but couldn't prove it?"

"No. I don't know. I should have done something to stop this."

"You're blaming yourself again, Phoebe," Owen said. His arms were crossed, and he stared at me with an intense gaze. It was a gaze that made me wonder if maybe he was simply acting all those times when he spaced out. "You might have a gift to hear lies, but you can't know everything, and even if you did, you can't control everyone. Tonya would have come here if you'd known or not. And if you'd told her not to come, she would have probably broken speed records to get here."

"Probably." Admitting it didn't make me feel any better.

Owen looked like he had a lot more to say, but there was movement at the top of the stairs, and we all turned to watch. Trevor came down first, his arms twisted behind his back, wrists cuffed. I found it difficult to swallow, my mouth completely dry. Even now, it was easy to see why Tonya had trusted him at first. He didn't look like a bad guy. He just hid it very well.

The paramedics came next, and that was when I nearly broke down. Tonya was on a backboard, her neck stabilized. Blood was everywhere, covering her new blue shirt, in her hair, and on her face. God. Her face. What I could see was swollen and discolored.

"Oh god," I sobbed, and stepped toward her. Nathan held me back so they could move her out of the lobby.

Tonya murmured something, but her lips were so swollen the words were unintelligible. I knew she had heard me. I shook Nathan's hold off and walked alongside her as they got her outside, managing to grasp her hand. She felt so cold.

Looking down at her from that angle, I could see the other side of her face. There was an impression of the *Nike* swoosh along the side of her face. I choked back the bile burning my throat.

"I'm here, Tonya. You're gonna be fine." I tried to keep my voice steady, but it still trembled.

Her lips moved again, and I could see tears pooling in her eyes. My hand slid from hers as she was transferred to the back of the ambulance.

"Are you family?" asked one of the paramedics.

"What? No. No. I'm her best friend." I looked at the paramedic. My mind was completely clouded. I tried to figure out what was happening. "Is she okay? What...? Can I ride with her? Please?"

There was a pause as if he was debating, and then he gave a short nod. I climbed up in to the back of the ambulance and looked back at Nathan.

"Call Mrs. Robinson!" I yelled before the doors closed and we took off.

The ride was surreal. Nothing like I'd seen on television. There was no frantic moving about, working on her, no blaring sirens, although the lights flashed occasionally. The paramedics were calm and monitored her. I took it as a good sign that maybe she just looked worse than she really was.

They asked me a few questions—about allergies, medical history, medication—and I answered as best I could.

Once at the hospital, I was directed to the nurses' station where I simply gave them Mrs. Robinson's phone number. After that, there was nothing to do but sit. I found a seat in the emergency room and texted the name of the hospital to Nathan and Bianca. They arrived a few minutes later.

"Any news?" Bianca asked, sinking in to the chair beside me.

"No. They took her back and made me stay out here. Did you manage to get hold of her gran?" I looked up at Nathan.

"Yeah. She sounded pretty upset. I guess she thought Tonya was with you. She should be here pretty soon."

I was going to end up banned from Tonya's house. Mrs. Robinson still hadn't forgiven me for covering for Tonya before, and now she'd think I was doing it again.

"I don't get it," Bianca said. She was slouched in the seat, staring straight ahead, a kind of deer in the headlights thing. "Why would she start seeing him again? She knew what he was like."

I didn't have an answer, and I glanced up at Owen, curious to see if his sudden ability to understand and explain people would be able to handle this.

"Maybe she thought he wouldn't do it again. Or maybe she thought she could change him." Owen's idea seemed so out there, so unbelievable, but, at the same time, scary and real.

"What an id—" Bianca cut herself off with a shake of her head.

We all knew what she'd been going to say. We'd all thought it. But who calls the victim of an abusive partner an idiot? They are the victim. Tonya was the victim, and nothing she did asked for this. She had wanted to see the good in him, despite everything he'd already done. She'd believed in him, and maybe, like Owen had said, she believed she could change him.

I knew Tonya better than anyone, but even I wondered how many times would he have to prove her wrong before she finally believed?

After what felt like hours of waiting, Mrs. Robinson came out to tell us Tonya was in the ICU and couldn't have visitors. She didn't go in to details, but I had seen the marks on Tonya's face and knew that it had been just a fraction of what she had endured. I arranged with Mrs. Robinson to pick up a few of Tonya's things from the house and bring them by the next day.

The drive home with Nathan was silent. I was completely drained and could do nothing more than stare out the window. He seemed to realize that I needed those moments to hold myself together.

It was after two in the morning when we pulled up to my house. Every light in the place seemed to be on. I'd already talked to Dad on the phone earlier, but I'd known he would still be up to make sure I got home okay.

"Thanks for the ride," I said, still feeling numb.

"Phoebs," Nathan turned off the truck and twisted, so he faced me as he spoke, "are we going to talk about us? Is there an us again?"

I thought over everything that had happened the past few weeks—of how miserable I'd been when we weren't together, and how crazy I'd reacted to everything. It was actually hard to believe he wanted to get back together. Before all of the Tonya stuff, being with Nathan had felt right. Easy. Like I didn't have to work at it. I wanted that back. I wanted to know that I had something in my life that wasn't complicated, or weird, or scary.

"I was angry with myself. Not you." I saw his eyebrow twitch. "Okay. Maybe a little with you, but mostly with myself and the fact that I didn't trust me, or my gift, enough. Besides, if Tonya really was there tonight, getting back with Trevor, then it just goes to show that knowing what kind of guy he was wouldn't have been enough to stop her."

Tonya had been so giddy when she'd been dating Trevor, loving the secret of him, loving the fact that she was hiding him from her gran. She'd even said that she'd thought his moodiness had been attractive at first; that it had shown her how passionately he loved her. Any time I'd mentioned how obsessive it was, she'd make it a joke, like I was jealous because Nathan wasn't like that. And she'd been a bit right. But now, I didn't want anything to do with that kind of relationship. I wanted my Nathan back.

"I want things to be simple again," I said. It was difficult to swallow, and tears pooled in my eyes. "I want us to just be us, and not a bunch of other crap. No drama. Just us together with no one else. Simple."

"I think I could manage simple."

He moved closer and framed my face with his hands. The

kiss that followed was the most gloriously uncomplicated kiss I'd ever had. It was sweet and gentle, and I felt like I'd gone back in time to New Year's, and we were kissing for the first time again. When it ended, I pulled back and gave him a slight smile.

"So the only question left is: can Vivian handle us?" I asked.

He groaned and tilted his head back. "That's gonna be the best thing about getting back together with you."

"What's that?"

"I'm not gonna have to hang around her, trying to make you jealous anymore."

"Are you serious?" I asked, giving him a gentle whack on the arm.

"God. The entire time I was dating her was hell. Did you honestly think I wanted to hang out with her again?"

"Nathan, you dated her for a year!" I felt mildly bad for Vivian, to think that her one-time boyfriend hadn't even liked her, but that sympathy died pretty quick when I remembered how she'd treated me since ... well, since forever.

"Yeah, well, it's kind of hard to break up with someone who never shuts up," he explained. The smile he wore dimmed as he put his sexy-serious face on. "I'm glad you finally called."

"I'm glad you waited," I said, and before I could say anything else, he leaned in for another quick kiss. It ended too soon, with him sliding back to his side.

"Your dad is peeking through the blinds," he said when I scooted closer to him for another kiss.

I dropped my head to his chest in frustration, then moved back and grabbed my purse from the floor. Nathan hopped out of the truck, came around to help me out, and we held hands as we walked to the door. I didn't want him to leave. For a few minutes, he'd managed to consume my thoughts, and I knew once he was gone, the image of Tonya's battered face would return.

"I'll call you tomorrow," he said, letting go of my hand when we reached the porch. He brushed a light kiss on my cheek, then stepped back so I could go up the steps.

Dad met me at the door and folded me in to a giant bear hug, squeezing me hard, as if trying to force the sadness from me. Over my shoulder, he waved to Nathan and then walked me inside. We went in to the kitchen, and I sat at the table while Dad poured a mug of hot water from the kettle and then added a hot chocolate mix.

"I see you and Nathan have made up," he said over his shoulder.

"Yeah. We talked and..." I shrugged. As happy as I was about being back together with Nathan, it felt wrong to be in a good mood about anything. My thoughts of Nathan drifted away, and those of Tonya came crashing back.

"You want to talk about what happened with Tonya?" Dad asked, setting the mug in front of me. I'd known this was coming as soon as I'd called him from the hospital. There was no way Dad would let this go undiscussed.

"No. Yes. I don't get it." I wrapped my hands around the mug and watched the steam wafting up. My shock was wearing off, and in its place was anger at Trevor and at Tonya. "Why would she go back to see him? Why would she lie to me again?"

I knew it wasn't right to blame Tonya, but part of me did. She was the one that had made the decision this time, completely aware of what kind of a person Trevor was.

"Relationships are hard to understand. Especially abusive ones. Sadly, for Tonya, she's finding things out the hard way."

"But why? If Nathan ever hit me, I'd be gone so fast. No. I'd probably kill him first."

Dad sighed and leaned back against the counter, crossing his arms. "Tonya isn't you. No matter how much the two of you seem alike, she has seen and experienced things in her life that have caused her to think differently about this. Ms. James hasn't exactly been a good role model for her daughter. I know her grandmother tries, but there's only so much she can do. Tonya's father was never around, and her grandfather died before she was born. She hasn't had any positive male figures in her life."

"She had you."

He smiled and shook his head, coming to the table and sitting across from me. "It's not the same thing. I'm her best friend's dad. I think you'd be surprised to know how little she cares about what I think."

Considering Tonya was usually the driving force behind me skipping school, or sneaking out at night, I was pretty sure I knew.

The image of her on the stretcher, both eyes puffy and already circled in deep blue and purple bruises came to mind. I rotated the mug around and around, trying to erase the picture, then lifted the hot chocolate and took a small sip, burning my tongue in the process. But it was nothing compared to what Tonya must have felt. The worst part was I didn't know how to help her then, and I knew even less how to help her now.

"I don't know how to make her see how wrong she is about this." My mug thumped against the table as I set it down.

"You can't," Dad said, and laid his hand one my forearm. "All you can do is be there for her."

Every bone in my body felt completely useless, and my eyes filled with tears. Dad got up to wrap me in his arms. A sob burst out as I began to cry. I felt totally helpless, and I hated it. Helplessness was debilitating. I hated that I was crying, instead of kicking Trevor's ass.

"There has to be something more," I said, sniffling as the tears finally slowed.

"Be her friend. She has a lot of other people helping her, too. You don't need to do anything other than be there for her."

It sounded so easy. Yet, it was exactly what I thought I'd been doing the past few weeks, and it obviously hadn't been enough. My head spun at the realization of how quickly she'd gone back to him. I squeezed my eyes shut, attempting to calm the dizziness threatening to overtake me then pushed my chair back.

"I think I'm going to crash. I'm exhausted."

Dad nodded and gave me a kiss on the top of my head. "I'll see you in the morning then, sweetheart."

I carried my mug downstairs, and even made it to my room before Lily and Chloe were on me. Lily kept herself from getting too close, lingering in my door, and shifting from one foot to the other. Chloe, on the other hand, wrapped me in her arms.

"Phoebe, I tried to call! I swear! As soon as I saw what was going to happen, I called your cell, but it kept going to voicemail. I'd been getting random flashes of things, but nothing made sense, and then I was grabbing something from your room earlier and it just hit me. I was seriously freaking until Lily calmed me down."

I tried to remember everything Chloe had mentioned over the past few days, and the pieces fit right in to what had happened. Nathan coming to talk to me at the theater, us in front of an apartment in San Diego, the hospital, me needing Nathan. She'd been right about everything, even if it hadn't all made sense at the time.

"It's okay. You warned me the best you could." I sat on the edge of my bed and gave Chloe an understanding smile. "I'm going to head to bed. I need to go over to Tonya's place in the morning to pick up a few things."

"Let me know if I can do anything. I might not be Tonya's biggest fan, but no one deserves what happened to her." Chloe came over to give me another hug, and then left.

Lily moved to follow her, and then paused, her hand shaking as it rested lightly on the edge of the door. "I'm glad you're okay."

For a moment, I thought she was going to cry, her eyes were so sad and tired, but then she pulled my door closed behind her and went back to her room.

I did try to sleep. But it was impossible. Every time I closed my eyes, I saw Tonya, and all the rage and disbelief came back. I lost track of the number of times I threw off the covers, only to pull them on again. Anything to distract me. It was nearly four in the morning when my door creaked open. Soft footsteps padded across the room.

"I'm sorry," Lily whispered, and I knew she didn't realize I was awake, so I kept my eyes shut.

Her hand hovered over my arm, a heat radiating from her that was a sign of her gift. Then she lightly touched her hand to my arm. It was always the oddest sensation when Lily healed. All my negative emotions vanished, sucked out of me, and there was nothing in its place but an overwhelming sense of calm.

My breath rushed out of me, and my already closed eyes grew heavier. There was a slight movement of air as Lily moved away, but I didn't hear her leave. I was already asleep.

CHAPTER 15

THE NEXT MORNING, CHLOE drove me to the movie theater, and I picked up my car. For once, she kept her mouth shut and let the drive past in peace. I knew she wanted to say something about her visions.

The silence in the car was unnerving. I wanted to reassure her nothing was her fault, and that I would forgive her anyway, but I couldn't say those things. Not because I wouldn't have meant them, but it would have made everything seem so much more real. With every passing moment, it was easier to pretend that Tonya was fine and that the night before had never happened.

I drove over to Tonya's place and used the key Mrs. Robinson gave me at the hospital. It was weird to be walking around their house alone. Almost like I was snooping. Feeling awkward, I went straight to Tonya's room. I pulled out some slippers from under her bed, and a few shirts and her jogging pants from her dresser. I wasn't sure if she'd be able to wear anything other than the hospital gown, but I wanted to fill the backpack I'd brought. Her *iPad* and chargers went in the bag next, and I considered taking her laptop, but she'd showed off how she could do everything she wanted on her *iPad*, so the computer stayed where it was.

The last thing I did was pull her diary out from behind her bookshelf. She'd always been paranoid that her gran would find it. I moved to place it on top of everything and then faltered. Had she written about getting back together with Trevor? I wanted to know what she'd been thinking when she'd decided to go see him, and, most importantly, how she could have possibly forgiven him. I wanted to read it.

The cover flipped open, and I sat down on the corner of her bed, thumbing through until I reached the end of her entries. I slammed it shut. No. I couldn't read her diary. That was a massively wrong thing to do. If it was Chloe's, then I'd do it for a laugh. But this was Tonya, and she was obviously already having problems trusting me if she'd been lying to me about Trevor.

Then again, could I trust her to tell me what was going on? I opened the book and immediately slammed it shut again. I fell back on to her bed, totally frustrated. I wanted to read it, but I knew I shouldn't.

A vibration in my pocket cut off the warring parts of my brain. I still had to figure out how to get it back on to ringing. I pulled it out. Nathan's name flashed on the screen.

"Hey. What's up?" I asked.

"Just seeing how you were doing."

"Fine. I'm at Tonya's, grabbing a few things. I'm going to take them up to the hospital this afternoon. Do you want to come with me?"

"Can't. I'm working the day shift today. Give me a call when you get home, though, and maybe I can come over to study tonight."

I laughed at his wording. Study was his code word for making out he used whenever his parents were within hearing distance.

"Maybe. I've got some really hard biology questions I need help with." I couldn't resist teasing him. "Are you any good with anatomy?"

He coughed, and I giggled again. It was easy being with Nathan. I realized I had missed that more than anything. Well, maybe not as much as I'd missed our 'study' sessions.

"I gotta go," he said. "I'll talk to you later."

We hung up, and I put the cell phone back in my pocket. I glanced down at Tonya's diary. Before I could reconsider and think of all the reasons why I should read it, I dropped it in to the backpack and zipped the bag closed. Just as much as I needed Nathan and me to be simple again, I needed it with Tonya, too. Invading her privacy wasn't going to help me do that.

Later that afternoon, I went to the hospital by myself. I'd hoped Lily would come, maybe make things a bit better for Tonya or at least Mrs. Robinson if we couldn't see Tonya yet, but she gave me some excuse about Dylan needing her help with something. It sounded plausible, but I hadn't been Lily's sister for seventeen years without knowing she had an extreme aversion to hospitals.

Mrs. Robinson had called earlier and given me Tonya's room number. When I reached the right floor, I found her in a family waiting room. She was curled up in a chair, head arching back in what looked like the most uncomfortable position ever. I gently tapped her knee. Her eyes fluttered, and her mouth tipped into a small smile before she seemed to realize where she was and why.

"How's she doing?" I asked, taking a seat across from her.

"Well, they moved her out of intensive care, but they ran tests all morning, making sure..." She paused and took a deep breath. "Making sure there's no permanent damage."

In all my worries, I'd never considered permanent damage, but from what I'd seen of her, physical and mental damage wouldn't be surprising. I looked down at my feet, seeing the bag full of her things. I'd packed it like she was on a sleepover; not like her life was going to change forever.

I picked up the backpack and held it out to Mrs. Robinson. "I grabbed a few clothes, her *iPad*, and some other stuff."

"Thank you, sugar." She took the bag, and it promptly fell to the floor. She looked old. Much older than the mid-fifties I knew she was. She stared at me so intensely I barely suppressed the urge to squirm in my seat.

"Did you know she was going to see that boy?" she asked bluntly.

"No!" I sat up straight and looked her right in the eye, something Dad had always told me to do when I told the truth. Shifty eyes made people doubt you. "I swear, Mrs. Robinson, the last time I heard Tonya mention him was the day after the movie incident. She told me she never wanted to see him again."

"So when she told me she was going out with you and Bianca Friday night...?"

"She told me you wouldn't let her go."

"Lordy. These two girls of mine will be the death of me," she whispered under her breath, then looked back at me. "I guess I knew, as soon as that Nathan boy called last night, asking if she was there."

"I'm sorry. If I'd known..."

"I know that, sugar. My girl's got a mind of her own, and when I started laying down the law about this boy, I should have known she'd do something crazy." She shook her head. "I suppose you want to see her?"

I sat up. "Can I? I wasn't sure, since..."

"Oh. She can have visitors. I'm just taking a break." She handed the backpack to me, and I took off for Tonya's room.

Seeing her was almost as shocking as it had been the night

before. While the blood was gone, swelling and deep bruising had settled in, making it nearly impossible to recognize her. She didn't hear me come in, completely engrossed in something on her tray table.

"Hey," I said, then repeated myself louder when she didn't respond.

Her head jerked around, and her lips tilted up on one side. "Hey. I didn't hear you come in. Were you standing there long?" she asked.

"No."

She shrugged. "I can't hear too good out of my left ear."

"Oh. Is it...?" I did some lame gesture toward my ear, not wanting to say permanent.

"They think it's just the swelling right now. Hopefully, it'll get better, but the doctor said it might not."

"That sucks." I pursed my lips and wandered over to the dresser to inspect a vase of flowers. It was harder than I thought it would be to look at her. Not because I was grossed out, but because I hated to think of her feeling any of the pain associated with those marks.

"What sucks is I'm gonna miss school," she said, and I nearly fell over in shock.

"Did you really just say it sucks to miss school? As in our high school?" I stared at her as if she'd grown horns.

"Phoebs, I'm gonna be stuck in a freaking hospital and then at home, watching soaps with Gran for days. Not that I don't mind catching up on all of them, but, seriously, they're not the *Real Housewives*. It's only been a day, and I'm already going insane watching that junk already." She raised a hand when my mouth opened to say something. "I know. I must be crazy anyway for doing what I did."

"I was so not going to say that!" I said.

"Really?"

"Yes. No! I mean..." I stammered to a stop.

I didn't want to lie and say it hadn't been crazy, but I didn't want to hurt her feelings either. Four months ago, I'd have told her she was bat shit crazy for going to see Trevor. Now she just seemed so much more fragile, as if my words could suddenly add the weight of the world to her already bruised shoulders.

"Girl, chill." When she smiled this time, both ends of her mouth tipped up. "Just make sure you keep me filled in on all the good stuff going on. Gran still has me grounded off the computer. And, apparently, she had some tech geek at the computer store block pretty much any page I'd want to go to."

"Well," I said, dumping the contents of the bag on her lap, "Vivian is gonna go ape shit tomorrow."

"Please tell me it's because you got over your stupid self and are back with Nathan."

"Ha ha. No, I didn't get over myself, but, yes, Nathan and I are back together. I think." I sat in the chair beside her bed and slouched back. "I figured I'd let him suffer enough."

"Please," she said, rolling her eyes. "I think everyone was suffering along with him thanks to your sparkling personality when you're single."

"Gee. It's nice to know there's no permanent damage to your snide side." I almost smacked myself for saying the words as soon as they left my mouth. How could I make a joke about what she'd gone through?

"It's okay, Phoebs. Seriously." She shifted on the bed and placed her *iPad* on the tray that hovered over her legs. "I'd rather have you making fun of me than listen to Gran nag me about making better choices and loving myself enough to not let someone hurt me."

"Uh. Kinda sounds like some good advice," I said.

"Tell me that after you've spent hours listening to her rant. God. I am so ready to go home. Maybe then she'll back off a bit. She, like, freaked out every time she came in here today."

"Can you blame her?"

"No, but I don't need you to start on me. Trust me, this," she gestured to her face, "is not something I'm going to repeat."

I made some lame comment, and, somehow, the conversation was steered back to Vivian, which was even lamer, but at least it was safe. I didn't have to think about how I hadn't even realized that Tonya would do something so stupid, and she didn't have to think about how she had done something so stupid.

When there was nothing left to say about Vivian and her little posse, a heavy silence settled around us, forcing me to think and speak the words I needed to.

"Are you really okay?"

Her hand, which had been messing around with the screen of her *iPad*, faltered and began to tremble. Tears filled her eyes. I watched her struggle to hold them in until I couldn't see for the ones gathering in mine.

"No."

Her answer was heartbreakingly honest. I got up from the chair and leaned in to hug her. She latched on to me, clawing at the back of my shirt, trying to keep me from moving away. I kept in all the other questions I had for her and just held her, rubbing her back like Nanna had always done for me.

"I thought I was going to die. Everything happened so quickly. We were arguing. Something stupid." Her words came out in bursts, between sobs she didn't try to hold back. "School ...or something. I called you...from the bathroom. I thought I'd locked it."

"It's okay. You're okay." I whispered the words, trying to soothe her.

"But I'm not okay. Every time I close my eyes, I can see his foot coming at me. I can feel it smashing my face."

"Your face is gonna heal. It will be okay."

"But I'm not. Why was I such an idiot? What the fuck was I thinking, right?"

I didn't know what to say. I wanted to say it didn't matter, that she was safe and it was over, but I knew that wasn't true. It wasn't over because, according to Dad, they were going to press charges, and Tonya would have to be in court. And, most importantly, it did matter why she'd done it. There'd been a time when I thought Tonya would never let herself be so disrespected by some guy. Now I knew she'd let it happen multiple times. What if she went back again? Would she survive next time?

I pulled back so I could look in to her eyes and know that she was really listening to me. They were dull and defeated— so close to lifeless. "I don't know why this happened to you, but I know that you didn't deserve it. You are awesome, Tonya. You're funny, and everyone likes you."

"Chloe doesn't."

"Yeah, well, do you really want to judge yourself based on my cheerleading sister, who has been known to hang with Vivian?"

"True." She cracked a slight smile.

"You're my best friend for a reason, girl, and it's not just because you can work my cell phone for me."

"I know. It's 'cause I tweet for you, too, right?"

"What? I have a *Twitter* account?" I ignored the fact that I had checked it only days ago and seen Trevor's tweet.

"Yeah, for about a year. I try to update it every few days."

"Gee. Thanks," I said with a roll of my eyes. "So what do I tweet about?"

"Oh. The usual. How hot Nathan looks, how Vivian is a skanky bitch, how Nathan is so sexy when he's stripping for you."

"Yeah, but what did you tweet before we were dating?"

"That was before. Now it's the juicy stuff about your sex life."

"Are you serious?! No wonder Vivian tried to take me down."

"You know it! Maybe I'll start tweeting about our Mickey."

"Micah," I said.

"What?"

"That's the guy's name. Micah. He's hot, but has a stick up his ass or something. I haven't seen him talk to anyone since you first pointed him out to me."

"Oh. Well, I think I'm done with dating for a while anyway." There was another awkward pause until she spoke again. "Gran talked to my therapist, and she wants me to go to some support group."

She lifted her *iPad* to show an info pamphlet, and I picked it up, holding it as if it would burn me. Seeing the words domestic violence across the top made me realize just how crazy things had gotten. Tonya hadn't been attacked by a complete stranger. She had loved Trevor. I might not have understood why, but I knew she had and now there would always be a part of me that would constantly wonder if she would go back to him again.

"Will you go with me?" she asked.

I looked up, startled at the idea. "Is that allowed? I mean, isn't it only for people who've been..."

"I don't know," she said with a shrug. "I just don't think I can go alone. Not yet. So, will you?"

"Yeah. Of course. I mean, if I'm allowed." I didn't want to, but, at the moment, I would do anything to help Tonya stay away from Trevor, including going to a support group. Including using my lie detecting skills on her whether she liked it or not.

We talked for a few more minutes. Then Mrs. Robinson came in and said Tonya needed to rest again. I tried not to laugh when Tonya rolled her eyes in annoyance. But it was a relief to leave. As much as I wanted to be there for Tonya, hospitals had always kind of creeped me out. They were too white and clean, and way too organized. I loved the look of chaos. It made me feel like what was going on inside of me was actually under control.

* * *

Dad was in the living room when I got home. I flopped down beside him on the couch, needing a few father-daughter moments. I wrapped my arms around him and laid my head on his chest.

"Hey. You okay?" He smoothed a hand over my hair.

"Yeah." I squeezed him harder, and he gave me a sideways look. "What? I can't hug my dad?"

"Of course, but it is a rare occurrence," he said doubtfully. "You girls used to be attached to my hip. Now none of you wants to spend any time with your old man."

"Aw. Dad, you're not old. Yet." I eyed his graying hair and laughed as he wrapped an arm around my head and rubbed his fist on the top of it. I used to hate it when he did that. Mainly because he'd follow it up by calling me 'boy'. Now it didn't seem so annoying.

"So, what's up?" he asked.

"I went to see Tonya. She's gonna be okay." The words were slightly muffled against his chest.

"Ah. Well, I'm glad she's doing better. She's got a battle coming up if Mrs. Robinson gets her way."

My head lifted. "What do you mean?"

"There are a lot of steps Tonya needs to take if she wants to keep him out of her life. Abusive relationships are difficult to get out of."

"Do you think she'd go back to him?" That was my greatest fear.

"I don't know. I would hope not, but she's not only been physically abused, but mentally and emotionally as well. And she's already gone back once."

I sighed and lowered my head again. "I don't know what to do for her. She wants me to go to a support group with her. I said I would."

"That's a start. Be there as her friend. It will be good for her to know that she has someone who loves her enough to do the hard things like that. It might just give her the strength to break free of him. I think it would be good for you, too."

"Me?"

"So you can learn the signs of abuse and learn how to get out of an abusive relationship."

"Dad, Nathan would never do that to me."

"I'm not saying that, but in a few years, you might be at a different place in your life..." He cleared his throat, maybe realizing I didn't want to think of a time when Nathan and I weren't dating again. "And you'd learn how to talk to Tonya about what happened, and how to help her not make the same choices again."

I let that sink in for a minute, wondering if maybe I needed to think about more than my discomfort with hearing details of abuse. "So, you really think I should go?"

"Yes."

"I think so, too."

* * *

Nathan didn't make it over that night, but he came by the next day after school. Dad had come home early, so our 'study' session became a lot less fun. I curled up against Nathan on the couch and let myself bask in the reassuring warmth flowing from him. After weeks without him being around, it was heaven to just sit there and snuggle.

He put on one of *Bruce Willis*'s older movies, but even the blasts of machine guns and explosions didn't faze me. That was the awesome thing about action movies. I didn't have to pay attention to the entire thing. Just my favorite parts.

Lily came in at one point, and for the first time since I'd gone completely mental and broken up with Nathan, she didn't look as if she were about to die in agony. But there was still a strain pulling at the corners of her mouth and darkening the skin around her eyes, which, with her pale complexion, didn't help her out at all. Whatever she'd been going through, it was bigger than me and my love life. Something more was bothering her, and I wished I had her ability to know exactly what people were feeling.

I watched her for a bit before I was distracted by the feather-light touches of Nathan's fingers along my arm. Glancing up at him, I smiled, loving how the tingling sensation he brought to life reminded me who I was with. I had Nathan back, without having to apologize—because I definitely don't remember having to do that—and life felt like it was getting back to normal. Except for Tonya.

Lily shifted in her seat and looked over at me, her hands slowly curling into fists. I wanted to just ignore her, but she'd looked almost peaceful only moments before. I gave her a slight, though reluctant, nod.

"I don't know how you watch this stuff."

She rose from the recliner. As she walked by us, I reached out my hand, letting hers brush across my skin. Tonya didn't completely disappear from my thoughts, but the worry and pain I had been associating with her vanished. I took a deep, calming breath and snuggled closer to Nathan.

"You okay?" Nathan asked, staring down at me.

I loved his stormy eyes. Most of the time I didn't notice people's eye color, but with his, I couldn't not notice. They didn't change color spontaneously or glow in the dark, but they definitely twinkled just a bit when he thought something was funny, or right before he kissed me. They were twinkling now.

"I'm better than okay," I replied, and followed it up by reaching behind his head and pulling him in for a short kiss. "I'm perfect."

His eyes practically sparkled. "Oh. I don't know about that. Perfect is pretty steep praise. I think you could use a bit more practice."

"Oh really?" I leaned away from him and crossed my arms over my chest.

"Just a bit. Then again, maybe I'm wrong. Let me test you out again." He moved in quick, pressed his lips to mine, and I forgot about trying to prove myself, or about pretending offense. Instead, I let myself drown in the taste of him. He'd been in my dad's thin mint chocolates.

"You know," I said as we parted for air, "you really need to stay out of my dad's candy. He doesn't need another reason to want to kill you."

"Hmm ... so I have to either give up the chocolates or kissing you? Wow. That's a hard one."

I punched his arm lightly. "I suggest you make a quick choice. Before I decide you don't get either."

"Okay, okay. I'll lay off his candy." He gave me a quick peck on the cheek and then turned back to the movie.

I glanced at him, watching the way his eyes made tiny movements as they took in the on-screen action. He tugged me closer, and I relaxed in to his arms with a smile, thinking of how close I'd come to losing him for good. If Tonya hadn't called, if she hadn't gone to Trevor's, there was a chance that I would have shoved my foot—okay, feet—back in my mouth after seeing Nathan and Vivian together at the theater. I felt a nudge of guilt as Tonya came back to my mind, but it was done. There was nothing I could do to change her situation.

"You know I'm sorry, right?"

He looked at me, an eyebrow cocked in surprise. "Excuse me? Did I just hear you say sorry?"

"Ha ha. This is serious. I'm sorry I blamed you."

"What brought this on?"

"I just..." The words froze in my throat. Admitting I was terrified of how close I'd been to losing him would leave me open to that horrible vacuum of emptiness I'd been in without him.

My silence brought a smirk to his face.

"I know," he said. "You couldn't stand to be without this hotness again." He flexed his biceps, and then squeezed me close while we laughed.

When my giggles finally settled, I cupped his face in my hands and kissed him, trying to put everything I felt in to it. I wanted him to feel everything I wasn't ready to voice yet.

We stayed pressed to each other, taking in the other's breaths until the sound of the door at the top of the stairs opening drew us apart. Nathan's wandering hands came back to mine, and I slid my fingers through his.

"I'm sorry, too."

"What for?" I asked.

"You were right that I didn't believe you. Well, I did, but I didn't. When it was stuff that wasn't in my face, I didn't have to believe it. Then when I finally saw Trevor in action, I realized that you'd been right. I hung out with the guy, and he seemed so cool."

"He was. I just wish I'd trusted my gift enough to not have been sucked in to that side of him."

"We all were." He pressed his lips to my forehead, and I let my eyes drift closed, relaxing in to the feel of his arms.

* * *

I woke an hour later when Nathan shifted under me. I looked up at him. He wore a decidedly guilty look on his face and was staring over my head. I twisted around and found my dad gazing at us with an eyebrow raised. I shot to my feet, heat flooding my checks. I rarely blushed for anyone but Nathan, but having Dad catch me sleeping on top of my boyfriend was definitely a blush-worthy moment.

"Hey, Dad. I...we—"

"Nathan, I think it's time for you to be heading home. It's a school night, and it's getting late."

Nathan stood and rubbed a hand over the back of his neck. "Yes, sir."

I grabbed Nathan's hand and dragged him toward the stairs. Once Dad was no longer visible, I gave a giggle, which got me a dirty look from Nathan.

"Phoebs, it's not funny! Your dad is going to kill me."

LIE TO ME

I gave a full-blown laugh this time. We stepped on to the porch, and I turned to wrap my arms around him. "He won't kill you. Now if we'd been naked..."

"Hmm ... I think I might be willing to take that risk." He wriggled his eyebrows and leaned down to kiss me. I met him halfway and pressed closer to him.

"That's good," I whispered when we pulled apart, "because Chloe said..."

"She said what?" No missing the hope in his voice.

"She said..." I paused and gave him a sweet smile. "She said, we'll be waiting a long time."

He groaned while I snickered at his frustration. I finally ended his wordless complaint with my lips. After a brief kiss, he moved back.

"I suppose I'll just have to get by on my dreams of you and your hot pink panties," he said, and dodged my hand when I tried to playfully pinch him. "I'll see you in my dreams."

He took off for his car, and threw me a wave when he climbed in. I waited for him to drive away before I went back inside, making it to the top of the basement stairs before my dad's voice stopped me.

"Phoebe, I'd like to have a talk with you."

I turned back and went in to the living room where Dad sat in his recliner.

"Sit down," he said.

I barely held in my groan. This was not going to be a conversation I liked.

"Nathan is a good kid, and I know you like him a lot, but you've only been dating a short time."

Oh dear god. He was going to give me 'The Talk'. This was going to be worse than I'd ever imagined.

CHAPTER 16

I SWIVELED MY DESK chair around, letting my eyes blur for a moment, the English essay I'd been writing forgotten on my computer screen.

School without Tonya was weird. She'd begged her gran to let her stay home until all the bruises were gone, but news about what happened had spread pretty quickly. It died just as swiftly. Mainly since no one had really known Trevor, and Tonya wasn't the most popular girl in school. Only our group of friends and my sisters knew what actually went down.

With Tonya gone, and Nathan and I back together, I'd almost expected Vivian to attack, but she hadn't. For the first few days, I'd been on edge, waiting for her to strike. But nothing. I was hoping she'd finally given up on the idea of Nathan dumping me and going back to her. Tonya still held out hope that Vivian would bring back a little of the drama. Although, she didn't mention fighting again.

I'd gone with her to a couple of support groups in the two weeks since she'd asked me to go with her, and I was glad I'd stuck to my word about going. It was hard to hear the things the people there described.

I'd sat silent, simply listening and thinking about how difficult it must be to tell another person the things they were sharing, yet they did. Tonya hadn't spoken at any of the meetings other than to introduce herself, and I was almost relieved. I didn't want to know everything Trevor had done, and I think me being there was one of the reasons she didn't talk. Dad said she might be embarrassed about me knowing, and that, sometimes, it's easier to share those things with people who know nothing else about you.

She mentioned she'd been to another meeting on her own, and I was glad because, as much as I wanted to support her, she had to take the steps by herself. All she needed to know was that I'd be there to catch her if she needed. And I would be.

Going with her had helped me understand the cycle she'd fallen in to, how she could have stayed with Trevor, and then gone back to him, even after what he'd done. And it made me appreciate Nathan's imperfections all the more. He was late, a lot, and he didn't call that often, and there was his obsession with chocolate, but he respected me, and I thought he might actually love me.

So many times, those three little words had hovered on the tip of my tongue. Usually after he kissed me. But I always kept them in. I wasn't a touchy-feely kind of person, but Nathan always managed to make me go all gooey inside, almost to the point that I wanted to say them.

The very idea of love had me squirming with nerves. I sprung from my chair, paced the room a few times, and then headed down to Lily's room. I pushed her door open and flopped, stomach down, on to her bed.

"Hey?" she said, staring at me from her computer desk, clearly confused by my abrupt presence.

"Hey." I grabbed a magazine from her nightstand and began turning pages. It was some boring thing on art news. How did they even make a magazine about art news? At least it had some pretty pictures.

"Did you need something?" she asked.

I tossed aside the magazine and grabbed another from the overly organized magazine basket on the bottom of her nightstand. "No. Just thought I'd spend some quality time with my favorite sister."

"Um. Okay."

She turned back around and resumed her typing. She must have been working on her English paper. Even though I had English at a different time than her and Chloe, we all had Ms. Garcia, so we had pretty much the exact same assignments. Although, Lily usually didn't leave things to the last minute, and with the paper due in the morning, she was probably doing some extra credit work.

I glanced at the rapidly flipping pages before me. This one was slightly better with hot guys every few pages. My eye caught the word love, and I stopped. A love quiz. It was so stupid. Love. How do you put everything you feel for a person in to one little four letter word?

It wasn't a word I'd thought of before Nathan. At least not in connection with me. I read the questions on the page. *Favorite color? What are his dreams? Does he open the door for you?* Is that really how I was supposed to define my feelings for Nathan? Did I even have to? He hadn't said he loved me. Shouldn't he go first? If I said it first, would he just do a pity return? Then again, what did it matter who said what first? Or even if we said it at all? It wasn't like I was Lily. She was one of those emotions people, always wanting peace and love and understanding.

"Nathan asked me to junior prom," I said. "I'm going to try and get Tonya to go shopping with me. She always finds the best stuff. It's totally unfair."

I looked up at her nodding head. She'd stopped typing and was gazing at a picture, which, from my viewpoint, looked to be of her and Dylan. I wish I could figure out what she saw in him.

"I think we'll try and go in to the city. The stuff they have in town is horrible. I saw Vivian trying on some of them, and she completely skank-tified them." I turned a few more pages, leaving the stupid love quiz behind. "We're probably going to go next weekend. I think it's still too early to buy something. I mean, junior prom is over a month away, but Tonya is refusing to do last minute shopping with me. Hey. Why don't you come with us?"

At her lack of response, I sat up and scooted over to the edge of the bed. I waved my hand in front of the photo. "Yo, Lily? You still with me?"

"Are you and Nathan in love?" she asked, still staring at the picture.

Sometimes, it was scary how the twin, or I guess the triplet, thing worked. Then again, maybe she'd been reading my emotions or something and decided to make me think about it all over again.

"Yeah. I mean, I guess we are. We've never said it, but it's there, you know?" I gave her one of my half smiles. I wondered if my answer seemed as lame as it sounded. Maybe I was a freak for not having told him yet. "Do you think that's strange? Should I tell him?"

"No. Not unless you want to."

She glanced at me and tried to smile back. I rolled back on to my stomach, scrunching one of her pillows under my chest while mussing up the comforter with my legs. I could practically see her calculating how many seconds it would take her to fix the bed once I left.

I considered what she'd said. It wasn't that I didn't want to tell him that I loved him; it was just that it didn't seem that important to say the words. But maybe it was. Maybe he was waiting for me to say them first. But how?

"How did you tell Dylan?" I asked.

She looked back at the photo, probably reliving the glorious moment. She would have made it sweet and all roses and puppy dog tails. As she took her time answering, I decided right then that I would tell Nathan when I really wanted to. Anything Lily had done would just be too ... well, too not me. I would tell him. Soon.

I glanced at Lily. She still hadn't answered my question, and she had a freaky look on her face like she was about to tear herself apart. She'd been acting so strange lately.

"Lils? Come on. How did you tell him?"

She put down the picture.

"I didn't."

"What?"

I nearly fell over in shock. She'd been dating Dylan forever. How could she never have said I love you? I'd only been with Nathan a few months, and I was pretty sure I loved him. No; I knew I did. So how messed up was Lily?

ABOUT THE AUTHOR

ANGELA FRISTOE grew up in Alberta, Canada. She dreamed of becoming the next Dian Fossey or Jane Goodall until she realized she wasn't all that keen on the outdoors or animals. Instead, she went into education and focused on helping struggling readers. Angela lives on Vancouver Island with her family where she is pursuing her writing career while continuing her work in the education field.

www.angelafristoe.com

YOUNG ADULT BOOKS
BY ANGELA FRISTOE

A Touched Trilogy
Lie to Me
Heal Me
Watch Me

The Woods of Everod
Waken
Rising
Book 3 coming soon

The Vitares Chronicles
Fate's Legacy
Book 2 coming 2019

Songbird